Winter

of the

Wolves

Winter of the Wolves

James N. Frey

Henry Holt and Company   New York

Published by Henry Holt and Company, Inc.,
115 West 18th Street, New York, New York 10011.
Published in Canada by Fitzhenry & Whiteside Limited,
91 Granton Drive, Richmond Hill, Ontario L4B 2N5.

Library of Congress Cataloging-in-Publication Data

Frey, James N.
Winter of the wolves / James N. Frey. — 1st ed.
p.   cm.
I. Title.
PS3556.R4474W56   1992
813'.54—dc20   91-30139
                                         CIP
ISBN 0-8050-1764-X

Henry Holt books are available at special discounts
for bulk purchases for sales promotions, premiums,
fund-raising, or educational use. Special editions
or book excerpts can also be created to specification.
For details contact: Special Sales Director,
Henry Holt and Company, Inc.,
115 West 18th Street, New York, New York 10011.
First Edition—1992

Book Design by Claire Vaccaro
Printed in the United States of America
Recognizing the importance of preserving
the written word, Henry Holt and Company, Inc.,
by policy, prints all of its first editions
on acid-free paper. ∞

1   3   5   7   9   10   8   6   4   2

main

FOR SEBASTIAN

The First Lesson of History is that evil is good.

—RALPH WALDO EMERSON

The first time I saw her she was riding a bike up the hill on the Creek Road. It was fall, the best time of the year in the Adirondacks. The leaves of the maple, birch, and beech trees had just changed and both sides of the road were ablaze with reds and browns and yellows. The air was crisp and fresh, and the wind gusted cold from the northwest.

I came up behind her in my old Ford Bronco and the first things I noticed were her nice round behind and her fine, rust-red hair shimmering in the Indian summer sun. She was wearing a red sweatshirt and a pair of tight shorts, and her legs were slender but muscular as she pumped away on the pedals. She turned and glanced at me and I saw her freckled face and large brown eyes. She was, I guessed, about thirty. I was forty-three. The arithmetic wasn't right, I thought, but that didn't stop me from wishing it was.

I hung back for a few moments just watching her ride. Prince, my black Labrador retriever, was in the passenger's seat,

1

his head out the window, growling at the slowdown. He liked to speed along with his face in the wind. The redhead turned every once in a while to give me a smile. She had a nice smile. Like Katharine Hepburn when she was young.

I followed her down the hill to where the old covered wooden bridge crosses the creek and kept behind her as she rode across the bridge and started up the long hill on the other side, where she again turned toward me and with a motion of her head invited me to pass. She was straining, red-faced, sweating, as she pumped the pedals against the hill.

Passing her, I went over the hill and down the other side toward the town of Amber. To the north, I could see snowcapped Blue Mountain and Mount Kempshall, and Mount Marcy further in the distance.

At the bottom of the hill, just before the town of Amber, there was a pond full of reeds and cattails off to the right; some comedian of long ago christened it Amber Lake. The road curved around the pond, past a dozen clapboard houses set back from the road with swings and dogs and kids in the yards, and on into the center of town.

Up ahead was the white clapboard Community Church on the right, surrounded by a cemetery of old gray stones, which sat at crooked angles to one another. Next came the Amber Inn and Jenny's Diner, then the small red-brick post office. Across the street was Maxie's Convenience Store, a small concrete block building about the size of a two-car garage. Further down were a couple more bars—Willy and Martha's and the Amber Tavern— then the Texaco station, the Arco station, and the IGA at the edge of town.

The road through town was pockmarked with potholes, which nobody seemed to mind because it kept the traffic down.

Most of the young people moved away from Amber to find

jobs. Albany. New York City. California. Amber was a quiet town that would never amount to much; it was a town where people dressed in faded flannels and old jeans and nobody gave a damn. It had made a pact with history never to be mentioned even in passing. Just the kind of place I wanted to be then, a place full of peaceful, normal people, who didn't have anything more on their minds than the weather. A town where a man could forget who he used to be.

I left Prince in the Bronco, which seemed to be okay with him. He lay down in the back to take a nap. I went into the post office for the mail. Only thing I got was an advertising circular for a hardware store in Albany addressed to "boxholder." When I came back out I looked for the redhead on the bicycle. I thought she'd be riding by. I waited for a few minutes and she didn't show. She must have turned off some place.

I got in the Bronco and drove back up the Creek Road to go home. I didn't see the redhead along the way.

3

The next morning, Prince woke me at dawn with a growl. Rain was pelting the roof.

"What is it, boy?" I whispered.

He growled again and trotted off. I rolled out of bed and followed him into the darkened living room. I pulled back the curtains and looked out. In the pale morning light, I could see there were no cars in the driveway that ran up the ravine from the main road to my house. It was raining hard; there were big puddles down where my driveway met the road. The piles of fallen autumn leaves were flattened by the rain.

I scanned the woods at the top of the ravine and detected no movement in the trees. "Nobody there," I said to Prince.

He snorted, lowered his head as if he were a little ashamed of himself, and went back into the bedroom. I figured he must have heard a car going by. Not many cars went by my place, especially that early in the morning.

The house felt cold and damp. I lit a fire in the Franklin

4

stove to take the chill off and sat for a while in the living room smoking a cigarette, watching the water cascade off the porch. The burning hickory smelled good in the damp morning air. My living room was small and cozy and it didn't have a whole lot of furniture, just a chair, a small couch, a coffee table made of a cross section of a huge tree. I had a couple piles of books here and a few boxes of them in the bedroom. I didn't own a TV or a stereo. Or have a goddamn telephone, either.

I was on my second cup of coffee when I heard a car coming. I went to the window and caught a glimpse of it as it glided by. It was a new model; one of those rounded, aerodynamic jobs. It cruised by slowly, as if whoever was driving it was looking for something. Whoever was in the car wasn't just the electric company man looking for a meter to read, that was for sure. My instincts told me I had unwelcome guests.

I got out my sporting rifle, a Marlin bolt action .22 magnum with a six-shot clip and a Leupold 12x scope, slipped on a pair of jeans, a shirt, a slicker, and a pair of boots and went out the back door, holding the rifle and a half-full box of shells in my hands. Prince came alert, sniffing the danger in the air. I told him to stay. For once, he obeyed.

Going up the hill behind my place, I circled around on a small ridge that ran back down to the road alongside my driveway. Along the top of the ridge there was a stand of pines that gave me good cover. The rain, now mixed with sleet, was still coming down hard.

The driveway to my house ran from the road straight up a horseshoe-shaped ravine about two hundred and fifty feet long. The small, white, clapboard house was at the head of the ravine surrounded by pines, with a wooden stairway that went from the driveway to the house. From my position I had a good line of fire in three directions and a couple of good escape routes: up over the hill behind the house where there was plenty of cover, or out over the ridge to the north.

It was cold and miserable in the rain. The smoke coming out of my chimney invited me back inside. But I waited. Whoever was in that car had been looking for something. It might have been just a bill collector looking for a deadbeat, or a repo man looking for a vehicle to recover, but I didn't think so.

A half hour later it was fully daylight and still raining hard and I was still in the trees, waiting. The car came back. A charcoal gray T-bird, two men in it. Through the scope I could see they were wearing trench coats over suits and ties, and one of them was a guy I knew from the outfit where I used to work—the Exchange, it's called. The Exchange does work for the CIA, Defense Intelligence, the State Department; it's not officially a part of the government, not exactly *not* a part of it, either.

The Exchange man's name was Lawrence Langston. I didn't know the guy with him; he was young, a trainee, no doubt, learning the ropes. He was blond and built well with square shoulders and a muscular neck. He had a kind of determined face, but he looked scared too. His mouth was curled in a way that always gives away fear.

He had every right to be afraid. When I left the Exchange I told them I never wanted to be bothered again. Ever. And if I was bothered, I might kick some ass.

Langston parked the T-bird across the road and the two of them got out. The young blond guy pulled a small automatic and checked it to make sure it was loaded. He stuck it in his coat pocket but kept his hand on it.

If they were planning to dump me, they were going about it all wrong. They should have brought two dozen guys with assault rifles and flack vests. Or they could have paid the price and got themselves a real shooter who knew what he was doing. Somebody who could whack me before I even got a sniff of him.

Anyway, they'd never pick a clown like Langston for a job like that. The Exchange was loaded with clowns, I guess, because its bosses were all ex-government men who hired other ex-government men, and so it had become just as bureaucratic and bungling as the rest of the damn government.

Langston and his pal crossed the road and started up the driveway on foot, slipping in the mud, getting it all over their nice clean pants. Langston had put on a little weight since I'd seen him last. His face looked puffy. Booze-puffy. Both of them wore hats with wide brims, which the rain ran off in back. They came up the driveway about three-quarters of the way and stopped near my Bronco. Langston put his hands up to his mouth and yelled:

"Croft! Thomas Croft!"

I guess he wanted to make sure that I wouldn't think he was trying to sneak up on me. Prince barked in return from inside the house.

Langston said something to his companion. Then he yelled again: "Thomas Croft! We've got to talk to you!"

I was waiting to make sure it was just the two of them. Patience, patience. Maybe they were just a couple of dodo birds sent to decoy me. A long shot, but possible. You never know for sure what a clown like Langston will do. I wasn't in any hurry to find out what they wanted.

"Your life may be in danger!" Langston shouted. His voice echoed up the hills.

I still didn't answer him. He gave a little wave and the blond guy took off toward my house on the run. He went around my Bronco parked at the top of the drive, then up the stairway to the top of the hill and around the house, ducking under the windows.

He ran like a running back, head down, swiveled-hips. Langston just stood in the middle of the muddy driveway, the rain streaming off his hat. A couple of minutes went by. Prince kept barking his ass off. I hoped Blondie wouldn't break the door down and kick the dog.

I didn't move. You have good cover, you don't blow it for anything, not even to save your dog.

I did a sweep of the area with the scope. No more cars. A minute or so later Blondie came around the house shrugging his shoulders. Langston waved his hands and yelled, "Croft! Thomas Croft!" Then he waved to Blondie, who jogged back down the stairs to him. They started back for the car together.

I took aim at Blondie's hat and shot it off. The hat sailed through the air like a frisbee. The crack of the rifle echoed off the surrounding hills.

In those parts, a gunshot is as common as a bird chirp. Especially in and around pheasant season.

Blondie dropped straight down in the mud with his gun out, aiming along the ridge of the hill, but my cover was good and he couldn't find me. Even if he saw me, with that little automatic he couldn't have hit me in a hundred tries. The jerk. Where the hell were they getting their goddamn recruits?

Langston figured out that he'd been had. He reached into his coat and took out a chrome-plated automatic with his thumb and forefinger and dropped it in the mud. He said something to Blondie, who got to his feet and dropped his little automatic in the mud, too. I could see it pained him; the curl of his lip folded over severely. They both put up their hands. Blondie had mud all over his nice clean trench coat.

I let them both stand there for maybe five minutes, just to let them stew a bit. The scowl on Langston's plump face got bigger. He said, "Come on, Croft, show yourself!" He kept saying it, over and over. The blond guy's mouth got tighter, his eyes angrier. Nobody likes being made a jackass, even if he is one. Finally I stepped out of the trees. "Hands on top of your heads," I said. "Lace the fingers real tight now." They both obeyed. I climbed down the hill, careful not to slip, keeping my rifle pointed at them.

"Don't you recognize me, Tom?" Langston said. "Lawrence Langston. This here's Bill Vanders."

"Glad to meet you, Mr. Croft," Vanders said. He started to take his hands off his head to shake mine, but I gestured with the rifle for him to put them back. Langston sighed like I was really trying his goddamn patience.

"What the fuck you want, Langston?" I said, keeping the rifle pointed at Vanders.

"Can't we talk in the house?" Langston said. "It's a little unpleasant out here in the elements." His voice showed exasperation. He had been a desk man most of his life; his idea of a tough situation was having his coffee get cold.

"What's this shit about my life being in danger?" I said.

"At least permit us to put our hands down."

"Not a chance."

"I was always square with you, Tom," Langston said. He said this with a sincere squint, like he really goddamn meant it.

"Maybe I just don't like the way you guys operate."

"Nobody ever confused us with Goodwill. You knew that when you joined up."

I said, "Haven't you heard, Langston? The Cold War is over. Peace has been declared."

"The Soviets have collapsed but the game goes on. There are plenty of other players. Lots of opportunity. The New World Order means everything's up for grabs."

"You said I was in danger."

9

"Gray Wolf is going to kill you."

Gray Wolf was the code name of an old pal of mine, a guy I'd worked with on and off for years. I said: "That's bullshit."

"He's gone over."

"You're a liar."

"It's true. He went independent. Gunned our station chief in Paris."

"You're full of shit."

"Two weeks later he did an Israeli diplomat in Cairo. Iran paid the freight for that one. You must have seen it in the paper. Got him at the Cairo Hilton giving a speech to a Lions Club from Illinois."

"I don't read the papers. The world can go screw itself, what do I care?"

A stream of water ran down Langston's nose. He slanted his head so the water would run off the side. "We want you to get him," Langston said. "A one-deal contract. Fifty grand, plus expenses. The Director says you're to have every assistance we can render."

The Director ran the Exchange. Nobody knew who he was. He probably wasn't even one guy. He was a committee or a board of directors, some bullshit like that.

"You got dozens of shooters," I said. "You don't need me."

"We sent two," Langston said. "They both came back in boxes. We need somebody who knows Gray Wolf, somebody who can outthink him. That somebody is you."

"The answer is no."

Langston smiled, a humorless, cynical smile. He only smiled on one side and it made his pudgy round face look sinister. He took a couple steps to the side, where the mud wasn't so deep. "You always were a difficult son of a bitch, Croft," he said. "Time you smartened up. Gray Wolf's sure to figure we're going to send the best man we got to get him, and that's you. Soon as he figures it out, we both know what he'll do."

I was looking at Langston, about to tell the jerk he didn't know Gray Wolf half as well as he thought he did, and that's when Blondie made a grab for my rifle.

I planted my feet and brought the stock of the rifle around over his outstretched arms and smashed it into the side of his head, making a crunching sound. The blow spun him halfway around and I bent him with a kick in the groin, then jabbed him twice quickly in the face with the stock and dropped him with a kick in the belly. He groaned and fell face-first into the mud.

I guess he'd felt humiliated standing there with his hands on his head and had to do something manly, no matter how stupid it was.

Langston stared at him for a long moment, then shook his head. "Notre Dame, first string. No shit, the guy was runner-up All-American."

"Pick him up and haul his ass out of here. And tell the Director and anybody else who hasn't got the message, when I quit, I quit for good."

Langston shook his head. "Can't figure you, Croft, no sir, I really can't. Top of the business, knocking down a quarter of a million a year for a few dozen jobs you could do sleepwalking. Hard to figure. What was it? Word's around you quit on account of the Benevides job."

"I quit because the Exchange is fucked."

Langston looked up at the house, then at me, the wind blowing the rain into his face. "You got a big problem, Croft, only you don't know it. You let the killing of an ant get to you. Benevides was an ant."

"He was a man."

"Okay, so you had a pang of conscience. Maybe it isn't right to kill an ant. Maybe there isn't any right and wrong, I'm past caring whether there is or isn't. But okay, you got fed up and quit, I can see that. Sure. We all have got to take time off once in a while. Rest up. You let the Benevides thing become personal. It happens to the best of us, letting things get personal. You took it personal and so you got hot about it and you quit. But you got to face it, you'll be back. You're one of us forever whether you like it or not. Want to know why? Because it's what you are. You're one of us. I mean you're a player. You'd never go over to the other side, so where does that leave you? The CIA and State won't take you, not after the shit you've done. They'd be afraid of the blow-back. One day you might end up on the cover of *Time* magazine. So you have to stay in the shadows, and that means you've got to stay with us."

"Get the fuck out of here."

"You mind if I take our weapons?"

"Leave 'em."

"They'll take them out of our paychecks. What the hell you got stuck up your ass? What'd I ever do to you?"

"You're a fucking worm. I hate crawling, slimy things."

He glowered at me for a long moment, then helped Vanders to his feet. I'd hurt Vanders pretty bad. He was shaky on his legs and could hardly stand up. Maybe I busted something inside. Blood ran down the side of his face and down the front of his trench coat. The creep gave me a hurt look like maybe I ought to feel sorry for him.

Langston put his arm around him and the two of them went down the driveway, slipping on the mud, and crossed the road and got into the T-bird and tore off down the road. I didn't figure they'd be back. Langston was a messenger boy; he'd have to go file a report. He'd say I was uncooperative, openly hostile. That I attacked them without provocation. But then, what the hell did I care what they said in their report?

I went inside, shivering, and threw some more wood on the fire, took a hot shower, and put on some dry clothes, all the time thinking about Gray Wolf and what a dangerous son of a bitch he was.

I first met Gray Wolf on another rainy morning; one in September 1971 at Gau Li, Republic of Vietnam. I was a master sergeant in the Special Forces at the time.

I'd been working with SOG, Special Operations Group, doing recon along the Ho Chi Minh Trail, looking for arms caches for a month or so, and before that I had been in the hospital for a couple of weeks with infected leech bites on my legs.

Colonel Sanderson, my commanding officer, had called me into his hooch that morning and said he was sending me to Gau Li on an important mission and I was to report to a Lieutenant Fairweather. A chopper picked me up. First we flew south to a fire base and picked up a lurp named Jackson. Lurps were long-range reconnaissance guys. Jackson was wearing his lurp tiger-striped fatigues.

Jackson, a cracker from Georgia, had a stubby build. He chewed tobacco and enjoyed killing. You could tell by the eyes. He looked out at you with a vacant kind of stare like he had no soul. Except for the eyes, he was maybe nineteen. The eyes were old eyes. War does that to a man.

Gau Li wasn't much of a place. A few dozen sandbagged bunkers and a helipad on a small hill pockmarked with shell holes. It overlooked the Mekong River right across from Cambodia. Somewhere up the line there was some artillery fire, but at Gau Li it was quiet and sultry hot under a gray sky. It had stopped raining and the jungle all around us was steaming. We were taken directly from the chopper to a small mess hall in one of the bunkers that also served as a briefing room. Dimly lit with kerosene lanterns, it had sandbag walls and a low ceiling. It was cooler in there and smelled of cooking, earth and decay, and old sweat.

A couple of guys were waiting when Jackson and I came in. Copperfield and Smyth, they said their names were. Both real hard cases. Copperfield was black and a master sergeant. Two tours, he said. He had an ugly, jagged scar on his right cheek. Smyth was a big white guy, didn't say much. He stuck close to Copperfield.

The four of us had coffee, a smoke. We talked about how fucking hot it was, what we were doing there, where the best whorehouses were in Saigon. Then the man who would one day be Gray Wolf came in smoking a cigar, grinning. Sandy blond hair cut short; big, even teeth; he looked like a college kid who worked out a lot. He had strong arms and a thick neck. Hazel eyes. He said he was Lieutenant Fairweather. His fatigues were clean and pressed. He could have just stepped off a goddamn recruiting poster. He looked like he thought war was a tennis match at the club. Made my stomach turn.

"I'll get right to it," he said. "We've got pretty good intelligence that General Giap is making an inspection tour of training camps operating along the Si Ni. That's this little river, right

15

about here." He pointed to a speck on the map about twenty miles into Cambodia. I knew the area, I'd been there before. We weren't officially fighting in Cambodia. Officially we were honoring Cambodian neutrality. What a laugh.

General Giap was North Vietnam's best tactician, one of the cofounders of the Viet Minh after World War II; he supposedly had masterminded the siege of Dien Bien Phu, which broke the back of the French in 1954.

Lieutenant Fairweather looked back from the map and smiled. "Giap'll be at the camp for one day. Today. He's coming in at 1200 hours by river, he'll inspect the troops, pow wow with some local commanders in the evening, and he'll leave by 0600 tomorrow. He'll take this trail along the ridge of the valley."

"So what's our mission?" I asked.

"To kill Giap," he said.

"Just the five of us?"

He nodded and smiled, like we were all being invited to a beach party.

We four looked at each other. Jackson said, "How many men will Giap have with him?"

Lieutenant Fairweather shrugged. "A company. A hundred men, maybe a hundred and fifty. Ordinarily he wouldn't expose himself in the field like this, but this particular unit he's visiting was pretty hard hit last month at Vi Lim and they've got a lot of new recruits. He's going there to bolster morale."

"How good is our intelligence on this?" I asked.

Lieutenant Fairweather grinned. "As good or as bad as it usually is."

"Which means fucked," Jackson said.

"Yeah, but if it's right, this could be good," Copperfield said. "You get this General Giap, you really done something. They talk about you forever."

Smyth nodded. I got the idea that whatever Copperfield said was all right with him.

"If you're dead, what do you care?" Jackson said. "Are we volunteering for this?"

Lieutenant Fairweather said, "I've picked you guys myself. You, Jackson, are the best point man in 'Nam. You can smell your way there and back again. Smyth, you can handle an M-60 better than anybody. You're worth ten men. You cover us once we get Giap. Copperfield, you're ferocious in a firefight. Croft, you have the privilege of pulling the trigger, because it's said that you never miss."

My father had taken me shooting every weekend since I was ten years old, knocking off tin cans until the gun got too hot to hold. I was rated third best in the army in Vietnam; the two top guys were good target shooters, but they weren't worth a damn in the field. Shooting men is not the same as shooting targets. Some guys choke when they're shooting at human flesh. You can't be a good shooter in the field if you think too much about it.

"And what's your job?" I asked the lieutenant.

"I'm the brains of the operation."

Copperfield laughed. He didn't try to hide it.

"Listen," Lieutenant Fairweather said, "we're going to deal the gooks a bigger blow tomorrow than if a division had been wiped out. We're going to cut off the head of the snake. You're all going to be in the history books. Now, who's coming, and who's a candy ass that wants to stay behind?" He was a cheerleader.

Jackson's eyes got a faraway look in them. I guess he was imagining all the kills he was going to get. "I always wanted to shoot me a general," he said.

Smyth said, "Whatever Copperfield says is okay."

"Why not?" Copperfield said. "Might be a kick."

"You and me, Copperfield, are gonna get along," Lieutenant

Fairweather said, giving him a pat on the shoulder. "How about you, Croft?"

"Okay."

I was a soldier then, I went along with things.

"We pull out at 1800 hours," Lieutenant Fairweather said.

Since I was going to do the honors of letting the hammer down on the general, I was issued a single-shot Anschutz international match rifle with an adjustable palm rest. A slick weapon. It had a thumbhole through the stock to give you a better hold, and it came with a Kahles 4x scope. I test-fired the rifle and set the scope before we left and packed it away with my gear. They gave me six bullets to test-fire and one exploding round to do the job. And they gave me a dozen pictures of the general so I could recognize him. He wouldn't be wearing insignias, so he'd be hard to spot.

Lieutenant Fairweather said, "We get one shot. It better be good."

"You want the right eye or the left?" I said.

He laughed. "You're okay, sport."

We took off in the chopper on schedule. The plan called for us to be dropped off four miles from the site where we were to intercept the general. We were to make our way up over a small mountain and spend the night in concealment along the ridge just above a narrow ravine where the general would be certain to pass. That was where we planned to get him. We would retreat up the mountain and call in air strikes to drive off the pursuit. Once we made it back across the ridge, we'd be picked up by chopper and returned to our base.

As soon as we took off in the chopper, I noticed Lieutenant Fairweather changed. He no longer made jokes or laughed or slapped people on the shoulder like some high school kid going into a football game. He was all business. His field gear was immaculate and his uniform was freshly washed like a kid straight from the Point, but he seemed to know what it was about. He sat studying maps and chewing gum. His muscles were tense, his eyes alert. At first I thought it was fear, but then I realized he was just concentrating intently and I began to suspect that he had the same passion for the work that I had.

We took light packs and lots of ammunition and a half-dozen grenades each, smeared burned cork on our faces. Smyth, the big man, carried the M-60. The chopper dumped us in a small jungle clearing and went out low. It was just getting dark. The setting sun painted the tops of the trees orange. Jackson checked a map and compass and we all had a look at the map so each man knew where he was and where he was going. Each man knew his job. If part of the team went down, the others would see that the mission was completed, if feasible.

Jackson seemed to have eyes that saw in the dark. He led us up a narrow trail and over a rocky ridge. Frogs croaked in the jungle around us. Occasionally, a bird screeched.

We made it down the other side of the ridge. Here the jungle was so dense we had to hack our way down the mountain. We swung around a couple of open places where artillery had wiped out the jungle and the soft earth was burned clear of foliage. A crescent moon hung on the eastern horizon. About midnight we came to the top of a cliff overhung by shrubs and moss and vines. Across the face of the cliff opposite us, General Giap would be coming down a narrow trail for his meeting with death.

I felt that fate had smiled upon me. I felt I was about to step onto the stage of history and do something that would make my whole life worthwhile. I had a momentary flash in my mind of the Russian tank that rolled over my mother in 1956. This was going to make things even.

While the other members of the team rested, I crawled

around in the moonlight and tried to find the best firing position. I found a clump of trees on an outcropping that would give me a clear field of fire for a hundred fifty yards. The trail narrowed as it moved along the face of the cliff and the footing was treacherous. They would be moving slowly. It was perfect.

I spent an hour camouflaging my firing position and then retreated up the hill and rejoined the team. They had been busy setting up defensive positions to fall back to as we made our retreat over the mountain. Copperfield was worried about the open places where the artillery had burned away part of the cover, and suggested the chopper pick us up on this side of the mountain, but Lieutenant Fairweather said it was too risky, and he was probably right. We ate some field rations, but didn't smoke. Lieutenant Fairweather passed out amphetamines to keep us alert.

We waited. Copperfield and Smyth watched the rear; Jackson scouted a little village just west of our position for signs of the enemy. He came back about 0400 and reported sighting some VC, but he couldn't tell how many or which way they were headed. We thought it must be some other bunch moving supplies. The war at that time had cooled off from the year before and the enemy was rebuilding.

At dawn I went down and got into my firing position. From this position I couldn't see any other members of the team. I had beef jerky for breakfast, then assembled the Anschutz and loaded it with the exploding bullet. My mouth was dry. I felt anxious, but clearheaded. This was not just another job. Five guys were about to knock off the enemy's biggest general. And the gods had chosen me to pull the trigger.

0600 came, then 0700, then 0730. No General Giap. No North Vietnamese. Nobody.

At 0815 a couple of peasants bending under a couple of big

sacks of rice came up the trail. They chattered with each other as they went. It was getting hot; even the monkeys and birds stopped screeching and hooting. At 0900, Lieutenant Fairweather crawled up next to me and said he'd been trying to reach headquarters, but couldn't. His breath smelled sour from the amphetamines. He was going to the top of the mountain to try again. He crawled away.

I waited. About noon I saw the silver vapor trails of a flight of B-52s heading north on a bombing run.

I ate more beef jerky and watched the clouds roll by. A yellowish brown bamboo viper slithered across my boot. Sweat rolled down my face. At 1400 Lieutenant Fairweather came back. He looked worried.

"Something's not right. They say they want us to hold our position until 1500 hours, then pull out."

"Why, what are we waiting for?"

"I don't know. Something's fucked up. I sent Jackson to have a look up the trail."

"They think the general is still coming?"

"I'm not sure he was ever coming."

He crawled back into the jungle. I sat and waited, getting angry. Another army screwup. The Three Stooges were running the war, I was sure of it. Still, I kept hoping the enemy column would appear any moment and I'd get my shot at Giap.

Suddenly I heard gunfire, maybe a mile to the east, up the trail, signaling my date with destiny had been canceled. If the general was on that trail, he'd be heading for cover. The mission was a bust.

I headed into the jungle, back up the mountainside. More rifle fire, closer now. I found the trail we'd come down and started running. Lieutenant Fairweather was coming toward me.

"Jackson's in trouble," he said. "He ran into twenty, thirty gooks heading our way. There's another gook patrol coming up from the village."

He turned and headed up the trail. Off to our right I could hear Smyth's M-60 firing in bursts. Then a grenade explosion. We raced up the mountain and around a clearing; on the other side we took up a firing position behind some fallen trees with some pretty good cover. Out of breath, we sucked air into our lungs.

Then Lieutenant Fairweather said, "Copperfield and Smyth are supposed to rendezvous with us here."

"I think we got to get the fuck out of here," I said. Just then a North Vietnamese regular came into the clearing. He was young and stupid. He waved at half a dozen others to follow him. They came in our direction. They hadn't seen us. I guess they figured they were ahead of us and were going to take cover where we had taken cover. I took aim at their leader with the sniper's rifle and pulled the trigger. His head burst like a water balloon.

Lieutenant Fairweather opened up with his M-16. He got four; the other two disappeared into the jungle. A moment later we heard more firing, then it was quiet.

"They must have run right into Copperfield and Smyth," I said.

"Yeah," he said. "Wonder who finished who."

One of the men Lieutenant Fairweather had shot lifted his head. I pulled off one shot with my M-16 and hit him between the eyes.

"Superb," Lieutenant Fairweather said.

Smyth came into the clearing. He had Copperfield over his shoulder and his M-60 under his arm. No pack, no ammo bag. Copperfield was riddled with bullets and obviously dead.

"Fuck," Lieutenant Fairweather said. He called to Smyth: "Over here!" Smyth lumbered up the hill. Lieutenant Fairweather

22

called Jackson on the radio and didn't get an answer. "We're pulling out, let's go." He turned to Smyth. "Leave him."

Smyth shook his head. "He's got a mother." Tears were coming down Smyth's face.

"You fall behind, we're not waiting for you," Lieutenant Fairweather said.

We moved up the mountain. Smyth fell behind. I told him to drop Copperfield, but he didn't. A half mile further up the trail, we lost sight of him. Ten minutes later, we heard gunfire.

"They must have got him," I said.

Lieutenant Fairweather didn't say anything; we just kept going. After a while, he said, "He deserved it. You don't owe any loyalty to a corpse. A corpse don't care."

When we got to the crest of the mountain, we heard a movement in the jungle beyond us. We dropped to the ground as machine guns suddenly opened up on us, bullets whizzing all around. We returned fire to make them keep their heads down, but the jungle was so thick we might as well have shot into the air. We were being fired on from the rear and both flanks. We sprayed bullets in all directions.

"All doors closed," I said.

I kept firing and slamming in clip after clip of ammo while Lieutenant Fairweather got on the radio. "Red Dog One, this is Rover, come in—"

"Keep shooting!" I said.

"Red Dog One, we need air support now!" He gave the map coordinates.

"They'll unload right on our heads," I said.

"You got a better idea?" he asked. I didn't. He called for the chopper and said we'd be at the pickup point in twenty minutes.

I just kept firing. A hand grenade sailed over our heads and exploded, knocking down a tree. Lieutenant Fairweather fired a whole clip in the direction it came from. "Come on, you mother-fuckers!" he cried. "We got enough for all of you!" He came to his knees, firing, bullets singing through the foliage above our heads.

"We ought to have company in about four more minutes," he said, throwing a grenade. We kept firing, but at that rate I figured our ammo might not last four minutes.

The enemy backed off and waited. They weren't stupid; they must have known that we would run out of ammo in no time. Then the F-4 Phantoms came in low and let go with rockets and suddenly the jungle all around thundered with rocket bursts. We got up and started running, pumping our legs as fast as we could. Trees fell around us. Flames everywhere. A piece of shrapnel caught me in the shoulder; I kept running.

We crested the mountain and fought our way through the thick foliage on the other side, bullets singing all around us. Suddenly Lieutenant Fairweather pitched forward. "I'm hit!"

I dropped down and fired blindly into the jungle behind us. I could hear the helicopter approaching half a mile away.

"Got me in the fucking lung," he said, coughing blood. "Get the fuck out of here, that's an order."

"Fuck you."

I grabbed hold of the back of his shirt and dragged him for maybe fifty yards, then lifted him by the waist and got him up over my shoulder. My other shoulder where I'd taken the shrap-nel hurt like hell, but I still had the strength in my legs. I kept moving.

The chopper swooped in low and I dumped Lieutenant Fairweather aboard. The door gunner on my side grabbed my collar and dragged me on board with one hand while spraying the brush with quick bursts from his M-60 with the other. The chopper took off in a cloud of cordite as both gunners chewed the trees and brush.

There was a medic on the chopper, who got to work on Lieutenant Fairweather. I lay back and smoked, happy as hell to have a ride, thinking about nothing except how good it was to be out of there.

They had a field hospital at Gau Li that wasn't much, but they patched me up okay. Lieutenant Fairweather was sent to a hospital ship. I didn't get a chance to talk to him.

I took a little R and R in Saigon before returning to my SOG unit. Saigon always depressed me. Too many whores, petty thieves, con artists. Too many off-duty GI paper pushers.

I was in the bar of the Quison Hotel getting loaded the night before I was shipping out when I saw Lieutenant Fairweather come in. He looked pale and shaky on his feet, like he might keel over if he didn't get back to his hospital bed. He came over to the bar and told the whore I'd been talking with to get lost. Then he climbed on the stool and ordered a beer.

"You look like you ought to be in bed," I said.

"I excused myself from that for a few days. Did you hear about Jackson?"

"No."

"He made it. All on his own. Got shot up pretty bad, but he made it back. Took him six days."

"He had the look of a survivor."

The bartender gave him his beer. He took a sip. "I was a fucking fool," he said.

"How's that?"

"I actually believed in this fucking war."

"It's your country's war, you've got to believe in it."

"Fuck my country."

"Something eating you, Lieutenant?"

"I've been doing some checking. Found out what our fucking bullshit mission was all about. There was an intelligence leak someplace up there at Gau Li. A colonel named Willows had this scheme to track it down. He made a few deliberate leaks just to see what would happen. Seems that the chopper pilot who took us up there had a Vietnamese girlfriend he was shacking up with. She was feeding info to the VC."

"So there never was going to be any encounter with Giap?" I asked.

"Giap is in Hanoi."

I took a drink. I didn't say anything.

"Well?" he said.

"Well what?"

"What are you going to do about it?"

"What do you mean?"

"We were royally fucked over. You just going to sit there and take it?"

"Okay, we were fucked over. They needed to get a spy. They got the spy. We were used. Isn't that what we're here for? To be used?"

"I don't look at it that way."

"How do you look at it?"

"Personal. I'll tell you something else. Colonel Willows is not in Gau Li; he's right here in Saigon, staying on the Rue de Bonaparte. Now, what do you say, Sergeant?"

"Why should I care?"

"Because he's got to pay. Nobody fucks me over, nobody."

"I say let it go, Lieutenant. It's over."

He signaled the bartender to bring me another beer, and left a bill on the bar. "Enjoy," he said, and walked away. He didn't mention anything about me saving his life.

The next day everyone was talking about it. A Colonel

Willows had been lured to a seedy hotel by a VC whore—at least everyone assumed she was a VC whore. Colonel Willows had been tied down to a bed, his voice box cut out so he couldn't scream, and his belly opened with a knife. He was just left there.

The famous Saigon sewer rats did the rest.

After Langston and Vanders's visit, Prince kept rubbing against my leg as if he could sense I was scared and wanted me to know I wasn't alone. I scrambled up a couple of eggs and made some toast and strong black coffee. I gave Prince a piece of raw steak and two doggie biscuits for dessert. The damn dog was spoiled rotten.

After breakfast I cleaned the two automatics I'd picked up in the driveway. Langston's was a 9mm Steyr GB, a double-action gas-operated job that carried eighteen rounds. Vanders's was a cheap seven-shot Walther PPK/S. I hid them away in a dry spot under a floorboard. Next, I cleaned the rifle and replaced it on the rack in my bedroom and put the shells back in the drawer.

Then I put on a heavy slicker, left Prince in the house, and drove over to Amber in a torrential downpour.

I figured I had to somehow get word to Gray Wolf and make him understand that I was out of the business for good and no matter how much money they threw at me I wasn't coming back. I figured if he got such a message, he would know I wouldn't say so unless I meant it. If I was going to come and get him, I'd just come. After all the years we'd worked together, he ought to know that much about me.

The problem was, I had no idea how to get hold of him. Players aren't exactly listed in the phone book. There weren't many people in the world he would trust. One of them was Cindy Ferris. He loved her. And she loved him.

She didn't know him as Gray Wolf, of course. His cover name was Gary Strong when he met her and that's the name she knew him by. He told her his old man was rich and had left him a bundle, so all he had to do was clip coupons and live it up. She bought his story too, because of the kind of guy he was. He acted like a goddamn playboy most of the time. He had a wild sense of humor, like a teenage kid, and you'd never have guessed in a million years what he did for a living.

He and I and a guy name of Philbin had rented a house out on Long Island one summer, some years back. We'd been doing some training of Contras down in Honduras and were taking a three-month leave. Gray Wolf was using his Gary Strong cover and I was Jake Mann. Cindy's husband, Wilbur, a famous Jewish comedian, was always off someplace. Vegas. L.A. Doing a show for the Community Chest. Cindy had salt-and-pepper hair and a big bust, and Gray Wolf later said she loved to make love until they both passed out from exhaustion.

When Gray Wolf met her she was just this housewife type, mousy and quiet. She lived to serve her husband and her kid, and the limits of her world didn't go much further than her hedgerow. Gray Wolf at first told me she was just another broad to him, but he would pace up and down all day when the comedian was home and he couldn't see her, grinding his fist into the palm of his hand. He went nutty over her, a goddamn mousy housewife who drank too much and giggled too much and didn't have a brain that you could detect with a microscope. Philbin, the guy who was staying with us, reported the affair to the Exchange, who gave Gray Wolf a hard time about it and sent him off to goddamn Afghanistan for a year and a half. Gray Wolf fixed Philbin up later with this whore who had penicillin-resistant gonorrhea.

Even when we "went on tour" with an assignment, Cindy Ferris would see him from time to time. I could tell when she was around; he'd have a kind of kidlike smile on his face. It was against the rules when you were on assignment to fraternize with a civilian, but Gray Wolf didn't give a damn about the rules.

I thought maybe Cindy would know where he was and could get a message to him. I used the pay phone at the Arco station in Amber to call her down in Southampton.

The rain was coming down like Niagara against the phone booth and made it hard to hear. I could still remember her number. I was always good at remembering things. Cindy's husband answered and told me she'd taken off on him and he didn't know where the slut was. He sounded drunk. Eight o'clock in the morning and he was slurring his words. "Gone," he said. "Gone. Gone. Gone. Gone." I asked him if she could be with someone calling himself Gary Strong and he hung up on me, which I took to mean that's exactly where she was.

Then I called Frank Webb, an old pal of mine who worked for the Exchange. He'd been my control for fifteen years. Besides Gray Wolf, Frank Webb was the only man on earth I ever trusted. He said if his men didn't trust him, he was finished, that as long as I was straight with him, he'd be straight with me. We kept that pact all the years I worked for the Exchange.

I got through to him at his home in Atlantic City. He loved gambling, so when he came back to the States that's where he moved. He was supposedly retired, but I'd heard he was still doing recruiting for the Exchange, dreaming up game strategies and contingency plans, and maybe even directing some field operations.

A woman with a fluttery little voice answered Frank Webb's phone. Asian accent. I asked for Frank and was told he wasn't there. She said, "Call tomorrow in morning." Click.

I stood there for a moment, trying to think of someone else I might call, but no one came to mind. A sudden and inexplicable wave of fear broke over me. I was on the outside now, on my own.

I sat in the Bronco smoking cigarettes and watching the rain dance on the hood for a long time, while trying to think of somebody else I might turn to for help. Bob Carpano, a big-time gangster I knew who owed me one, could get me a safe house, but I really didn't want a safe house. I wanted to stay where I was.

I couldn't think of anyone else. I'd been pretty much a loner all these years. My instincts said run, but I didn't want to run. I wanted a settled-down life, not an endless chain of hotels and motels and safe houses, name changes, never getting to know another human being. Amber was my home now, and, by God, I wanted to stay and be left alone.

But I doubted the Exchange would leave me alone. If they wanted me to put Gray Wolf down bad enough, they'd keep the pressure on.

Soon they'd be sending someone else with another offer, more money maybe, and when that didn't work, then what would they do? Threats, maybe. Some rough stuff. Whatever they did, it wasn't going to work. I was not going to put Gray Wolf down for them, no matter what.

31

I tried to think the way they'd be thinking. They'd grab your mother and hold a gun to her head to make you do what they wanted you to do. Anything. There were no limits.

And then it occurred to me that as they turned up the pressure they'd want to know if the pressure was having any effect, so they'd need some way to find out what was going on with me. They'd need somebody to get close to me to report back. *Operation feedback control.* They were always careful to have operation feedback control. Now who could that someone be?

It would have to be somebody new in town. It couldn't be just a hiker or a hunter or skier passing through. If they lingered, I'd spot them. It would have to be somebody living here, but they couldn't risk recruiting a longtime resident for a job like this. So it would be somebody new in town. Somebody who could get close to me. Somebody I'd want to get to know. The only person in town who fitted that description was the redhead I'd seen riding a bike the day before.

I drove over to Jenny's Diner. Jenny knew everybody in town and what they were up to.

Jenny's Diner was in a low, white, oblong building with a green composition roof. In late afternoon the rain had finally stopped. Inside, the place would seat maybe two dozen. There was a long counter with stools fixed to the floor and four tables with red-and-white checkered plastic tablecloths. It was overly warm inside, smelling of cigarette smoke, grease, coffee, and fuel oil.

I sat on one of the red vinyl-covered stools at the counter. Nobody else was in the place. The calendar on the wall said it was October twenty-first, but it was actually the twenty-fourth. People in Amber didn't give a damn about the date. They were perfectly content to let time—and the world—go by. That was okay by me. Nothing in the world I wanted more.

Jenny poured me some coffee.

I tasted the coffee from the heavy mug. Hot, strong, and bitter—as usual. Jenny was a washed-out blonde, forty maybe, a little on the heavy side. Rumor had it her husband beat her. If he did, she didn't seem to mind. Her pact with life said she would take what comes, good or bad, and she'd keep smiling.

"Say, Jenny," I said, "you happen to know a young woman, about thirty, red hair, rides a bike?"

She glanced back over her shoulder. "Freckles? Pretty? New in town?"

"Sounds like her."

"I know who she is," she said, brushing a lock of hair out of her eyes. "Her name is, let's see—Meredith. Meredith Keller-man. She rented a place out on the Hollow Road, right behind you on the other side of the old quarry. The old Brewster place. She's working with the theater people up at the crossing, helping them to put on plays. It's mostly for the skiers. Nobody around here goes to see dumb plays, not when they can just drive over to Heather Glen and go to the movies. Or rent them at the video store." She deftly flipped a pancake. "Any particular reason you're askin'?"

"No particular reason."

She said, "Them theater people go to Willy and Martha's most every night, oh, about ten. Seen them in there myself." She said it with a wink. I guess she thought I had romance in mind. I didn't.

I arrived at Willy and Martha's place a little before ten that evening. It smelled of peanuts and cigarette smoke; it was dim and warm and friendly. A long bar with a brass rail ran toward the back along the left side wall. The floors were bare and worn and marked with a million cigarette burns. An old stuffed brown bear stood in the corner. Nobody ever sat near it because it smelled musty and looked vicious. The jukebox played only country and western music, Willie Nelson, Hank Williams, Jr., Loretta Lynn—the old-timers. In the back room sat the best coin-operated pool table in the state, or so Martha and Willy claimed.

Willy was behind the bar. He was in his midthirties, tall, thin as a corn stalk, and had a stringy beard that he liked to tug on when he talked. And he liked to talk. He especially loved politics. He liked things aesthetically pleasing, he often said, and he found most things politicians did, like sending arms to the Contras, not very pleasing at all. An amusing guy. I never told him I knew some Contras, way back when Eden Pastora was with them, before the CIA tried to blow him up. Willy had it right. The Contras were evil people.

Willy's wife, Martha, was younger, dark and pretty, vivacious, and opinionated. Willy had been a poet, and Martha an artist, down in New York City, but there wasn't a hell of a lot of market for poetry that nobody can figure out and pictures that look like cat puke. So when Willy's uncle died and left them a chunk of money, they moved to Amber and bought a bar.

I took a seat in a booth by the front door. One of Martha's cat-puke paintings, entitled *Lust*, hung on the wall above the table. Two other customers huddled together at one end of the bar watching a cop show on TV, and a solitary woman sat at the other end sipping dark wine from a beer glass and talking to Willy. She nodded in my direction. I nodded back. I had a nodding acquaintanceship with most everyone in town. I'd been there since spring and they were beginning to think of me as one of them.

I was halfway through a pitcher of beer when Meredith Kellerman arrived. She wore a sheepskin coat and jeans and had her flaming red hair in a ponytail. She came in with two young guys, the three of them chatting and laughing. She didn't seem to notice me.

I knew right away the two guys with her weren't locals. One wore a tweed sport coat with a turtleneck and jeans and wire-rimmed glasses. Tall and intelligent-looking, he kept his head cocked back, superior as hell. The other one was shorter, in stylish baggy pants and wrinkled shirt, and had a dark cigarette dangling from his mouth.

The three of them went back to the poolroom. Martha followed them in with a pitcher of beer. The doorway to the back room was wide and I could see most of the pool table.

The tall, superior one racked the balls, and Meredith Kellerman took a look around and that's when she spotted me and looked surprised for a moment. Then she smiled thinly and turned back to the table, chalking her cue stick as if she knew how to do it. She bent over the table and stroked the ball with finesse and a self-assured air. She sure didn't seem like someone who'd be happy long in a little nowhere berg like Amber.

Working at a playhouse? Maybe. But doubtful.

She seemed to be the kind of woman who was good at attracting men. And the Exchange would know what kind of a woman I'd find irresistible. Here she was, as perfect as if she'd stepped right out of my imagination.

I watched her intently. She never glanced in my direction; she didn't seem nervous, she was just playing a game of pool and having a beer. I loved the way she got serious when it was her time to shoot. The way she kidded the guys when she ran a dozen balls in a row. The way she threw her head back when she laughed. The way she feigned despair when she missed a shot. The three played for an hour.

A couple of locals came in, laughing about one of them falling on his ass when he got out of the car. He'd torn his pants and everybody thought this was just a riot. The guys watching TV turned up the sound to drown them out. Willy quieted everyone down after a couple of minutes. Meredith Kellerman and her two friends finished playing and came out into the main barroom and sat down at a table, laughing and chatting and ribbing one another. The two men looked glum. I guess she'd beaten the pants off them.

Then the three of them got up and put on their coats and headed toward the front door. She broke away from her friends and angled over to me. Damn, if she didn't look good. Her freckles seemed like specks of cinnamon in the soft light.

"You're the man with the Ford Bronco, aren't you? You've got a black dog?"

I nodded. "Prince, his name is. I'm Tom Croft."

"Did you enjoy watching my ass?" She said this with a smile, joking around.

"I enjoyed it very much."

"It's nice to meet a connoisseur." She put out her hand and we shook. "Meredith Kellerman. I rented a house behind you— I'm moving in my stuff tomorrow actually. I guess we'll be neighbors. Stop by sometime."

"Might do that."

If she had been sent, she was doing it all wrong. She should be coy, letting me come to her, not the other way around. But maybe she figured if she did play it coy, I'd be even more suspicious of her. She didn't turn away from my steady gaze.

"Nice meeting you, Mr. Croft."

"Nice meeting you, Miss Kellerman."

She said goodnight to Willy and Martha and then went out with her friends.

She left a hint of perfume—faintly like jasmine—behind.

I stayed up late that night pacing in the living room, drinking scotch, watching the shadows of the flames from the fire in the stove dance on the walls. I couldn't get Meredith Kellerman out of my mind. Her arrival was too coincidental to be just chance. Her invitation to stop by was too . . . too unlikely. It wasn't just a neighborly invitation. She really wanted to get to know me.

She was with the Exchange all right, I thought. She was a player for sure.

I kept telling myself it was a certainty, although a part of me was hoping that she was just a civilian, just someone who happened to move into town, and I just happened to find her attractive.

37

How she looked, how she moved, how she spoke and threw her head back when she laughed, the easy, professional way she held a pool cue, the way her hair flew out behind her when she rode the bike—everything about her kept replaying in my mind as I searched for clues that would give her away, prove beyond a doubt she was a player.

After a while it occurred to me maybe she wasn't with the Exchange, maybe somebody else had sent her for quite another reason. Maybe Gray Wolf had sent her to check me out, I thought, to find out if I was a threat to him. She might even have been sent to set me up for a wet job.

A "wet job" is the euphemism players use for a killing.

Whoever she was, I had to know one way or the other.

I finally crawled into bed after three and slept fitfully until after eight. As soon as I'd fed Prince, I put on a pair of boots, my jacket, and a poncho and headed up the trail that ran behind my house. I took Prince with me.

I also took Langston's gun.

I walked east through a pine woods. Prince went off sniffing after a rabbit or some damn thing, barking happily as he went. I crossed over a barbed-wire fence and headed down the long hill to the Brewster place, which was Meredith Kellerman's now. I kept looking back over my shoulder. The woods were misted, as if the trees were giving off steam. The pine smell was strong and fresh in the air; the ground was soft and mud stuck to my boots.

It gives you a damn peculiar feeling thinking maybe a killer is stalking you. I'd once had a problem with the Bulgarians. They were mad over a little matter of one of the cryptography clerks who had been feeding me information during her lunch hour in a lavish private room in back of a butcher shop across from her embassy. They dispatched a top hit man name of Druzhien to get me. He chased me around Turkey for four days. When he caught up with me I was holed up in Istanbul in an old hotel in the old town along the canal. I watched him come in from the street, then I climbed into an old trunk and lay on my back in the dark. He figured I'd skipped out and he was looking for some clue as to where I might have gone. When he opened the trunk his eyes flashed open like he'd just found a live snake. I shot him in the middle of his forehead and dumped his body that night in the black waters of the Bosphorus and watched it float out into the Sea of Marmara.

They sent another guy after that, but Gray Wolf intercepted him at Haidarpasa Railway Station and garotted him. The Bulgarians gave it up. Their cryptographer clerk is now a computer programmer in Oshkosh, Wisconsin.

Okay, so I dumped Druzhien without working up a sweat, but I was young then, and quick, and now I'm forty-three, I thought, and not so quick, and Gray Wolf is a bigger load than Druzhien. And back in the old days I thought of it as a game, and I was the best, except for maybe Gray Wolf, and when you think like that, like you're James Bond or Superman, and you don't get jittery, your bravado is a cloak of invincibility. I haven't had any bravado for a long, long time.

I walked along some limestone cliffs at the back of an old quarry. Kids from town had etched their names and slogans and messages on the rocks. Immortality was now theirs: *Kim '58. B.J. loves K.T. Nixon sucks bricks.* Nice to know something is permanent. But I guess in a few millennia even these rocks will be melted away by the rain. Maybe a few millennia of fame is enough.

The cool mist felt good against my face. I was headed downhill now, through a little stand of birch trees half naked of leaves and looking miserable in the cold.

The path came out behind the old Brewster place, which

was surrounded by high, overgrown bushes. It was a small old frame house, with peeling white clapboard walls, big old windows, a gabled front porch, and a garage out back that leaned twenty degrees. Like most places around Amber, there was no grass, just weeds and pine needles and piles of leaves.

Cogswell Brewster had been something of a legend around Amber, a cranky old devil who lived alone for thirty years. He told everyone his wife, Agnes, had run off with a liquor salesman, but most people around Amber believed he killed her. He was never charged with anything, though, and Agnes Brewster never showed up again, alive or dead.

A thin wisp of smoke wafted out of the chimney and sat like a cloud over the house. I came down a path through the brambles along the side of the house and found Meredith Kellerman unloading boxes of household goods from an old yellow VW bus. She was wearing a green slicker and her shining red hair had been matted flat by the rain, but working in the drizzle didn't seem to bother her any. She sang "Puff the Magic Dragon" as she worked.

She suddenly stopped singing, bent over a box of pots and pans. Her back was to me. She straightened up, spun around, and looked right at me like somehow she knew I was there. She didn't look startled or even surprised. She just smiled. She had a player's cool, all right.

"Hello, Mr. Croft."

"Hello."

"I was just about to take a break and have some coffee, would you care to join me?"

"Sure," I said, approaching her. "Why don't you get the coffee going, I'll get this stuff."

"Let's both do it."

She and I carried in several loads of dishes and pots and pans and knickknacks and boxes of art supplies.

Her place seemed slightly larger than mine, with high-beamed ceilings. A couple of circular windows had stained glass in them, rather crude, but they gave the place a kind of old-fashioned charm. Meredith Kellerman's household goods, most of them anyway, were still in boxes in the living room. She had a lot of paints, brushes, canvasses, drawing pads, and the like. If this was just a cover ID, the Exchange had done a good job getting her ready.

Despite the fire in the kitchen stove, the place felt cold and damp, and I thought of poor Agnes Brewster, who was probably buried under the floorboards. If Meredith Kellerman was here to do a wet job on me, I might just end up under the floorboards myself, I thought.

When we had most everything in, she started getting the coffee ready while I finished up the last of the unloading. I managed a look at the registration of her vehicle in the glove box. It was registered to her at 110 A Hollis Road, Binghamton, New York.

I took the last load in and put it down in the living room. I took off my poncho and jacket and put Langston's automatic into my jacket pocket. Then I joined Meredith Kellerman in the kitchen.

The kitchen was cluttered, but the clutter looked a little better organized than the clutter in the living room and the room was warming nicely. Coffee perked on the stove; coffee cake baked in the oven. I took a seat at the kitchen table. She was busy setting out utensils and cream and sugar. She had put on a pair of red slacks and a pullover blouse, a white one with a wide collar. It wrapped tightly around her narrow waist and her breasts and I found myself wanting her. No player in his right mind would think such a thing, but still I wanted her the way a hungry man wants a blood-rare steak.

"The coffee's ready," she said. She poured me some into a heavy mug with a wide gold band around it. "Cream? Sugar?"

"Black," I said.

She poured herself some and sat down opposite me, piling up some cans of spices to make room. I was looking her over closely, searching for telltale clues that might give evidence as to who she really was. Most players, even women, have muscular shoulders from working out and martial arts. She didn't. She had a white spot on her left ring finger where she might have been wearing a wedding ring.

"You married?" I asked.

"No small talk for you, is there, Mr. Croft? You get right down to it."

"Sorry."

She smiled as if to say she wasn't really mad. Then she said, "Should I tell you where I lost my virginity? It was in a frat house at the University of Arizona. Alpha Phi Delta. The boy's name was Edgar. He's now an orthodontist."

I smiled. "Lucky guy, Edgar. I'm sorry, I didn't mean to pry."

"That's okay. I like being direct. I grew up riding horses, and with horses you have to always be very direct. It was good training for getting along with men. You have to kick a man sometimes, just like you have to kick a horse. And if you can't get the bit in the mouth, don't bother trying to get them to do what you want." She laughed.

She had a nice, easy way about her. Friendly and open. The guys in the Exchange personnel section really knew how to pick them, I thought.

42

She said, "Tell me about yourself. You're the town mystery man."

"Not much to tell," I said. "I used to be a wildcat oil man. Texas, Oklahoma, Mexico, Iran. I socked away a few bucks and now I'm retired."

She sipped some coffee, staring at me over the top of her coffee mug. "Rumor has it that you're some kind of gangster hiding out from the mob, or a spy hiding out from the CIA."

"Somebody's got a huge imagination," I said.

"I was hoping it were true. I've never met a spy. I was planning to wheedle all your secrets out of you."

"My big secret is, there is no big secret. What about you?"

She shrugged. "Not really much to tell. My maiden name was Todd, and I lived most of my life in a little town in Arizona. Bakerstown, outside Flagstaff. Could ride a horse when I was two and a half. Went to the University of Arizona, studied art at college, married a bad mistake named Larry Kellerman—who went back to Bakerstown and opened a photography shop. No kids. I'm free, white, thirty-one, and have a grant that pays me eight hundred and forty bucks a month to do scenery design for the Crossroad Players until next September, and that's all I plan to do."

She smiled her winning open smile, and her big brown eyes smiled too. If she was a player, she was the best. Nothing about her seemed out of place. She was perfect. Too perfect. I told myself the sensible thing to do was to go into the next room, get my gun out of my jacket, and use it to paint her brains all over the kitchen.

I did not do the sensible thing.

We finished our coffee and had some coffee cake hot from the oven, and then she showed me some charcoal drawings she'd made of some old men. They were good drawings, the kind that

give you a sense of the personality behind the face. I could see by
the look in her eyes that she was proud of them, and by the way
she turned the pages of her sketch pad, carefully, as if they were
fragile and valuable. She'd done the inside of Jenny's Diner;
she'd caught the friendliness of the place and I could almost hear
the hamburgers sizzling. She was an artist, it wasn't just a cover.
I began to think maybe she was real, but I quickly told myself
that was no way to think.

"I've got some work in oils boxed up," she said. "I'll dig
them out and show them to you if you'd like to see them."

"I've really got to be going."

I wanted to get started checking her out thoroughly. The
sooner I got started, the sooner I'd know. I put on my jacket and
poncho.

"I'm sorry," she said. "I forget sometimes that people aren't
quite so fascinated with my work as I am with showing it to
them."

"No, no, it's not that. I'd love to see more. I think your work
is wonderful. It's just that I've got some business to take care of."

"Why don't you stop by tomorrow? I'm off for a couple of
days. I could use the company."

"Okay, I'll do that."

She walked me to the door. "Come anytime, I'll be here
fixing the place up. But if I bore you with my work, you let me
know."

"I will. See you then."

I walked away calling for Prince, who showed up panting
and happy and full of burrs.

That afternoon I drove into Albany and for two hundred
bucks at a private detective's office I had a background check run
on Meredith Kellerman. The detective's office was huge and

bustling, with a half-dozen detectives and a dozen secretaries. They got what I wanted in half an hour, all by computer.

She had been a graduate student at SUNY, Binghamton; at least that's what the records indicated. But for a few bucks slipped into the eager palm of an underpaid clerk in a credit office, records can be manufactured. So I hired the detective to send a man to Binghamton and make sure she really had been a graduate student there.

And if she hadn't been?

That, I didn't want to think about.

The next morning it was clear, but cold and damp. I drove to the
Arco station and called Frank Webb. He answered the phone on
the first ring: "Yeah?"

"Tom Croft, Frank."

"Ole' Coldiron!"

"Not Coldiron any more, Frank. Just frail flesh."

"How's it goin'? How's the retirement? Bet you want to get
back in the saddle."

"I've got to see you, Frank."

A pause. "About our pal?"

"And other things."

"Where you at?"

"Upstate New York. I can be at your place this afternoon."

"I'll be waitin' on ya."

I took Prince with me and drove over to Route 28 and picked
up Interstate 87 south, down to where it becomes the New York

State Thruway in Albany. Along the way I thought about what a pile of manure I'd made out of my life.

I enlisted in the army when I was eighteen. I really had the fire then. Funny, but I could remember that day I signed up so vividly. I guess even then I knew that was the day that would determine my course for the rest of my life.

My father went with me and we were ushered into the recruiter's office. The recruiter, a gaunt, serious man, looked me over with his shrewd eyes and turned to my father and said: "He looks a little thin, to tell you the truth. I mean for the Special Forces."

My father nodded his large head and said: "Thin, but tough—was footballer in high school." His Hungarian accent was thick and he spoke slowly, leaning forward in his chair to get closer to the recruiter. "Tom, he made all-country two year. Tell him, Tom. How many yard you run?"

"Two thousand, nine hundred eighty-seven," I said. "Tailback for Central High. We won the championship last year."

I remember saying it matter-of-factly, calmly, letting the numbers speak for themselves. It was 1967, before the Tet Offensive, when everyone knew we'd kick ass in Vietnam and show the gooks who's boss. It was just another kind of football game.

The recruiter bit down on a pencil eraser, still eyeing me coldly. A slab of beef. I hoped the Clearasil covered the pimples on my chin. My sport coat pinched my shoulders, but I sat as erect as I could and didn't look away from the recruiter's cold stare. An air conditioner in a corner window rattled on while the recruiter filled out a form. It was hot outside, the hottest day in June on record, but the recruiter's office was as cool as death.

47

My father shifted his weight in his chair. He was wearing his best suit, a baggy brown one, and he had on a new tie, a red one with a floral pattern that looked oddly feminine. His collar was too tight and it gave his neck a bloated look. He was a barrel-chested man, stocky, and strong. "Look," he said to the recruiter. "We from Budapest. This boy, he throw a gas bomb at Russian tank. Six years old. Tell him, Tom. Tell them about your mother. He see tank crush her to dead. Tell him what you feel about Communists."

"I hate them," I said.

The recruiter smiled. He had a mess of medals and ribbons on his chest and stripes on his sleeves. I thought he must have killed a great number of Communists and I was in awe of him.

"Are you sure you want the Special Forces?" the recruiter said. "You can kill Communists in the infantry or artillery or armored. Every kid comes in here wants Special Forces— Special Forces, the elite, that's all I hear. Look, take the artillery. Kill Communists with a Howitzer. What's wrong with that? With a Howitzer you can kill them by the carload."

I know now he was having fun with me, but I didn't understand anything then. I hadn't been there and it was all in my imagination.

"I want to see their eyes when I do it to them," I said.

The recruiter looked startled. Then he smiled slowly and turned to my father and said, "Thin as he is, he will look good in a green beret."

And I could still remember him pulling out a manila folder and writing on the flap with a black marking pen: *Croft, Thomas C.*, which was the name I'd been using since coming to America. I remember how proud I was at that moment.

Thirteen weeks later I was sitting under a tree with Johnny-Lee Franks, a nineteen-year-old from Waco, Texas, having a smoke, when he got hit in the back of the head and the bullet came out his eye.

A few days after that we raided a Viet Cong training camp up in the Central Highlands. Four of us got sixteen VC with knives while they slept. Our knives were glued to our hands with blood and Johnny-Lee Franks was avenged and I thought I was a real mud-fucking bad ass. We celebrated with two sixpacks each of Budweiser the King of Beers when we got back to camp. Had a hell of a party.

Five and a half years after my father and I visited the army recruiter on that hot June day, I'd kicked a lot of ass and seen many men's eyes before I'd killed them, and collected a foot-locker full of medals.

I'd been to places like Apbia Mountain in the Ashau Valley, a mile from the Laotian border, where after the battle there was so much carnage they called it "Hamburger Hill" and even made a movie of it. I never saw the movie.

A month after we took it, the brass decided it wasn't such a prize after all, and we abandoned it to the Viet Cong. Later that year I was at the fire base at Ben Di that was under rocket and mortar attack for eighty-one straight days.

My body paid the price of glory. I collected shell fragments in my left leg and buttocks in early '68. I took pieces of a grenade in my right arm and neck during the Tet Offensive down on the Mekong Delta at Vinh Long, and suffered second-degree burns on my back when we got bombed one night with our own napalm. This was about the time Nixon and Kissinger were talking that peace-with-honor crap.

In January '73 I met Frank Webb in the officers' club at Bien-hoa, which was a huge army base. The officers' club was in a deep concrete-and-sandbag bunker and even had air conditioning. Jason Tanner, a full bird colonel I'd known a couple of

years, introduced Frank Webb to me and said I should get to
know him.

Webb, in his fifties then, stood six-three and was a muscular
two hundred pounds, broad-shouldered, raw-boned, and always
wore his fatigues buttoned to his neck and snakeskin cowboy
boots on his feet. He hunched a bit and had a habit of running his
finger along the side of his nose when he was thinking. His face
was red with perpetual sunburn and he sweated a lot in the sun.
He always had a half smile on his lips and a guarded look in his
eyes, but I liked him. He seemed to know what I was feeling and,
like me, he raged against the sellout.

I was between assignments at the time, doing some training
in the latest James Bondian night scopes and listening devices,
getting drunk a lot.

We did a lot of drinking together, Webb and I. He was
supposedly a journalist, but I never saw him taking notes or
asking questions of guys coming back from the fighting, so I
knew right from the start he was working for some intelligence
outfit or other, and I knew by the kinds of questions he'd slip into
a casual conversation that he was feeling me out. He wanted to
know if I subscribed to the principles of the Geneva Convention.
Then one night, after I'd known him a month or so, he asked me
over to his room at the Colonial Hotel. The hotel had been hit by a
rocket and was partially burned, but the rest of it was okay and
the food was good. He poured us both a drink and asked me to
have a seat.

"Got a question for ya, Tom." He had a hard Texas drawl and
a way of looking at you when he asked you something that seemed
to be searching out your soul.

"Ask away."

"What you figure on doin' when this is over?"

"Go home."

"And do what?"

I shrugged. I was casual about it, but the truth was I had no idea whatever. If the army didn't want me, I didn't know what I'd do. I never could see myself as a salesman, a truck driver, anything like that. I was a soldier, born and raised to fight, and that's all I knew or ever wanted to know.

"How you feel about carrying on the fight?"

"Don't get you."

"The global thing. This war ain't over. It's just beginnin'. There's Africa and Latin America, the Caribbean. Cambodia's about to blow sky high. Then Thailand, Burma. The Mideast ain't gonna settle down for two hundred years."

"Who are you? CIA? Defense Intelligence?"

"Fuck, no. Being some sorry-ass bureaucrat is no place to be. The Congress can get to those boys. The fucking liberals— Senator Church and his hatchet men—are fixing to get their teeth into those guys and tear their hearts out. We got something else going here, something Congress can't touch because we're gonna be like the wind, invisible. We're calling ourselves 'The Exchange.' We're exchanging defeat for victory. We're gonna open a new offensive, we're gonna reinvent warfare."

I didn't know what to say. I didn't quite believe it. After a moment, I said: "How you going to get funded?"

He shrugged. "We'll get a little here and a little there. Some government money's being sent our way out of the black Pentagon budget. Some private people are behind us. Big people. Don't you worry, you'll be paid eight hundred a week to start and you'll have a good pension. We're gonna take care of our boys. You interested?"

"What kind of action?"

"A little of this, a little of that." He winked.

I stared at him for a long moment. "You want a shooter, don't you?"

"You aren't against shooting your country's enemies are you?"

"We won't be at war."

"Nobody declared war here. Shit. I thought you was a man who kept the big picture in mind. That's why I'm talkin' to you. Right now we figure to be supplying and training freedom fighters from Nigeria to Tibet. If we gotta take some pro-Soviet politicians out along the way, we'll do it. If the CIA can't deal with something because of political sensitivities, we'll do it for them. Democracies can't wage war anymore. You got TV here, you bring it into people's homes, civilians can't take it. War's got to be taken out of the hands of the politicians. We know you're right for this, Tom. We know you want what we want—the total collapse of the Soviet Empire. You with us or not?"

"I've got seven months more to go on this hitch."

He reached into his pocket and took out some papers and slid them in front of me.

"Your discharge is all arranged, Tom. You sign on with us, you can quit anytime. We want our people to be with us because they want to be. All you got to do is sign right here and you're out of this shit."

I thought of the other recruiter and the day I'd seen him with my dad and how I'd felt like I wasn't a boy anymore. This was different. I was part of a defeated army, which is a terrible thing, like being a walking dead man.

"Tom," he said, "I promise you, if you go with us, we'll give you something better than money, better than promotions, better than anything."

"What's that?"

"We're going to make you feel like a man again, and proud to be an American."

With no sense of sin, I signed.

Prince and I crossed into New Jersey and got onto the Garden State Parkway going south, down through Newark and over to the Jersey shore, down past Shrewsbury, Long Branch, Asbury Park. We got off the parkway at Port Republic and drove on a narrow county road through green rolling hills over to Pomona, about ten miles north and west of Atlantic City.

I'd been to Frank Webb's house a dozen times. It was situated on a cul de sac in a heavily wooded suburban area; lots of fir trees growing around the house gave it a nice country feel. It was a large, gray-shingled house with white shutters. I parked the Bronco on the street and left Prince inside. He was lying down for his nap so he didn't seem to mind. A blast of wind off the Atlantic blew my jacket open. I started up the circular drive and heard, "Hey! Over here, boy!" It was Frank Webb, waving to me from a side door. I jogged up the drive and shook his hand, while he slapped me on the shoulder. "Good to see ya, boy! Come on in, it's freezing out here."

Frank Webb seemed as friendly and warm as ever, and genuinely glad to see me. His hair was snow white now and his drinking man's face was lined with tiny red veins. He still hunched a bit and he'd grown paunchy and dragged one foot because of an old war injury, which made him seem rather clumsy. He was seventy-three or -four now and looked it, with deep wrinkles and a pallid complexion. He was wearing a plaid shirt and jeans and snakeskin cowboy boots, just like he always had. It was all part of his country-boy facade, which was part theater, part comic book, part real.

I followed him through the kitchen, where an Asian woman, probably Vietnamese, with salt-and-pepper hair and wearing a green robe was vigorously chopping vegetables with a wide-bladed knife. I took her to be a servant, but she might have been his wife. Frank Webb had had four wives that I knew of, and treated them all like floor mats. The woman didn't look up from her work as we passed through.

The dining room and living room had no carpets. Chinese paintings covered the walls; they were mostly landscapes, the kind that show big mountains and rivers and tiny people. The furniture was old and heavy, Early American stuff. The place had a disorganized feeling to it, like people were just moving in and hadn't quite figured out where everything should go.

Webb showed me into his study and closed the door. The study was oak-paneled and messy. Books on the floor, the desk, the window ledge. He cleared the junk off a couple of leather-back swivel chairs and eased into one of them. He crossed his legs and ran his bony hand over the stubble on his cheeks. He said, "Tell me what's going down."

"Can we talk here?"

"Guy comes in and sweeps for bugs every day. Shielded walls in this room. Safe as anywheres."

I sat on the other chair and settled back. He was looking at me, waiting, his eyes searching my face. This was hard for me, asking for a favor.

"You wondering if I'm still your friend, even if you're out of the game, ain't ya?"

"That's not it, Frank."

"You got to trust me, you got nowhere to go and no place to hide, Coldiron. That's a fact."

"Got a visit from Langston."

An eyebrow went up, but he didn't say anything.

"He wants me to do a wet job on Gray Wolf. Says Gray Wolf'll be coming for me if I don't get him first."

Webb folded his hands on his lap, just staring off into space, thinking. Then he nodded. "If he got word you were lookin' to do him, he might come for you quick. What'd you say to Langston?"

"Told him no."

"What you want from me?"

"Can you get a message to Gray Wolf?"

"Me? How would I do that?" He flashed his innocent ole-country-boy expression.

"You know people, you've got contacts."

"You want him to know you ain't gunning for him, that it?"

I nodded.

He rubbed his chin, crossing his arms on his chest. Then he reached over on his desk and picked up a pipe and lit it, blowing blue-gray smoke toward the ceiling.

"Even if I could somehow get a message to him, I don't think I would, Tom. You ought to kill Gray Wolf. We've only had three agents defect in the history of the Exchange, and they all paid the full fare for the trip. Gray Wolf has got to be put down."

"But not by my hand."

He was quiet for a moment, then he said: "Would you like a bit of lunch, some tea?"

I shook my head.

His pipe was out. He relit it and a grin crossed his lips. "Gray Wolf was always a hoot, wasn't he?" Webb said. "Remember the time he put a live chicken in General Cummings's luggage? Fearless, he was. A player's player, though, I give him that." He sucked some more on his pipe and thought things over. "Look, you've had some time away from it now. Time to think it over. Time to be missing it just a tad. How about coming back into the fold and at least help us get him?"

"Nope. I came here as a friend, Frank, needing your help. You going to give it to me or aren't you?"

He looked me over for a few moments, then he shook his head slowly. "Gray Wolf knows what a loyal son of a bitch you are to the Exchange. He just might not believe it even if I could get a message to him."

"Coming from you, he'll believe it."

He smiled and nodded. "I'll see what I can do."

"I'll give you the number for Jenny's Diner up there in Amber. Leave a message there, Jenny'll send somebody out to let me know."

"You don't have a phone? Jesus Christ, man, next thing you'll be a Trappist monk."

"I can do without a telephone," I said with a grin, "but monks have to do without real essentials."

Frank Webb laughed.

"One more thing, Frank," I said. "There's a woman I met in this town where I've been staying. She calls herself Meredith Kellerman. Redhead, about thirty. Works for a little theater group. Came on to me friendly. Could you find out if the Exchange planted her to keep an eye on me?"

"The Exchange's got no cause to be worried about you, you ain't about to go over to the other side."

"Maybe for feedback control."

"Not possible."

"What makes you say that?"

"I know all the woman players—I teach tradecraft to the new people, and the Exchange doesn't have a redhead about thirty. She could be a free lance, but I doubt they'd use a free-lancer for that kind of duty, they couldn't control her backstory."

"See what you can find out anyway, okay, Frank?"

"Will do."

He walked me out to the car, putting his arm around my shoulder. "They wouldn't be bothering you, my friend, if they figured you were burned out. You're at the top of your skills. Maybe a little slower than you once was, but a whole lot smarter. You know what a good agent costs to recruit and train? They'd go way out into deep water to get you back."

"They're not getting me back, not now, not ever."

He just smiled like he goddamn knew better. Then he said, "If Gray Wolf has got it in his head to kill you, you better watch your ass. He's one deadly son of a bitch."

Frank Webb was right about Gray Wolf being a deadly son of a bitch.

Once, he was sent on a mission to the Greek Cyclades in the Aegean Sea, to a small, private island between Mílos and Santoríni. I was back in the States at the time being treated for an eye infection.

The Exchange had been working with a Greek gangster, Socrates Kronis, on a deal in Switzerland involving the theft of some rocket launchers to be dealt for a schematic of a Mig 25A the Iranians got hold of. The job was botched somehow and some Exchange men ended up sentenced to long stretches in a Swiss prison. Kronis blamed the Exchange, the Exchange blamed Kronis.

The Exchange sent an assault team of four men to Kronis's little island to inflict some pain on him. I don't know what their orders were. To pull his fingernails out or something. As it turned out, Kronis killed three of the Exchange men and took the fourth as a hostage. Kronis lost a couple of bodyguards in the shoot-out, but personally didn't get a scratch.

A week later, Kronis and a couple of big shots from the Exchange sat down under an acacia tree in a public park in Athens and made a peace treaty. Kronis agreed to give up his hostage, and in return the Exchange was to pay him one million dollars. Neither the hostage nor the million meant all that much to either the Exchange or to Kronis; the gesture was symbolic.

Gray Wolf and another Exchange man named Peterson arrived by speedboat from Cyprus one June morning with two million dollars in large bills in a red gym bag. They had no weapons. That was part of the deal. No weapons.

Gray Wolf and Peterson drank a skin of resin wine on the way and so arrived slightly drunk. They didn't expect this to be anything but a pick-up and delivery job. They pulled up to the small dock where a half dozen of Kronis's men met them. Kronis's men searched Gray Wolf, Peterson, and the boat. They were thorough men, some of whom had been smugglers and so they knew all the possible hiding places.

The leader of the six was a pint-sized, pale-faced man in his fifties. When they were through with their search, he said Gray Wolf and Peterson should follow him.

Gray Wolf said he'd rather not take the time to socialize, that he'd like to start back.

That's when they produced guns.

They forced Peterson to carry the bag of money up the long stone steps that went from the beach up the side of a white stone cliff. On top of the cliff was a sort of pasture, with sheep and donkeys grazing in the afternoon sun. Further up a small hill were a citrus orchard and an olive orchard. They went along a trail past the orchards and more pasture to a set of whitewashed buildings with red-tile roofs and blue doors. The cluster of buildings was surrounded by a whitewashed stone wall forming a small compound. From there, you could see the sea all around, shimmering blue-green in the afternoon sun. Peterson told me later it was a magnificent view, but he was too frightened at the time to appreciate it.

The little man told them to stop and sit down on the ground. Then the little man went into the compound, leaving Gray Wolf and Peterson to swelter in the sun. From inside the compound Gray Wolf and Peterson could hear a man shrieking.

After a while the gate opened and a man in a white suit and a broad-brimmed hat came out. He was followed by a group of perhaps eight to ten men. A couple of them were carrying the Exchange man, Conners. He'd been bullwhipped. His shirt was shredded and the flesh on his back had been peeled back to the bone. He was pale and shaking in shock.

The man in the white suit was Kronis. He was pudgy and dark complected, with a large bushy mustache and dark eyes full of malice. Gray Wolf smiled like nothing at all was wrong.

Kronis asked if he was Gray Wolf, also known as Gary Strong. Gray Wolf said he was. Kronis said he had heard of his exploits and knew of his reputation as one of the most feared players in the game. Gray Wolf thanked him with a bow.

Then Kronis gave a signal and his men grabbed hold of Gray Wolf and pushed his face into a bucket of pig shit one of the men had carried from the compound.

He did this to humiliate him, and to humiliate the Exchange. Peterson said Gray Wolf merely smiled at him, a forced smile with no warmth in it.

Kronis and his men all had a good laugh. They made Gray Wolf pick up Conners and take him to his boat. It was a twenty-six footer used for smuggling, a custom-made wood job with twin turbo charged engines, 180 horses each. Very fast. Gray Wolf and Peterson sped away with Conners. Kronis's men followed in their speedboat, but they couldn't keep up with them, so they turned back.

Soon the island vanished into a dot on the horizon. Gray Wolf cut the engines and checked on Conners. He was dead. Gray Wolf dumped his carcass overboard. Then washed the pig shit off his face, slowly, carefully, without speaking. Peterson told me he was more frightened in that moment than he had been sitting under the guns of Kronis's men. He said Gray Wolf's eyes were like a ferocious animal's, terrible to see.

Gray Wolf took a bottle of retsina out of a kit bag and opened it and drank half of it down and announced he was going back as soon as it was dark. Their boat was wood, he said; it would not be picked up on radar.

Peterson was a desk man, he'd had almost no field experience. Peterson protested, saying they had no weapons. Gray Wolf said no matter, he was going back and if Peterson didn't like it, he could swim for it.

Gray Wolf sat in the boat drinking wine and staring and not speaking until long after dark, then he got up and started the engine and headed back to the island. The last mile or so, they drifted on a friendly tide. They landed in a small, isolated cove and beached the boat. Gray Wolf told Peterson if he wasn't back by dawn to get the hell out of there and slipped away into the night.

There were at least twenty men on that island and most of them were hard cases, men in the rackets who knew guns and fighting, and were not easy marks.

Peterson waited and heard nothing but the sound of the waves for the next five and a half hours. Then he heard gunfire that lasted fifteen or twenty minutes. All was quiet again for another hour, then there was some more gunfire on and off for an hour. Forty-five minutes later Gray Wolf came limping back to the boat. He'd taken one in the arm and another in the shoulder. He had an assault rifle strapped to his back and was dragging the bucket of pig shit.

Kronis's head was in the bucket.

The day after I got back from seeing Frank Webb it turned colder. Snow clouds formed over the mountains to the north and east, and an icy wind drove the last remaining leaves of autumn from the trees. I loaded the woodbox in the back of the house from the three cords of wood I bought from the village woodsman for twenty-eight dollars a cord.

Just a few days before it had seemed like summer, and now it was winter and not yet November. The merchants would be happy. The skiers would be coming now in droves.

It started snowing just before noon, a fine dusting of it that looked like sprinkled sugar on the gold and red and brown leaves blanketing the ground around my house. I had little to do except to watch it snow and wait to hear from Frank Webb. I hung sheets over the windows as a precaution against getting sniped at, and took to carrying a gun. It didn't make me feel very safe.

At noon I ate a tuna sandwich sitting in the semidarkness, listening to a fire crackle in the Franklin stove. I had a small cognac and lit a cigarette. Prince came into the room and I patted him on the head and he went out again. Easy guy to please.

I started thinking about my predicament with Gray Wolf. It was the Benevides incident that ended my association with the Exchange. Something I normally wouldn't have even been involved in. It was the thing that woke me up and made me realize what I'd become.

I snatched Miguel Benevides one night when he was working late in this massive brick building where he worked for the Ministry of Defense of his goddamn mudhole of a country. He came out of the building about midnight, wearing a baggy suit with a vest. The vest was unbuttoned, his pot hung over his belt, a newspaper was tucked under his arm. I followed him. He took a green and gold streetcar at the corner, the last one of the day. I followed the streetcar for eight miles and saw Benevides get off. Then I drove around the block and waited for him to come walking by on a dark stretch of street. His street. I was close enough to his house to smell his wife's cooking.

Benevides was a procurement officer. A goddamn clerk. He was getting seventy American dollars a month from the CIA to sell his country's secrets, and he'd been delivering them as regularly as the Staten Island Ferry comes to Manhattan.

But what the hell, he had six kids and a procurement officer down there didn't make but fifty bucks a month American. Of course there were bribes from gun and tank manufacturers to supplement his salary and what we were paying him, and he lived a hell of a lot better than all but a tiny fraction of his countrymen. Miguel Benevides was corrupt as hell, but no more corrupt than any of the other fifty thousand bureaucrats in his banana republic who were on the take.

Over the years he gave the CIA plenty for their seventy bucks a month. But then one day he stopped selling, saying he thought his superiors had gotten suspicious. His superiors were probably on the take too, so why shouldn't they be suspicious? No, that wasn't the real reason. We knew the real reason: the Soviets had turned him. That's why I snatched him that warm June night.

I took him to a safe house, a filthy, dirt-floored, tin-roofed shack outside a small coastal town.

Benevides was small change, and ordinarily the Exchange

would have given the job to a new man, but the guy they had scheduled to do the job was caught running a printing press into Cuba and wasn't expected to return to duty. I'd just come off a job in a nearby country training men to work as urban combat teams—death squads, they're sometimes called—so I was available. I didn't care for interrogation, but orders were orders, so I did it.

Benevides was fifty, dull-witted, and corrupt down to his socks. We knew he'd sold a particular repair manual for an antiaircraft gun to the Soviets for fifty-five hundred bucks American money. I was supposed to get out of him the name of the agent he sold it to, where the drop was, and the like. The Exchange already knew most of this but wanted him to reveal the information to break him. To make him ours again.

When you break a man, that's what happens. He becomes yours. Totally and forever. It's a strange phenomenon. Once the will is broken, the man no longer has a will of his own, it is given to the men who break it. The Communist Chinese broke our men in Korea by the hundreds.

When I started interrogating him, I gave him a small burn with a cigar on the back of his pudgy hand. He messed his pants. He started to sweat. I thought he'd break in five minutes. But he didn't. He had it in his head that not betraying the agent who'd turned him was a matter of honor and he was a man of honor.

So I tied him to a chair and a young trainee from his country's secret police with a taste for this sort of work beat him with a riding crop. The trainee was a born sadist. He loved his work and had a natural talent for it. He knew by instinct how to deliver the most pain, and how to inflict the fear of its coming. After two days Benevides' face looked like a purple bag full of marbles. He said nothing. I called in an experienced technical assistant from the Exchange to give him electric shock, an old-timer who was bored with the whole process but knew what he was doing. Still Benevides would not break. His tongue turned black. He shook and sweated constantly and stunk like a rancid garbage can, but he would not break.

A strange thing happens when a man resists torture. He comes to have an affinity for his torturer. The psychologists try to explain it by saying that it's an escape mechanism or something. What they haven't explained is what sometimes happens to the man doing the torturing. He can come to feel his victim's pain. Everything that Benevides felt, I felt. Every time he screamed with terror, I felt the terror wash through my body.

I pleaded with him: "Damn it, Miguel, you sold out a thousand times to us! You've given us everything. How can you think of yourself as a man of honor?"

He gave me the twisted look a tortured man gives his tormentor. I could see in his eyes that he knew that if he gave in we would own his soul.

"You do not understand . . ."

"I don't understand what, Miguel?"

"You do not understand the first thing about what it is to be a man."

"Tell me," I said. "I want to understand."

"I sell information, but it was never anything you would not find out a hundred other ways."

"Okay, so what?"

"My family is large and I want an education for my children. But what you want now, this man's name, I will not give it. If I give it, you will kill him. I owe him silence. That is what you will get from me."

"You're being a fool, he would give you up in five seconds!"

"No matter, I will tell you nothing." He shut his eyes tight and would not look at me.

After that he refused to speak. I pleaded with him. I told him we already knew the man's name, so it didn't matter, we only wanted him to say it. I promised he could go home to his wife and children. The technician turned up the juice and put the wires on his testicles. Benevides opened his mouth and screamed until the tin roof shook, but when the current was turned off, he still would not speak. He took it again and again. After an hour or so, he choked on his thickened tongue and died.

That afternoon I fired off a telegram to the Exchange command notifying them that I was no longer in their employ.

A few days later I got together with Gray Wolf and tried to make him understand it.

We met in New Orleans, at the Andrew Jackson Hotel in the French Quarter. It was summer and hot. I remember his shirt was dripping with sweat as he paced up and down, as he tried to convince me that it just wouldn't be the same without me, that I couldn't run out on *him* like that.

That's what he said over and over, that I was running out on him.

I told him I wasn't running out on him, I just couldn't do it anymore, something had snapped in me. I'd gone off to war to fight the great evil of Communism and ended up in a dirty shack torturing a corrupt government clerk. He said I was an idiot, that we were a team, and half the team couldn't just quit. But I'd already made up my mind, I said. When you tell yourself you're no longer a player, that's it. You've lost your edge and you're done.

The next morning we had breakfast in a little restaurant on the Rue de Royal across from Preservation Hall. He came in wearing a new white suit with a white hat to match, one of those wide-brimmed southern-plantation-owner jobs. He dropped into the chair next to me, tilting his new hat on the back of his head, flashing his big toothy grin like I'd been forgiven everything, like he'd figured something out in the middle of the night and everything was going to be okay.

We ordered the spicy "Ragin' Cajun" omelet and coffee. While we ate he told me he had finally come to accept my decision and he wasn't going to bug me about it anymore. He wanted to know if I had enough money, where I was planning to go, and what I was planning to do. It was all so restrained and polite and not at all like Gray Wolf usually was around me.

When I got in the cab to go to the airport, he said that a player couldn't have a friend who isn't a player. Then he told the cabdriver to drive on.

In the shower I got to thinking about how things might have turned out differently if I'd taken other paths than the one I'd taken. I thought about Rita O'Tool, a woman I once knew. I hadn't even thought of Rita O'Tool in a long time. She was a redheaded Mex-Irish fireball who could drink and sing and dance all day and make love all night and be ready the next day for more of the same. Rita had big dreams for us. She wanted to marry me and settle down and raise corn and pigs and *chicos*. I was nuts about her, but at the time I was playing James Bond and hooked on the excitement. God, what an idiot I was.

I heard a knock at the back door and Prince started barking like hell.

I had Langston's automatic in a plastic bag hung around my neck. I drew the gun out, rolled out of the shower, and opened the window to a blast of cold air. Meredith Kellerman was standing on the small back porch in a green parka, hands in her pockets, exhaling puffs of vapor. She had no hat or earmuffs on. Snow was blowing around her like a veil.

I yelled at Prince to shut up. He did, even though he gave one last yelp to keep his self-respect.

Meredith Kellerman said, "Have I come at a bad time?"

"I'm sort of in the shower."

I thought she might say she was sorry to have interrupted me and she'd go away. But she didn't move. She just stood there shivering and looking at me with those brown eyes, smiling. After a long moment, she said, "If you ask me in, I'll promise not to jump you." She rubbed her hands together.

She looked damn good standing there with bright red cheeks. But even though Frank Webb said she wasn't with the Exchange, I still couldn't be sure. They could have a parallel organization he knew nothing about. Or she could be a player on somebody else's team. Or maybe she was who she said she was.

I knew it was dangerous, but I figured maybe I ought to let her play her hand and see what cards she had. No cover was perfect. I figured she'd trip herself up someplace and then I'd blow her backstory wide open.

I said, "Be just a minute."

I slipped on a robe and went into the living room and checked the street. No footprints in the fresh snow. No tire tracks. She must have walked over the hill from the back side. I checked both sides of the house. Nobody else around. I stashed the gun under the floorboards, then I opened the door.

"What's going on in here?" she said, patting the dog. "So dark!"

"I was taking a nap," I said lamely. "I didn't sleep well last night." I pulled the sheets off the front window and threw some more wood into the stove.

She took off her parka and tossed it on the couch. "Cozy little place," she said. "Typical bachelor digs. Messy."

"Prince and me call it 'manly.'" I was trying to be goddamn witty, but it probably sounded dumb as hell.

She laughed. She seemed amused.

"I'll get dressed," I said.

I went into the bedroom and put on some underwear, jeans, a T-shirt, a bulky sweater, heavy wool socks, and some shoes, and ran a comb through my hair, then went back out into the living room. She was sitting on the couch leafing through a biography of Napoleon Bonaparte. Gray Wolf gave it to me years back. He loved Bonaparte.

"'Men are moved by two levers only'—according to Napoleon," I said. "Fear and self-interest."

"Not the men I know," she said. "Their levers are located elsewhere. Maybe he should have asked a woman, women know what moves men."

"Bonaparte didn't think much of women. He said they were machines for making babies. He said it would be a merciful deed by a protective divinity to rid us of love—something like that."

She put the book down and said, "I wouldn't have figured you for a bookworm."

"I'm no bookworm, but I have spent a lot of time in hotel rooms and I can't stand TV, so I read. Want some coffee?"

"No thanks. I've come to ask you a question." She dropped the book on the stack next to the couch.

"What question?"

"What was it I said or did that made you rush off the other day?"

"I had an appointment, that's all. I suddenly remembered it." I knew that sounded goddamn lame.

"Let's have a brief review of our relationship, all right? The

70

first time I lay eyes on you you are admiring my *gluteus maximus* out there on the Creek Road, and when I see you that night at the bar and I accuse you of same, you do not wilt and deny it like most of the termite brains that inhabit these woods would. You are obviously a man of the world, well traveled, got a little tread worn off, but what the hell. I think to myself, well now, here's someone I'd like to get to know. And I think you were thinking the same about me."

"I was," I admitted.

"So when you came over and helped me move my stuff in, I said to myself, hey, gee, he just might like something about me besides my bottom, and so I ask you in, we sip a little coffee, exchange pleasantries, start to get to know each other a little bit, and then like Marley's ghost, whoosh, you've vanished. Now I must have said something. Was I coming on too strong, is that it?"

"I don't think you were coming on at all."

"You just aren't used to opening up to women, is that it?"

"Nothing of the sort. I just had to go make a phone call. An important personal matter. Really."

"Then you said you'd be over yesterday. But you didn't come."

"I was out of town. Something's come up. I'm having a few problems—nothing I can't handle, but they do need my attention."

"Well, okay." She stood up suddenly and reached for her parka.

"Hold it, hold on there," I said. "What's the matter?"

She crossed her arms and stood with her legs apart, looking at me. "You want to know what I think? I think you're attracted to me, but you don't want to have anything to do with me because you're an emotional basket case. You're afraid of letting yourself become involved, probably because you've been burned recently."

She couldn't have been further off the mark if she'd been aiming for the stars and hit her foot. But I nodded and said, "You're right."

"I knew it," she said, with an easy smile. She brushed her hair back from her forehead. "As soon as I saw you, I knew that you'd been damaged. For a long time I felt just the way you're feeling. I didn't want to have anything to do with a relationship. But life is meant to be lived. I don't know about you, but I have to be with people. What do you say, let's be friends?"

She put out her hand and I shook it. Then she looked at me sharply for a long moment. "Oh no, I had you all wrong, didn't I?"

"What do you mean?"

"You never got burned by a woman in your life. At least not recently."

"Do you probe everyone's psyche like this?"

"Not everyone's, just the ones that interest me." She shook her head like I was just too much of a problem to unravel. "Oh, well, give me time, I'll get it right. In the meantime, let's take a drive up to Blue Mountain, I know a great place to have lunch. They call it a bistro, but it's really a hamburger joint. The greasiest french fries in the Adirondacks." She had a gleam in her eye, a devilish gleam for liking greasy french fries.

"Okay," I said. "What could be better than a greasy french fry on a cold afternoon?"

We left Prince there with a canful of dog food and a full water dish, which irked him a bit. He wanted to go. He started whining and yapping as soon as he saw me get out the can opener. I went into the bedroom and got on my scarf, knit cap, and sheepskin coat.

The coat had a big pocket I had especially made to hold a gun and that's where I put Langston's automatic.

It was snowing harder as we headed north on Route 28, like in a Bing Crosby Christmas movie. Big flat flakes swirling down to earth. I drove the Bronco and she sat in the passenger's seat huddled in her green parka. She had a little blackberry brandy in a silver flask and we passed it back and forth. I said we had to get it straight right off the bat that I was a smoker and if she didn't like it, she better not nag me to quit. I said I'd divorced five wives over the issue already.

She said she liked a man who smoked; it showed a recklessness, even fearlessness, in the face of an almost certain, hideous death. She laughed.

"You put it that way, it does sound courageous," I said.

"Anyone can quit," she said. "It takes a remarkable person to persist in his pleasures in the face of statistical certainty."

"Absolutely," I said. I took another drink of blackberry brandy.

On the way to the bistro, we stopped by the little theater where she'd been working as a set designer. I guess she was proud of it and wanted me to see it. The place was on a corner lot at the crossroads just outside Heather Glen. Nothing else there. The old Cities Service Station across the way had been boarded up for years. The playhouse itself was once a one-room school. It was white and had a bell tower and was set back from the road a little ways up a hillside surrounded by scattered pines and kids' swings and teeter-totters. We had to trudge through ankle-deep snow to get to the place.

Inside, it was cold, musty. Folding chairs, maybe fifty of them, filled about half the room. No curtains or blinds on the tall narrow windows. In the center of the room stood an old-fashioned Franklin stove and a stack of wood. The stage wasn't even a stage; it wasn't elevated at all, it was simply the front of the room, blocked off now by a large, purple curtain.

"Performances on weekends only," she said.

"What's the play?"

"It's called *The Meaning of Death*."

"Not a comedy," I said.

"You're right about that. Would you care to see my design?"

"Sure."

"Wait right there." I waited. I was standing in the center aisle near the Franklin stove. She disappeared behind the purple curtain. After a moment she called: "You ready?"

"Ready."

Suddenly the curtain shot open to reveal the image of a man pointing a gun at me. I dropped to one knee as I drew my gun and started to squeeze the trigger—but caught myself in time and slipped it back inside my jacket before Meredith saw it.

It wasn't an assassin. It wasn't even a man. It was a horrible figure on the backdrop of the set. The figure was kneeling with a spear of some kind aimed outward, toward me. The figure's face was not quite a living man's, and not quite a skull, but rather a mixture of the two, with an angry, demonic expression. It was lit from the rear, giving it the illusion of depth, so that viewed in a certain way the face seemed alive, alive and feminine, and darkly beautiful.

Meredith came out from behind the curtain. "Well, how do you like Herman?"

I said, "It's frightening. Yet it's so beautiful."

She came over to me and took hold of my arm. "I wanted you to see it because it's going to come down. The director thinks all the audience is seeing is my pal here, and not the play."

"I say 'so what?' "

She touched her finger to my cheek. "You know, you're sweating. Are you all right?"

"Jungle fever," I said. "Had it since I was a boy."

"No, really, what's the matter?"

"I'm ravenously hungry, that's what's the matter."

She studied me for a moment and I knew she didn't buy it, but finally she smiled and said, "I'm hungry too. Let's get out of here."

The Olde English Bistro you'd think would be in Tudor style with leaded windows, shutters, something like that. No chance. It was a cinder block building sitting close to the road. We pulled up at a little after two in the afternoon; the wind had picked up and turned nasty, swirling the snow into a frenzy.

Inside the bistro were a few rough-hewn tables coated with polyethylene. The waitress was a perky blonde dressed in ruffles and a low-cut blouse, lots of cleavage. She took our order on a pad, her lips moving as she wrote. I ordered the "Beefburger Surprise," which promised mushrooms galore, and Meredith chose the "Mountaineer," which was topped with blue cheese. We both ordered beer and french fries. We were the only customers in the place. A huge kid's drawing of a witch and a pumpkin covered one wall. Halloween was a week away and already it was snowing.

"I finally figured you out," she said.

"Oh?"

"You're in the government protected witness program. You're a Mafia kingpin turned against your former cronies."

"You got me." I made my fist into a gun and pulled the imaginary trigger.

She smiled. "Everyone loves a mystery. And everyone is entitled to their secrets. That's what makes people so interesting. 'The proper thing for man to study is man,' or something like that. Alexander Pope. Ever read Pope?"

"Never heard of him."

"What college did you go to?"

"Never went to college."

She smiled at that like she didn't believe me. "Funny, you look like a professor."

"So I've been told."

"Are you a writer, or something like that?"

"Sorry—nothing like that."

"Do you call intellectuals 'eggheads?' " she asked. "My father never said the word 'intellectual' in his life without prefacing it with 'so-called.' "

"Smart man, your father."

"Do you ski?"

"No."

"You should try it, it's exhilarating."

"I've had enough exhilaration in my life."

"Were you in Vietnam?"

"I was."

"In the thick of it?"

"The thickest of the thick."

"Still have flashbacks?"

"No flashbacks."

"Would you like to kiss me?" She smiled an impish kind of smile.

I looked around. The waitress had vanished. "What makes you think I'd like to kiss you?"

"You wouldn't like to kiss me?"

"I didn't say that." She had me feeling like an adolescent

76

again. I took a cigarette out and started tapping it on the table to pack the tobacco tighter.

"Well, would you like to kiss me, or wouldn't you like to kiss me?" She leaned over and rested her chin on her hand, grinning.

I kissed her. Supple, sweet, soft. I drew back; she kept her eyes closed. "You'll do," she said.

"Do you give grades?"

"B+. How was I?"

"I'm still evaluating."

"I want to know everything you ever did and every place you've ever been," she said, sitting up straight. "Where would you like to start? How about Vietnam? What was it like?"

"Bam, bam, bam, whoosh, boom, boom, boom."

"That's all?"

"That's all I remember."

"Did you get wounded?"

"A little."

Her eyebrows went up. "Not in any important places?"

"No." I laughed.

She wiped her forehead in a mock gesture of relief. Then she said, "You don't think I'm too forward?"

"No."

"Yes you do. You like your women sweet and demure. Like a southern belle. Wah Bret, Hoooney, I do so love the way you comb your eyebrows."

We both laughed.

Our order came. As promised, the french fries dripped with grease. Meredith ate them like they were a great delicacy, swishing them around in ketchup and holding them over her mouth and lowering them in. The burgers were thick and overdone, served on stale buns, and the beer was warm, but I didn't give a damn.

Nothing she said or did was setting off any alarms in my head. Even the best players give themselves away with small inconsistencies in mannerisms, in their backstory, in their eyes when they look at you. I saw none of those things in her and I started feeling at ease. I began to worry about what she was going to think when she found out who I really was and what I'd done with my life. Someday, I thought, I'd have to tell her. I wasn't going to live a lie.

Once back on the road it was quickly obvious the snowplows and salt trucks would soon lose the battle against the falling snow. It was piling up as we headed back to Amber. Luckily, I had heavy snow tires and four-wheel drive. There wasn't much traffic: a few locals, a few skiers.

We passed the blackberry brandy back and forth again and sang Christmas songs. It was still a long way to Christmas, but they were the only songs we both knew. Mostly I just hummed along because I have both a lousy voice and no memory whatever for lyrics. I hadn't sung Christmas carols since I was a kid. But she had a superb, throaty voice and knew every damn carol ever written.

"Belt it out," she kept saying between songs. "It doesn't matter if you mess up the words, you have to catch the spirit of it! Once again: Over the meadow and through the woods, to Grand-mother's house we go . . ."

We sang till we were hoarse. Then she slid over next to me and put her arm against my shoulder and curled her feet up under her.

Above Heather Glen there was a large field alongside the road. A couple dozen kids were sliding down a hill on sleds and flattened cardboard boxes. It was a steep hill, maybe a hundred and fifty feet high. Where they'd been sledding, the snow was packed down and slick, forming a sort of twisted track.

78

Meredith asked me to pull over. We got out in the cold wind and stretched our legs and watched the kids, who were yelping with joy. Meredith tilted her head back and caught snowflakes on her tongue. The kids had piled some snow in a mound, three or four feet high, at the bottom of the hill and were sailing over it.

Meredith found a discarded, flattened, cardboard box some kid had been using for a sled. "This I gotta try," she said. "Come on, there's room enough on this for both of us!" She headed up the hill.

"I know my limitations," I said.

A kid on a sled in a bright blue snowsuit came down the track, leaning into the curves, then plunged down the straightaway and hit the hump at the bottom, flew twenty feet through the air about five feet off the ground, and came in for a perfect landing. A bunch of kids at the bottom cheered. Another kid followed, this one on an aluminum saucer; he hit the first curve and dumped over. The saucer shot down the hill, hit the hump, sailed almost to the road, and landed flat against a snowbank. The kid stood up looking like a snowman, but he wasn't hurt.

Now it was Meredith's turn. She waved to me from the top of the hill. The kids looked on with incredulity. A couple glanced at me as if to say, *is she nuts?*

And I nodded, as if to say, *damn right.*

She lay belly down on the cardboard and had a couple of kids give her a push to get started. I covered my face in mock horror, looking through the cracks in my fingers. Keeping the cardboard rolled up in the front, she leaned into the turns and slid around them, dragging her feet. Thankfully, she was moving far more slowly than the sleds, but still fast enough to go sailing when she hit the hump at the bottom. At the steepest part of the run, she put her head down and let out a horrible yell: yiiiiiiiiiiiii!

She hit the hump at an angle and rose up in the air; the cardboard twisted, then separated from her. She looked like a diver about to do a belly flop; then she hit, the snow around her exploding in what looked like a shellburst.

I ran over to her; she was rolling on the ground holding her stomach, simultaneously laughing and groaning.

A big kid in a khaki jacket and I helped her to her feet. She brushed herself off and caught her breath. "That was wonderful," she said, her face flushed and happy. "I got the wind knocked out of me! Your turn," she said to me.

"Come on, mister, give it a try," one of the kids said. He handed me his sled. "Don't be a chicken." I turned to give it back to him, about to say that I was neither a chicken nor an idiot, and the next thing I knew, whammo, I got hit in the head with a snowball. I turned around to see that it was Meredith; she was busily packing another as she headed for cover, four or five kids running with her. They took up positions behind a thick, fallen tree.

Not one to ignore a call to arms, I packed some of my own and started raining snowballs in a high arch, like mortar, on her fortified position, a couple of kids helping me. Soon the kids, squealing with joy and yelling battle cries, had divided themselves into two small armies of six or seven each, half with me, half with the renegade, Meredith Kellerman.

They had the high ground and better cover. We were in trouble. First thing, I put the small kids to making snowballs, since they didn't have enough arm to strike the enemy without venturing into the no-man's land between the belligerents. Then I sent two of my best boys on a flanking maneuver. They withdrew up the road and circled back of us, then climbed the hill and came around behind the enemy, where they could bomb them without fear of retaliation. Then with my remaining force of two small kids and one big girl with an arm like an NFL quarterback, we made a frontal assault.

The enemy, suffering direct hit after direct hit, broke ranks. First one little kid in a red parka headed for the woods, then another ran toward us and joined our side, then two more headed for the woods. This left Meredith and three others, and they could see all was lost. They suddenly bolted and scattered. Meredith tried to cover the retreat by firing at us, but she was getting hit now every few seconds and she finally had to duck down behind the fallen tree trunk. "Uncle! Uncle!" she yelled, waving a white scarf.

My side passed congratulations around, patting each other on the back. Then one of the kids cried, "Let's hit the hill again!" and off they went with their sleds.

Meredith said she had enough, that every muscle in her body ached.

On the way back to Amber in the Bronco, she bubbled excitedly about the snowball fight, and like most defeated military strategists, composed her memoirs, blaming everyone but herself.

"If only they'd held fast when you began your assault, we'd have beaten you back! And then three of my men turned tail and ran, and another went over to your side! Traitors! Cowards!"

I, of course, merely stated the obvious. She had the high ground. She had launched a surprise attack. She had the best fortifications. At the opening of hostilities she had all the obvious advantages.

"How could we have lost?" she said, shaking her head in mock despair.

"Superior generalship on our side," I said.

Strange I should have said that; it was one of Gray Wolf's favorite expressions.

The fire crackled in Meredith's old stove, flickering through the Pyrex window in the front, casting long shadows on the walls. I was feeling warm, relaxed, happy. It crossed my mind that Frank Webb might be trying to get in touch with me, but at the moment I didn't care.

The room smelled nicely of burning pine. Meredith made some Irish coffee and we sat on the couch in the living room and watched the flames and the shadows they made. Outside, slowly, day faded into night. We sat there in a dreamy state, not saying much.

She'd done a lot with the place in a day. She'd put down a braided, circular, maroon-colored area rug in the living room. The couch was thickly padded and comfortable. Practical. It wasn't new, but it was in good shape. On the walls were some paintings, mostly in the modern, abstract mode, the kind I can't stand. But she did have some nice watercolors of fields of flowers, mountains, a couple of little girls playing in a sandbox.

She said she'd done the watercolors herself. She beamed when she said it.

If she was a player playacting, she was the best I'd ever seen.

"Would you like to hear some music?" she asked.

"Might break the spell," I said.

"Might at that."

I stretched and let my body sink deeper into the sofa, and we smiled at each other and watched the fire again for a while. I remembered my old training days at Camp Perry, "the farm," where they train American espionage agents. An instructor name of Harrison told us that, whatever we did, we could not have a relationship with a woman. There were three kinds of women: co-workers, civilians, and members of the opposition. Fraternization with female co-workers was not allowed. A civilian could not be told anything, and therefore could not share a player's life. If the woman was a member of the opposition, she would ruin you. Have sex, lots of it, Harrison said, but never get involved. That was rule number one.

To hell with rule number one. I had another Irish coffee.

After a while Meredith said she thought she'd make a little something for dinner. Would I stay?

"Love to," I said.

She cooked up a quick meal of veal sausage and eggs, served with chunks of hot, buttered french bread and some good, strong Costa Rican coffee. We ate hungrily in the living room on a card table set up near the stove. For dessert, she heated some apple pie and served it with a wedge of sharp cheese.

While we ate she talked about her art and how hard she tried to be a serious artist, to make serious statements, but she could see I didn't know what the hell she was talking about. She tried to explain. She said that good art speaks to you, and when it is really good it speaks in a strong voice that reaches right inside you and sets off a bomb that blows the top of your head off.

I said her set design blew the top of my head off and she said she was glad.

After dinner she disappeared into the bedroom for a few moments. I could hear her clicking on a stereo. Big band music started playing, soft, melodious. A lot of brass and a nice mellow sax. The speakers must have been hidden in the rafters someplace.

She came back into the living room. "Dance with me," she said.

"Bulldozers don't dance," I said.

She did a couple of twirls; she was graceful and lithe. She took my hands and tugged at me. "Come on, nothing to it."

We were both in our stocking feet. "I haven't danced since high school," I said.

"Shame on you."

She showed me the basic square step and a couple of variations, saying "One, two, three, four" over and over again. There wasn't much to it. I took her in my arms. Her body was firm, yet supple. She felt good and smelled good, with just a hint of perfume. As I moved to the music she moved with me, as if my mind were directing both of us. She pulled herself closer and rested her head against my chest and I was in a dream, lost in the music and the movement together, and time seemed to stretch out; time seemed to just melt into the dream and all I knew was the music and Meredith and me and then we were kissing each other and her lips were warm and giving.

And we kept moving around the floor to the music, to the dance of the flames in the stove and the shadows on the wall and the smell of pine wood burning and we were lost in it all and without my knowing how we got there, we were in the coolness of the bedroom and slowly undressing each other in the darkness, and then we were in the bed and I was running my hands over her breasts and flanks and buttocks and we were kissing, and we were rolling, still moving to the music, and it seemed like I was floating weightless on the music and I entered her smoothly and we moved together, swimming in the dream.

Afterward, we lay there, holding each other, floating on each other's joy. After a while she raised her head and kissed me on the cheek and said, "Promise me you won't turn into a jerk." I said I promised. Then she put her head down on my shoulder and a few minutes later she was asleep.

I lay there for a long time in her warmth, listening to the soft music and the crackling of the fire. I drifted off to sleep after a while, dreaming of having her forever and ever.

But there, in the back of my head, was the voice of Harrison the trainer: *Love is death.*

I awoke to a kiss. It was dawn, and gray light filled the room.

Meredith said, "My director and I are meeting with backers in Albany this morning to see about bringing our play there. I'm late. Go back to sleep."

"How about dinner tonight?" I asked.

"If we're back in time, I'll stop by your place. No later than, say, eight."

"Nine," I said.

"All right. If you don't see me, I'll be over tomorrow morning bright and early. How's that?"

"Good enough."

I watched her get out of bed, naked, and fumble in the semidarkness for her robe. She had nicely formed breasts, nicely proportioned to her small waist. She smiled, watching me watch

85

her. She said, "And you said bulldozers couldn't dance." She laughed gently, then blew me a kiss and headed for the bathroom. A moment later I heard the shower going.

Throwing back the covers, I discovered it was cold in the room. I got up, put on my jeans and shirt and my heavy wool socks, and did some push-ups and sit-ups and some stretching exercises. I felt like a high school kid ready to run a football up and down the field.

I was jogging in place when she came back into the bedroom already dressed, running a comb through her hair. She had on a bright yellow pullover, a dark skirt, and a brightly colored Gypsy kerchief around her neck. I stopped jogging and stretched out my calf muscles and did some twists, all the time watching her. She put a little lipstick on, made a few quick strokes with an eyebrow pencil, and then came over to me.

"I've really got to run," she said. "The coffee's on. There's some raspberry turnovers in the fridge, just pop them in the toaster oven." I stopped exercising so she could kiss me on the cheek. I lifted her up, kissed her on the throat, then lowered her down again and kissed her on the mouth, holding her tightly to me.

She laughed, throwing her head back. "Later, sweetheart." She eased my arms from around her, then brushed a shock of red hair out of her eyes. She slipped on her boots and parka and whisked out the door.

It had snowed again overnight and the snow came halfway up to her knees. Out of habit I looked around for tracks in the snow. There weren't any. I watched Meredith use a broken-off old broom to brush the snow off her VW bus, then get in, crank it up, and drive off, leaving parallel tracks in the fresh snow. She stuck her mittened hand out the window and waved good-bye to me just before she disappeared over a little rise in the road.

I went into the warm kitchen. The coffee she made was strong, but not bitter. I heated a raspberry turnover and ate it slowly with a fork. I washed and dried the cup and plate after I was finished—just to let her know how damn domesticated I could be—then went back into the bedroom and put on my heavy sweater. I figured to go home before going to Jenny's Diner to see if Webb had left a message for me. Prince would be getting pissed off by now, not having his servant around to wait on him.

I was just about ready to put my boots and sheepskin coat on and leave when the old ghost of suspicion visited me again.

It just made good sense to find out all I could about her, I told myself, even if the odds were a million to one that she was a player. Ten million to one. I ought to at least have a look around.

I went upstairs and checked the upper rooms. Not much there. Bare floors, nothing on the walls and windows. A couple of rooms that could be used for bedrooms, but weren't used for anything. Another room had some canvases and boxes of old schoolbooks stored in it. Mostly art and design books, most stamped USED—State University of New York, Binghamton, Bookstore.

Downstairs there was the bedroom. Nothing in the drawers except the usual stuff: underclothes, blouses, sweaters, costume jewelry, cosmetics, mementos. *Resist Reagan* campaign buttons. She had a small rolltop desk that wasn't locked. Inside were a few letters from friends addressed to her in Binghamton. I glanced at them; they contained the usual crap: jobs, lovers, places they'd gone, places they had dinner, plays they'd seen, books they'd read. Blah, blah, blah.

In one drawer were half a dozen loose photographs showing her with an older couple: her parents, I suspected. The woman looked just like Meredith, only a little thicker around the middle. The man was wearing a cowboy shirt, but he had a well-groomed, businessman's appearance. Nice even teeth. An honest, forthright face, an outdoorsman's face. In the background in one shot was a boxy, ranch-style house with a '61 Olds in the driveway. That was the one with the wedged taillights set in horizontal fins, low to the ground.

Looking through all that stuff made me feel guiltier by the minute. Funny, I'd been doing the dirtiest kind of work for over twenty years and except for Benevides never felt guilty about a damn thing, but going through Meredith's stuff I felt guilty as hell. Maybe I was returning to the human race.

I locked the door when I left, got the Bronco started, and drove on home, feeling like scum.

When I pulled into my driveway and turned off the engine I sensed something was wrong.

It took me a moment to realize what it was: Prince wasn't barking.

I jerked Langston's automatic out of my coat pocket and took a quick look around. There was nobody in the trees that ran along both sides of the driveway. No tire tracks in the snow in the driveway.

Steam in the Bronco's radiator hissed, but otherwise it was quiet. I kept searching for some telltale sign, some movement, something. I scanned the ridge to my left and right, then the house in front of me. The wind gently stroked the pines along the ridge to my left.

On the path and stairs leading up to the house I could detect faint footprints, partially filled in by snow. My heartbeat quickened. I started the Bronco up again, put it in reverse, and backed down the driveway. At the road, I stopped for a moment while I thought things over, letting the engine idle.

Somebody was in there, I figured. And I wanted to know who it was and what he or she wanted.

I put the gearshift in low and hit the accelerator, heading straight for the house, then turned off at the last moment and shot up the embankment to the right. I bounced over the top of the rise and drove into the trees along the side of the house. I stopped the Bronco and rolled out of the cab and ran up the embankment and into the trees.

I found a thick tree and dove behind it, catching my breath.

Anybody laying for me would have to come after me. In the woods, a rifle wouldn't do much good because the person would have to get close to me. And close in, the automatic would be less unwieldy than a rifle. I was always good at this kind of thing; if anyone wanted to play, I was ready.

I crawled through the snow, keeping my head down, and moved back toward the house, detecting no movement whatever. I could see where the footprints led around the house to the back door. There were two sets, one going in and the other going out, but that's an old trick. The intruder could have gone in and come out, then gone in again, stepping in the original tracks.

I waited a few minutes. Nothing happened. No sound at all except the wind whistling through the tops of the pines. I crept closer, burrowing through the snow under the lowest branches of a pine tree, and took a look. The rear door seemed slightly ajar and I could see where it'd been jimmied around the lock. This wasn't Gray Wolf's doing. If he'd come to call and he'd broken in, there would be no way to tell. He could get in and out of Fort Knox without disturbing the dust on the gold bars.

I stayed right where I was for maybe an hour. My fingers got stiff with the cold. My feet went numb. It was a pretty good bet that whoever had gone in there hadn't gone in to say hi, how are ya, how ya like the weather? Most players are men of action, they can't stand just sitting around waiting. They have to move, do something. I kept waiting and listening, but there wasn't a sound. After a while my ass got sore and my feet got cold.

Finally I crawled back out from under the tree and, in a crouch, moved down the side of the building. The windows were still covered with sheets just the way I'd left them. I moved down the side of the house to where I had the wood stacked. I took hold of a chunk of wood and threw it through the window.

The glass tinkled onto the floor. Then it was quiet again.

I stayed crouched behind the woodpile for a long time. Finally I reached in the broken window, unhooked it, and climbed in. My feet crunched on the broken glass. I crossed the room and opened the door. I could see part of the living room and part of the kitchen. Nobody. No dog, either. I called out:

"Anyone in here, you better say something, because I'm armed and I'll shoot to kill."

No one said anything.

I stood up and went into the living room and checked behind the sofa: nobody.

It occurred to me I might have been visited by some transient who had wandered by. That happens a lot in the hill country. Somebody breaks in just to get out of the elements and to get a little food.

I stayed close to the wall and switched the light on in the kitchen and peeked in. A thin line of snow had blown in from the crack in the door. And next to it were some red spots. I looked to my right and there was Prince lying on the floor in a pool of blood.

I went over to him. His head was twisted and his jaw was open and just below it was a gaping slash across his throat. His gleaming dead eyes stared up at me.

91

"Bastards," I said.

I just stood there staring for a while, trying to figure out who would do this. Gray Wolf might have done this as a warning to stay out of it.

I checked around to see if whoever it was left behind any other surprises. I pulled open all my drawers and opened all my cabinets with string so I could stand back in case they were booby-trapped. I took it slow and easy. I didn't find anything else.

I carried Prince outside to an old shed with a dirt floor. I used a pick to break up the frozen floor, then dug Prince a grave. It took me a couple of hours to dig it, and when I was through my arms and back ached and I was wringing wet with sweat. I laid Prince in the hole. I started to shovel the dirt on him, but I stopped. He was only a goddamn dog, but he was still a friend. Some words needed to be said. Some farewell.

I didn't know what to say. I stood there for a long stupid moment of silence. Then I shoveled the dirt into the goddamn hole.

I boarded up the broken window, took a shower, put on some clean clothes, and drove to Amber and asked if anybody'd seen any strangers in town. No one had. Then I went over to Heather Glen, which has three motels. At each motel I said I was looking for a stranger. A man traveling alone. He ran over my dog, I said. The staff were glad to help.

At the first motel, they said all they had were couples, and all of them were skiers. Except for a lady selling hair care products. She'd been coming there for years.

At the second place, they said they hadn't quite finished sprucing up the place for the skiers' rush, and so had only two guests. College students.

At the third place, the Heather Glen Hostelry, the clerk said they had had a stranger the night before, a quiet man in his fifties. The clerk was an elf of a man with a potbelly and pink cheeks. He'd seen me around, so he took me for a local and was friendly. He described the stranger for me: curly black hair; big, dark eyes; a sort of slinky walk; thick accent. It sounded like a guy I knew name of Viktor Dukas who used to do messy little errands for Gray Wolf. He had booked the room for a week, but had only stayed one night and left early in the morning. I asked for his name and address. Stanley Frost, York Street, Syracuse. I got his car license number.

I tried information in Syracuse. No such person. I called the cops there, saying I was a deputy sheriff in Amber. They checked; no such street as York Street. I called the private investigators I'd hired in Albany and they ran the license through their computer. The plates had never been issued.

I went back over to Amber, to Willy and Martha's, and got a cold draft beer and sat in a back booth and tried to figure out what I knew, what I didn't know, and what to do next. Luckily there weren't too many people in the place. A young couple playing shuffle alley. A couple of old guys at the bar bent over their beers. Willy was watching a hockey game.

I was pretty much convinced it was Viktor Dukas who slit Prince's throat, and he did it on Gray Wolf's orders. When I'd first met Gray Wolf—when he was still just Lieutenant Fairweather— if you betrayed him he might have shoved a gun barrel up your nose and blown your skull cap into the ceiling, but he wouldn't have killed your dog.

The change happened one time when we were on tour in El Salvador.

We'd been helping out with some training exercises, showing the government's supposedly elite airborne unit some new house-to-house fighting tactics using sensitive listening devices to detect the presence of hostile forces. We were in the capital awaiting orders. The civil war there had just heated up. General Haig, Reagan's secretary of state, had called the civil war there part of a campaign coordinated by Havana and Moscow to support a Marxist insurgency, or something like that. Consequently, the capital, San Salvador, was crawling with American intelligence agents, official and, like Gray Wolf and me, unofficial.

We were staying in a safe house with a couple of CIA guys, who were all excited because they had some pretty good intelligence that the rebels, the Farabundo Marti Popular Liberation Force, were going to attack a military barracks that night.

Everyone was pretty eager for some action. The year before, Archbishop Romero, who was critical of Los Catorce, the fourteen families that ran the country, had been assassinated. The rebels launched an offensive, but failed to spark a popular revolt and had been driven into the hills. They'd stayed quiet. Nothing in the capital, San Salvador, at all.

This attack was supposed to be a show of force for an American TV film crew that was doing a documentary on poverty for "Sixty Minutes." They sure didn't have to look far to find it. Three-quarters of the people in the cities lived in hovels made of tin cans and packing crates, open sewers running down the streets. You could get all the workers you wanted for a buck a day.

I remember Gray Wolf saying that if I was a peasant there, I'd be a Communist, too.

"Not me," I said. "I know the Communists too well."

"You saw your children's bellies swell with hunger, even you would go into the hills."

I denied it. He laughed.

That night Gray Wolf and I got a few bottles of wine and walked down to the army barracks to see the show. It wasn't far, and it was a pleasant, warm evening in late summer. We sat down in the grass and waited for the attack. We were both in a good mood, enjoying ourselves. In those days, between assignments, life was a big party.

Before long the TV guys showed up and set up their cameras. The army showed up, too. They must have heard the rumors as well. Or maybe they were just following the TV guys. Everybody sat around and waited until way past midnight, smoking, drinking wine, chatting. The rebels never showed. The TV guys packed up their stuff and the army packed up their stuff, and everybody went home.

We couldn't find a cab, so we walked back to the safe house.

There were some security forces around checking papers all the time, but San Salvador was still open and everyone just went about their business.

We made our way along a wide boulevard. We were humming and singing, relaxed. Then we turned and went up Camino Alto, which was a narrow, cobblestone street. The Mediterranean-style houses sat back from the street behind walls and wrought-iron gates. There was a van parked next to the curb. I'd seen it earlier in the day, but didn't think much about it. As we passed by it, four guys in ski masks jumped out brandishing assault weapons, yelling in Spanish: "Get the CIA pigs!" Before I could get my gun out, I was clubbed into unconsciousness.

When I came around, I was in a clinic and they told me the rebels had Gray Wolf. I got hold of Frank Webb and he flew in and he got every damn security agent in the country out looking for him. They never found him, but the rebels finally figured out he wasn't the CIA man they thought they had, so they traded him for a few hundred handguns and a truckload of ammunition. They dumped him out of a car in front of the massive statue of El Salvador del Mundo in the hills on the outskirts of the city. He'd been beaten and starved, and somehow they found out—probably by trial and error—what secret fears he harbored.

They'd locked him in a cellar with rats. When we got him, he was as white as chalk and covered with rat bites. He didn't seem to know me. Spittle ran from his mouth. He kept mumbling, "Kill, kill, kill."

The Exchange put him in a good hospital for a while, then he took a rest at a resort in Panama. I visited him in November and he seemed okay and was anxious to get back to work.

We went on tour in North Africa that year. The change in him was a subtle one. We still drank, and laughed. But before, it was like a game to him. He loved the excitement of it, the danger.

After El Salvador, it was different. You could see it in his eyes when we had to put someone through an interrogation. It was no longer the excitement and the danger. What he liked was to inflict pain. Whenever I saw that look, I shuddered.

After a while, I got into the Bronco and drove around, still thinking of Gray Wolf. But when you've been a player for as long as I was, you try to think of all the possibilities. Unlikely as it seemed, maybe it wasn't Gray Wolf who gave the order and it wasn't Viktor Dukas who carried it out. Maybe the Exchange figured they'd get me to go after Gray Wolf if they sent some clown to pretend to be Viktor Dukas, have him stay in a local motel so I'd find him, and have him kill my dog so I'd blame Gray Wolf. The bastards were capable of anything.

Gray Wolf used to say we lived in a maze of mirrors, and there was no compass.

I started thinking about Meredith Kellerman, that maybe she was one of the mirrors in the maze. Damn. All indications pointed to her being just a civilian, but I had to know one way or the other. I stopped at a phone booth and put a call through to the PI I'd hired in Albany to go to Binghamton to check her out. He'd just gotten back, he said. He'd spoken to four people who had known her there and as far as he could tell she was just a graduate student in art, had a 3.8 average, and lived alone in an efficiency apartment. Her landlady said she was neat, quiet, didn't see her much. The PI checked with two professors and another graduate student, April Thorestein. Meredith Kellerman was definitely a graduate student there. She spent a lot of time doing set design work in the Drama Department.

It sounded good. I told him thanks and he said he owed me fifty bucks back on the advance. I told him to keep it.

I was 99 percent sure she was okay. But I had to know for sure, 100 percent. I just couldn't live with the doubt.

I went back to the house and packed a small bag, then drove to the Albany County Airport and took the first flight out for New York, where I hopped a shuttle to Kennedy and then took a United red-eye flight to Arizona, where she said she'd grown up. There, I figured, I'd learn everything I needed to know about her. No player would ever use their real childhood for a cover.

I rented a black T-bird at the Flagstaff Airport using a phony ID and drove to Bakerstown—east of Bellemont on I-40. I found a phone book at an all-night Union 76 station on Marcy Boulevard. There were nine Todds listed. The houses at the first four addresses didn't look anything like the house in the photo at Meredith's place. The fifth one was at 94 Sagebrush Drive.

The sun was coming up and the eastern horizon was etched in red as I turned off Morgantown Highway onto Sagebrush, which cut through a flat stretch of what was once hard rock desert. The houses were big and low, with red-tile roofs and landscaped with cacti, rocks, and scrub trees. A lot of the houses had high fences around them and most, I figured, had swimming pools out in back.

Number 94 looked pretty much as it had in the picture I'd seen at Meredith's, only it looked rather run-down. The name Todd was on the mailbox. No car in the driveway. The house had a four-car garage with two wide garage doors, closed up tight.

There was a light on in the living room, another one on by the side porch.

I drove on past. I felt like a jerk, checking up on Meredith like this. But working for the goddamn Exchange for twenty years had made me as paranoid as hell. Then again, maybe I just wanted to know her for myself, to get a feel of the places she'd been and the things and people she'd touched, to know with absolute certainty she was real. Maybe it wasn't all agent paranoia.

I continued down the road to where it dead-ended in raw desert with just a few tumbleweeds, barrel cacti, and dry washes. A billboard said, Another Weldon Homes Development Coming Soon. I headed back up Sagebrush and took a closer look at 94. The side of the house was pinkish gray in the dim morning light. The paint was peeling on the window frames and the cornices. Blown sand covered most of the sidewalk.

Just beyond the house was a curve where the neighbor's wall came almost to the street. I parked there, where I could see the house, but none of the neighbors could see me. I sat and had a smoke, keeping the hot tip of the cigarette cupped in my hand and slouching low in the seat so I could just see the house over the dashboard. It was getting lighter by the minute.

A car from one of the houses at the end of the street came by, heading for the main road. It was a big blue Lincoln with an elderly man driving. He had white hair, a scrawny neck, and was wearing a blue suitcoat. A few minutes later a Porsche roared by with a woman at the wheel who had short blond hair, gold earrings, painted lips, the kind that look like they belong on the cover of *Glamour* magazine.

I lit another cigarette off the one I was finishing. Suddenly I heard a noise like feet on gravel behind me and I swung around, jerking my gun out of my belt, keeping it low and out of sight. A middle-aged man wearing a bathrobe with a newspaper under his arm was marching toward me. He had short black hair and bushy eyebrows and at the moment his mouth was turned down in an angry scowl. I put the gun between the seat and the door on my left and pushed the electric button to move the window down on the right side.

"What are you doing here?" he said. "Casing the joint? We've got a neighborhood watch program, all suspicious characters are reported to the police. I've got your license number."

"I'm in real estate, scouting new listings."

"At this hour?"

"I couldn't sleep and I had an early breakfast appointment."

"The home is not for sale," he said stiffly. "Mrs. Todd decided not to sell the place. She's in Hawaii. She's coming back here to live next month. What is it with you real estate people, anyways? A bunch of lousy vultures."

"Even vultures have to make a living."

He grumbled something I'm sure was obscene and turned around and headed back across the street, his head tilted low in front of him.

I got out of the car. "Hold it there, mister."

He turned around and I crossed the street. His scowl hadn't changed. It could have been permanent on him.

"You lived here long? On the street, I mean?"

"Long enough."

"You know Meredith?"

"The Todds' daughter?"

"Yeah."

"Sure, I know her. Her name's Kellerman now. Moved back east someplace. Why?"

"I used to know her. My family owned a restaurant, she

used to come in all the time when she was kid. Just curious about how she's getting along."

"Beats me."

"What about Mr. Todd?"

"He passed away, oh, two, three years ago. You asked enough questions? I've got coffee to drink, toast to eat, and a paper to read." He marched toward the house across the street.

I got back in the car and sat there for a few minutes finishing my cigarette. No point in knocking on the Todds' door if no one was home. I started up the car and drove over to a Denny's and had their special Ranch Breakfast. Eggs, bacon, pancakes, coffee, juice, and an English muffin.

I don't know what it is about being in the game, but it makes you suspicious as hell whenever anybody gives you information you didn't have to beat out of them. There was absolutely nothing suspicious about the guy, what he wore, what he said, how he said it. I just had a goddamn feeling about him.

I bought a pint of pretty good scotch whiskey at a twenty-four-hour supermarket and rented a room at the Holiday Inn near the Interstate. I drank a little scotch, watched the morning movie—*Shane*, the great old western with Alan Ladd as a gunfighter trying to hang up his guns but can't—and tried to figure out what I was going to do next.

Taking a woman to bed once does not make her yours for ever and ever. But if I had to be honest with myself, the truth was I wanted her to be mine for ever and ever, wanted it even though I was plenty old enough to know that that kind of crap is a complete lie. There isn't any ever and ever. You like a woman and she likes you, you try to keep it that way as long as you can. Anything else is bull.

Shane kills the bad guys in the end, but gets shot himself

too. He sold his soul to become a gunfighter and, once you sell it, it's sold. I guess that's the message. Shane was a player trying to quit the business. It gave me a laugh.

I drifted off to sleep about noon after the scotch ran out and awoke late in the afternoon with a dull headache and cotton mouth. I brushed my teeth, then did some exercises, put on some jogging clothes, and went for a short run. Getting sweaty and out of breath always clears my head. I ran about five miles through treeless suburban neighborhoods loaded with RVs, snow-mobiles, boats, off-the-road vehicles, kids, dogs, and satellite dishes. I got back to the Holiday Inn a little after five. Then I drove to a nearby shopping center and found a hardware store.

I bought a flashlight and batteries, a pair of pliers, a screw-driver set, vice grips, tape, hacksaw blades, glass cutter, and some wire. The ruddy-cheeked check-out clerk in a red and white vest said, "Burglary tools." She said it with a smile, just joking.

"How'd you guess?"

She laughed and gave me my change with a wink. Must be a lively trade in burglary tools.

Next, I went over to K-Mart and bought a pair of black slacks, a black ski parka, black sneakers, and a cork fishing bobber. The check-out clerk here was an old guy, looked like he was clerking to supplement his income and would rather have been home with a Bartels and James. No wisecracks from him. He just rang it up and asked for forty-two seventy-five, charge or cash?

I locked my stuff in the trunk and went to Denny's and had the steak-and-lobster special. It wasn't quite dark when I got back to the T-bird. There was a cold breeze blowing from the south. I went back to the Holiday Inn, bought a newspaper at the gift shop, went up to my room, had a shower, took a nap, then read the newspaper.

About ten o'clock I went down to the lobby and got a Coke

out of the machine and took it back to my room. I sipped it as I changed into the slacks I'd bought and put on the parka. Then I burned the cork fishing bobber and wrapped it in a towel and put it in the pack with the tools. Sitting on the bed, I finished the Coke. Funny, but no matter how many times you do a bag job, it always gives you a little tingly feeling in the bottom of your gut.

I went back out to the T-bird with my tools in my knapsack and got in and headed for Sagebrush Drive. I listened to a little music along the way, a classical station from Fort Worth, Texas. A Handel chamber piece, very relaxing. The night sky was shot with stars, but no moon. That was good. I turned off on Sage-brush. Most of the houses had only a few lights on. No street lights. I drove past 94. The same two lights were on that had been on that morning. No car in the driveway. No car out front.

I kept going until I hit the end of the street, where I killed the lights and drove off the road and parked behind the billboard that said more houses were coming soon. I got out of the car and took a look to see if maybe somebody was out walking the dog or something and had seen me. No one around.

I looked up at the sky. A billion stars. Ten billion. There's nothing like the desert at night, it gives you the feeling you're standing on a grain of sand tossed on an endless beach. A chill wind gusted, smelling clean and fresh. I got back in the car and listened to the rest of the Handel and smoked a cigarette, all the time marveling at the stars. So goddamn many stars.

I took a few deep breaths to clear my head, then said to myself: Okay, it was time.

I put the burned cork on my face and got out of the car with my knapsack of tools and closed the door as quietly as I could. I stuffed my gun under the billboard. You get caught on a bag job, you don't want a gun with you. Since I wasn't going to steal anything, the cops couldn't get me for burglary, just illegal entry, which is a misdemeanor most places. But they get you with a gun, they can make a goddamn circus out of it. I started back up the road toward number 94. I could hear trucks going by up on the main road. Sound carries well in the high desert. Maybe it's the surrounding stillness. Somewhere, way off in the distance, a dog barked.

I kept to the center of the street where my feet wouldn't be making crunching sounds on the stones that collect along the side of the road. The house with the old guy and the young blonde was lit up like Broadway opening night; every damn room had the lights on and the drapes open. The old guy was pacing up and down in the living room with a drink in one hand and a small British flag in the other. I had no idea what he was doing. He paced with a sort of regal bearing, shoulders square, face front, while the blonde clapped her hands and laughed. The laugh was a cutting, sarcastic laugh that slashed through the night desert air and went out past me to echo off the rocks and canyons beyond in the dark. I felt sorry for the old guy.

I got to 94. I went around to the back of the house. Here was a fenced-in pool, no chairs around it. Looked like it hadn't been used in years. A burglar alarm, the old-fashioned kind with the outside gong and the little conducting strips around the windows, looked operational. That would be no problem. I checked around the doors and windows; they seemed to be shut tight. I went around to the front and checked around the front door. Here I found a key slot behind a potted plant. A second alarm system, probably one of those new microwave jobs that go off if there is any movement inside the house.

But from the sloppy way it was installed, I figured it must have been a pretty cheap lock switch. I took a look through the window and could see a small red light flashing at me in the darkness. That would tell the owner the system was on. Okay, the thing to do was just shut it off. I chipped away at the stucco around the slot and freed it. There were three wires attached: red, black, and white. I peeled back the insulation on the black one and the red one, then spliced a small piece of wire between them. No alarm went off, so I must have gotten the wires right. I peered inside. The red light had turned green, meaning it was okay to come on in.

Except that the old-fashioned gong system was still in place.

I went around back and took a look at the alarm again. The simplest thing to do with this type is to squirt shaving cream into the bell, which muffles the sound of the alarm when it goes off. I used that technique once in Panama and after I'd squirted a whole can of shaving cream in the bell the goddamn stuff leaked out and the bell just got louder and louder until it woke up the neighbor's three Dobermans and then all hell broke loose.

So I used the glass cutter to make a small hole in the sliding door to the bedroom and attached some wire to the window tape leads and the connection at the doorjamb. Then I simply reached in and unlocked the door and slid it open. The alarm didn't go off.

Inside, the place had a musty, closed-up smell to it. A few pieces of furniture were scattered around. There were boxes lying on the floor, half-filled, and closets half-filled. I went down the hall. The linen closet had been emptied. In a room that once had been a study of some kind, the bookshelves were empty except for a trophy with a girl riding a horse on top. It looked like somebody had been getting ready to move and then had changed plans halfway through.

Car lights traced across the walls and stopped. I dropped to the floor. The lights stayed on the wall. I crawled across the floor to the window and took a peak through the curtains. I couldn't see much past the headlights, but it looked like a pickup truck. I waited. Police? Private security? I could feel my heartbeat speed up. There was a time it wouldn't have—except for the thrill of it.

To avoid arrest, I'd knock some poor slob cop on the noggin, but I wasn't ready to kill. If necessary, I'd give up, get a good lawyer, post bail, and sail into the sunset. But how the hell would I explain it to Meredith? *Oh, yeah, I was just in the neighborhood so I thought I'd burglarize your mother's house.*

The vehicle in the driveway suddenly backed out into the street. Then I could see it was a pickup, and when it turned I could hear the rock and roll coming from the radio. Just a couple of kids turning around. They drove off down the street, the engine rumbling.

I waited a few minutes to see if the pickup drew any interest. A porch light went on across the street, then it went off a moment later. All clear.

I started going through the boxes in the living room, just browsing. Books, kitchen utensils, paints and canvas, and some old paintings, drawings. Mostly kid stuff. A lot of clothes. I opened each box, gave it a quick look, and put it back the way it was. Then I went into the bedroom. More clothes, a family Bible, and the family album. In the front of the album were old people in straw hats driving Model Ts. On the next page was a shot of a young couple. I figured they might be Meredith's mother and father. Then pictures of the house, and a little girl who had to be Meredith wearing cowboy hats and riding ponies. Damn, if she wasn't a cute little kid. I hurried through the album, but wished someday to take some time and look at all the pictures.

There were a couple of high school yearbooks called "Stallion Days." Meredith was there, a cheerleader and president of the Future Artists of America Club, which had four members. There was a picture of Meredith on a horse, smiling and waving. Someone had written over it: "Dale Evans rides again." And then

106

there was a wedding album with pictures of Meredith beaming and her gawky groom in a tux with a ruffled shirt looking sort of bewildered by it all. Wrangler Room, Mesa Hotel, it said in the background. There were old napkins with a wedding cake design, now yellow with age, tucked between the pages. Embossed on the napkins was, "Best to Larry and Rusty." Rusty must have been Meredith's nickname.

I had this sudden feeling of invading Meredith's privacy. I put everything back exactly where I'd found it. I left the way I'd come in, taking the wire with me. Then I went around to the front and repaired the wire, shoved the slotted key back into the hole, and filled the broken area with dirt from a potted fern by the door. At least the house would have some protection.

The only thing I had left to do in Bakerstown was to speak to Larry Kellerman, Meredith's ex-husband.

I found Kellerman the next morning. He wasn't in the phone book, but there was a Betty Kellerman, and when I called her she said she wasn't related to Larry, but she'd heard recently that someone by that name was running a camera store downtown. Kellerman Kamera, she said, with a *K*.

Kellerman Kamera turned out to be right on the edge of a renovated mall area that had brick sidewalks and new benches and litter cans and little patches of rock gardens. Right across the street from Kellerman's, though, it was still kind of seedy. There was an adult bookstore, and next to that was a vacant lot with a couple of bums lying in the sun sharing a bottle of hootch.

I walked on into Kellerman Kamera. Kellerman had put on weight since his wedding. He was six-two or -three and had a little belly on him. He had a tan, but his skin was mottled. I took him to be thirty, maybe thirty-two or -three. He looked a little worn out, as if lugging heavy cameras around all day was enough to put a man in an early grave. His shoulders sloped and he had bags under his eyes. I couldn't in a million years imagine him married to Meredith.

He was leaning on a glass case reading the morning paper as I came in. He folded the paper up and put it under the counter, then ran his hands down the front of his shirt as if he needed to spruce himself up before facing a customer.

"Help ya, pard?" he said.

Help ya, pard? God Almighty. I smiled and said: "Larry Kellerman! You don't remember me, do you?"

He looked at me as if I were a stale fruitcake and shook his head.

"Walter Fixx, I'm Meredith's cousin. I was at your wedding, what was it, eight, ten years ago? Out at the Mesa Hotel." I put out my hand and he shook it. He had the limp handshake of an eight-year-old girl.

"I sure am sorry about you two splitting up," I said. "If ever there was two people in love, it was you two. I am sorry, Larry."

"It was her fault," he said. A pitiful expression had descended on his face.

"I don't doubt it," I said.

"She changed after the wedding. Got real headstrong. Willful."

"That can happen. I've been sort of out of the country, out of touch, oh, six, seven years. My side of the family never was close to her side. I'm just passing through and stopped out to the house. Nobody home, seems like nobody's living there. Where's Agnes and John?"

"John Todd died a couple years ago. I heard Agnes was gonna sell the place and move to Hawaii. But she's changed her mind and is gonna be moving back any day now. That's the last I heard."

"And where's Meredith, what's she up to?"

"She fell in with a bunch of artists and actors and went off to graduate school in Upstate New York. Now I heard she's working for a year at a theater."

"You sort of miss her, don't you, Larry?" I gave him a reassuring pat on his arm.

He pulled his arm back. No reassuring pats for him. He said, "I wouldn't take her back if you put a .44 Colt to my head."

"I understand," I said. "Well, nice to have seen you again, Larry. I'm sorry things didn't work out."

"I ever see her again, I just might give her a big kick on the rump. That's what she needed."

I nodded. "You're right about that," I said. Never argue with an idiot. "Well, you take care, Larry. Be seeing you."

"Didn't ya want to see a camera or something?" he said.

"Already got one," I said.

I drove to the airport where I called Frank Webb. "Yeah?" he answered.

"Tom Croft. Things going well?"

"No, son, I'm sorry, but things are bordering on the horrific. Far as we can tell, Gray Wolf is in Algeria, and as you damn well know we ain't got a short piss worth of assets in that miserable dung heap."

"Okay, Frank, thanks for trying. One more thing. Do you remember a second-rate player name of Viktor Dukas?"

"A small bucket of cowshit. Yellow Wolf was his handle back in the old days."

"He's been up in Amber, I think, nosing around."

There was silence on the line.

"You hear what I just said, Frank? Viktor Dukas was nosing around here."

"Yeah, yeah. Hold it, I'm checking on something in this dang computer file." I waited a moment, hearing the clack of computer keys. He came back on the line and said: "The Exchange has got him down as having rolled over more than a year ago."

"Then he could be working with Gray Wolf?"

"More than likely he is."

"He slit my dog's throat."

Silence again. I waited. I heard him take a breath. After a moment, he said, "That's bad news, Coldiron. Gray Wolf is sending you a message. He must know the Exchange is trying to get you to put him down. I was you, Coldiron, I'd think hard on this one. He just might be saying he's coming. Maybe the best thing is for you to get him first. That would be the smart thing."

"I'm not going to mix it up with Gray Wolf. What did you find out about Meredith Kellerman?"

"She's a civilian. Some kind of artist, just got a degree at a university someplace. Forget where. I got a memo telexed on her yesterday. She grew up in Arizona, married once, no kids. A certified straight arrow."

Even though I'd been pretty sure of her, this made me feel even better.

I said, "Thanks for everything, Frank."

I got on the plane whistling a Hungarian folk song my father had taught me as a kid. I didn't remember the lyrics but it was about a happy cobbler who made a pair of shoes for a princess and she went off with him to live happily ever after.

In the air all I could think about was Meredith and how nice she looked, and how nice she smelled, and how much I liked making love to her. And I swore that I wouldn't hold it against her that she'd once been married to a ninny.

My flight touched down in Albany at 8:10 in the morning.

Driving back to Amber I thought over the situation I was in. My first consideration had to be Meredith.

Gray Wolf didn't believe in harming civilians. He wouldn't kidnap Meredith to get to me, but if she got caught in a cross fire, too bad. Which meant I had to tell her to stay away from me until I could somehow get things settled with Gray Wolf. It wouldn't be long.

Somehow, someway, I figured I'd get in touch with people who could get in touch with him. I knew people on the other side that owed me favors. If I could speak to him personally, I knew I could convince him that I was no threat to him whatever. He could forget about me, I could forget about him.

I also knew the Exchange was probably leaking it that I was after him to motivate me to go after him. They'd do whatever they deemed necessary to get me to go after him. That's the way they worked, they got what they wanted. No matter whose blood they had to spill.

The weather had changed; a warming trend had set in and a thaw was on. The sky was blue as blue gets. I drove right on through to Amber even though I hadn't eaten since the night before and my stomach growled all the way.

I swung by Meredith's place. Her VW bus was gone. She was working, I figured, but I slopped through the mud and slush of her driveway and knocked on the door anyway. No answer. I left a note saying I'd stopped by. I got back into the Bronco and drove up to the crossroads to the little theater, hoping Meredith might be there. She wasn't. A lot of fresh tracks in the driveway, but the place was deserted. I got back in the Bronco and drove on into town and parked in front of Jenny's and went on in.

Two old men in overalls and two women in flower print dresses and sweaters sat at the table in the middle of the place and were having a heated argument about something, punctuated with a lot of *gawldangs* and *bejezzuses*. Another old-timer in an oft-mended flannel workshirt and baggy jeans sat on a stool at the counter slurping coffee and dunking toast. He grunted a good morning to me, I grunted one to him. He went back to slurping. Nobody else but Jenny in the place. She stood leaning on the cash register looking bored. She perked up when she spotted me coming in. I sat at the far end of the counter on the last red vinyl-topped stool and ordered a stack of flapjacks and pan sausage and coffee.

"You're looking well," Jenny said, jotting my order down. "And I guess I know why." She winked.

"Why?" I asked.

"On account of somebody spelled K-E-L-L-E-R-M-A-N." She winked again and headed for the kitchen.

No safe secrets in Amber.

112

I picked up the Amber *Companion* that somebody'd left on the counter. It was a once-a-week local shopping guide which occasionally printed vindictive attacks on local politicians written by local citizens, often so scurrilous they were funny. *What's a matter with you flint-heads who are supposed to be running this town?*

Jenny put a mug of coffee down in front of me.

"You and Miss Kellerman sort of like each other, don't you?"

"How do you know all this stuff?"

She just winked and drifted off to pour some more coffee for the other customers.

She came back with my pancakes a few minutes later. Jenny made a little small talk about Amber's favorite subject, the weather. Wasn't it terrible that all the snow was melting? It'd be bad for the merchants; no snow meant no skiers. But she had every hope that it wouldn't last. I stopped by the cash register on the way out and paid her.

"I heard about Prince being hit by the car," she said. "The way people drive around here. What a shame. He was such a nice dog."

"He sure was."

I went back outside and walked over to the post office. No mail. So I drove back to my place.

My driveway was half snow, half sloppy mud. No fresh tracks around. I went up the driveway and around to the back of the house, where I took off my muddy shoes and went on in. The place was chilly inside and oppressively quiet. I started a fire and turned up the hot water heater. Didn't help that much. What was missing was that damn dog. How the hell did I ever let myself become attached to a dog? Stupid, really stupid.

I took a shower and put on a robe, then got a drink of scotch and sat in the living room looking out at the road, watching the drips fall off the roof. If Gray Wolf was coming for me, I doubt he'd do it here. He'd do it when I was distracted, doing something else. Something like making love to Meredith.

After a while I went into the bedroom and lay down on the bed and ten minutes later I was asleep. I had the strangest dream. Gray Wolf was getting married and there was nobody in the church except me, Gray Wolf, the minister, and the bride. When the minister said, "If anyone knows why this man and this woman should not be wed, let him speak now, or forever hold his peace . . ." I tried to speak, but nothing would come out. I stood up, waving my arms, trying to get the minister's attention, but I couldn't . . . and then the minister was saying, "I pronounce you man and wife." Gray Wolf turned to me, smiling his boyish grin, and then he pulled his bride to him and turned back the veil, exposing the twisted face of death that Meredith had painted at the theater.

I awoke with a start. Someone was pounding on the back door. I sat up, wiping sweat from my forehead.

"Tom! Tom, are you in there?" It was Meredith.

"Yeah, I'm coming, hold on."

I went to the back door and opened it; she was standing on the back porch in a short brown car coat with a bright yellow scarf around her head and she looked damn good. "I've been so worried about you. Why did you just disappear like that? Why didn't you leave me a message or something? And then someone told me your dog had been killed . . . what's going on?"

"I just had some business to do in Albany and I thought I'd be back, but then I got tied up. I'm sorry, but you don't have a phone."

"I'm going to get one, you can bet on that."

Meredith slipped her muddy boots off and came in on

stocking feet. It was already getting dark outside, so I switched on a couple of lights.

"I'm sorry about Prince," she said. "How did it happen?"

"Run over."

"That's awful."

She took off her jacket and tossed it on a chair and then she threw her arms around me and hugged me tightly, her head coming under my chin, her hair smelling freshly shampooed. We held each other tight for a moment, then I eased her away.

"I'm glad you came over. There's something I have to tell you."

"What?"

"We can't see each other for a while."

"Why?"

"Something's come up. It'll take me a few days to straighten it out."

"Why can't I help you?"

"It's hard to explain."

She looked at me for a long moment. "You're in danger, aren't you?"

I nodded.

"How much danger?"

"I don't know. A man might be after me to kill me—that's all I can say. I think he might have had Prince killed as a sort of bizarre challenge."

"You think he might hurt me?"

"If you're with me."

"Why don't you run?"

"I'm trying to handle it another way so I won't have to run. I don't think he's in the country. I don't think he's ready to make his move just yet. Otherwise he wouldn't have sent his lackey to try to shake me up."

She went over to the window and looked out at the muddy
driveway, toying with the curtain. Then she turned back to me,
and there were tears coming down her cheeks. For a moment I felt
a terrible sadness, yet I felt joy at seeing her tears because I
thought they meant that she felt as strongly for me as I did for her.

But then I suddenly flashed on something Harrison, my
instructor at Camp Perry, had said long ago: a female who's worth
a damn can turn on the tears at will. More men have been brought
to their doom by tears than by bullets.

I felt like I'd taken a hammer blow.

She was looking vaguely around the room. "Whatever it is
that's happening to you," she said, "I want you to not be afraid for
me. I want to be part of it. If you can't talk about it, that's all
right, too. I understand."

I didn't say anything.

She turned to me now. "You have such a strange look on your
face," she said. "What's the matter, what did I say?"

I didn't answer her. She came close to me, staring at me.
"What's wrong?"

"Sit down," I said. "I want to tell you something."

"Okay."

She sat on the couch, looking up at me, her hands folded in
her lap. She wiped the tears from her cheeks. The light on her
hair made it look almost blond.

"I'm not really the crybaby type," she said. "I'm sorry.
What is it you want to tell me?"

"I knew a man once . . . his name isn't important. Let's call
him Smith. He was working for Air America. A CIA proprietary.
He handled cargo movements. Guns, tanks, jeeps, ammo, things
like that. He fell in love with a woman. 'Sandy' her name was. A
real nice lady, I met her once. I liked her. But she was working
the other side of the street—selling information to the highest

bidder. Smith found out. He reported her to his bosses. Sandy was never heard of again."

She got this sort of cold, hard look on her face. Her mouth drew tight across her teeth. She stood up slowly, her limbs shaking. She walked to the door and put on her boots. "I get it," she said. "You think I'm an agent of some kind. You're in the spy business and you think I'm in it too. That I've been sent to lure you into some kind of trap. You told me that story to warn me, didn't you?"

I nodded.

"Now I know why you act strangely at times. Why you get these funny, distant looks in your eyes every once in a while. It must have been horrible for you to be around me, thinking such terrible things about me."

My throat closed up. She opened the door, but she didn't go out. Instead, she turned around and said, "You're right, I was planning to lure you into a trap."

I waited.

"But not that kind of trap. My kind of trap." She was crying again. "I'm no spy. I'm just me. Meredith. And I have no sinister designs on you."

She came over to me and held onto me tight. "And if somebody's after you and you're in danger, I want to be in danger with you. Please, please don't make me go away. If you do, I'll park my bus in your driveway and if this man comes, he's got to get through me first." She wiped her eyes and looked up at me. "How could you think such horrible things about me?"

"I'm sorry, sweetheart, I'm so sorry."

I kissed her, tasting the salt of tears.

"Promise you won't tell me any more stories like that again."

"I won't."

"Promise you won't go away again without telling me."

117

"I promise."

She wiped her face on my shirt. She kissed me again. "I never act this way," she said. "Honest. I don't know what's the matter with me . . . no, I do know. It's you. I've never felt quite this way in my life. It feels strange. It feels like I've taken a drug. I'm mixed up every which way."

"Me too."

We kissed again. We held each other tight for a long time.

"I'm never going to let you go," she said.

"I'm never going to let you go, either."

"I must look awful."

"You look beautiful."

"What do you say we go out and celebrate."

"What are we celebrating?"

"Us."

I threw on a pair of slacks and a heavy shirt, got out my sheepskin coat, and put on a pair of heavy leather boots. She went into the bathroom and washed her face. When I was ready to go, she was standing by the door, smiling. She took hold of my hand tightly like she never wanted to let it go.

We drove to Amber and had a few beers at Willy and Martha's. Meredith insisted on a game of pool. Twice she ran the table on me. A local shark in his seventies name of Lester Gorn, an Eight-Ball legend, played her for a beer and beat her twice, but both games were close. She tried like hell, taking her time with each shot, studying the tough ones from both ends of the table. She'd studied with a master, you could tell. She held her cue with the dexterity of a brain surgeon holding a scalpel. Old Lester had to slickly hide the cue ball a couple of times to keep her from winning. I think he'd rather have been run over by a truck than lose to a woman.

He chuckled when he won and toasted Meredith with the

beers she bought him. She was a gracious loser, congratulating him and bowing when he toasted her.

After the pool games Meredith said she was real hungry, so we drove over to Heather Glen and had dinner at Pine Acre Farm, a sort of roadhouse on the north edge of town. The steaks were thick and good, served on sizzling platters, and the french fries were cut thick and the skins had been left on them. The place was rustic, with a plain wood floor and a huge stone fireplace, and it was full of people out having fun. A bluegrass band played and when we weren't busy eating, we were busy clapping and stomping.

She said, "I could've had him, if he hadn't played dirty pool. Next time, I'll play peekaboo with him, see how the old coot likes it."

"All's fair in love, war, and pool," I said.

"I'll remember that." She stamped her feet and clapped to the music, having a ball.

After dinner we stayed and enjoyed the music and danced a little, but it was square dancing and neither of us knew what we were doing and it seemed like everyone else did. So we watched and clapped and drank beer for a couple of hours. We left when the band took a break. Meredith said she had something to show me, so she had me drive east a couple of miles on a narrow country road, then we made a turn off onto a fire trail. Tree limbs scraped the sides and the roof as we twisted up a hill and came out on sort of a flat edge of a cliff. Here we could see the valley below us with the lights of Heather Glen and Amber, and the cars going through on the main road above on the way to the ski resorts.

She turned some soft Benny Goodman stuff on the radio and we sat and smoked and sipped brandy from her flask. A crescent moon hung low in the eastern sky. Neither of us said anything for a long while, maybe an hour. Finally, she put her head on my shoulder and said, "I think I'm going to like having you around, sailor."

"Good."

"I want you to know I hate it when people call me Carrot-top."

"Okay, I'll never call you Carrot-top."

"Or Red."

"Okay."

"Or Rusty. They used to call me that when I was a girl, and I hated it."

"Okay. And you don't call me Chickenbrain. That's what my father used to call me when he was mad."

She laughed. And nestled up closer. After a while she said, "Take me home and I'll let you make love to me," she said. "Let's do it slowly. I've got this black silk thing with lace around here—" she drew a line low across her chest, "and here—" she traced a line across her lap.

"I can't wait to see it."

She turned her head and kissed me. "I am going to drive you wild."

We headed down the road back through Heather Glen and then over the bridge and up the hill to Amber. Meredith wrapped both arms around me and kept squeezing. "I'm never going to let go, you're going to have to get me surgically amputated."

Gray Wolf, the Exchange, my past, it was all a million miles away. I was dreaming the happy dream and didn't want to wake up.

I stopped at Maxie's and got a couple bottles of champagne. Maxie's best was nine bucks a bottle. When I started driving again, Meredith pulled my shirt up and started kissing me on the chest.

"Gives me the shivers," I said.

"Supposed to," she said.

I pulled into her driveway and there was a big black Lincoln Town Car with New Jersey plates waiting. Two men in it, the chauffeur in the driver's seat, the other in the back. Frank Webb, no doubt.

"I don't know anyone who owns a car like that," she said.

"I do. Go in the house, Meredith. Please."

She got out of the Bronco and dashed into the house. I waited for a moment before getting out. I was feeling cold all over. Frank Webb being here could only mean trouble. I was feeling fear and at the same time I was angry. I didn't like the idea of him being around Meredith. She was my new life and I didn't want any of the old filth sullying it.

I walked over to the Lincoln. It had turned much colder and the driveway was half frozen and crunched under my feet. The Lincoln's left rear window came down and there was Frank, sitting in the darkness sucking on a cigar.

"Emergency," he said. "Get in."

The chauffeur got out as I got in. Frank Webb was pressed up against the door on the other side and even in the dim light I could see his eyes; he was damn worried.

"What is it?" I said.

"Gray Wolf's on the move. He's in the States. We got a line on him in France yesterday. A toad of ours in Marseilles deals in false IDs and information. He cut a deal with Gray Wolf—papers, passport, that kind of thing—reporting everything to us. Gray Wolf knows I was trying to find him for you. He may have put two and two together and figures I was trying to find him so you could do him." He ran his sleeve across his forehead. It wasn't hot in there, but Frank Webb was sweating like a sumo wrestler. "The Exchange sent two more men to get Gray Wolf last Friday. Good men. He put them both down as slick as a lumberjack clearing saplings. We're in a big tub of trouble, my friend."

His voice was tight with fear. He knew what a deadly son of a bitch Gray Wolf was.

"Take it easy, Frank."

"I got a little money holed away, Coldiron. A hundred grand of it is yours if you do him. Call the Exchange, they'll kick in some more goodies, and they'll give you all the help you need."

"Gray Wolf wouldn't come for me just because you were looking to get word to him."

"Don't you think I know that? I been checking on it. Seems like somebody in the Exchange has let it out that you took them up on their deal and are on the hunt."

"Christ. Those bastards." I took a deep breath. "Give me the name of the son of a bitch and I'll ram his head through a keyhole."

"I don't know who it was, Coldiron. I'd give him to you if I did. But it was somebody in management, you can bet your ass on that."

I kicked the front seat. "I don't give a fuck what the chairman does or Gray Wolf does, or anybody does. I'm finished with all of it."

"What the hell you gonna do? Gray Wolf's comin', and he's gonna fuckin' blow you up!"

"I'll bury myself in the deepest hole I can find. Sooner or later, with the Exchange against him, he'll go down. I'll just wait him out."

"This ain't like you, Coldiron."

"There isn't any Coldiron anymore, Frank. There's only me. Civilian Tom Croft. And you want to know something? I'm scared and I'm running, Frank. I suggest you do the same."

He looked at me in the darkness and said nothing for a long moment. Then: "Where'll I be able to get hold of you?"

"No one will be able to get hold of me, Frank, I'm going to vanish off the face of the earth."

123

I got out of the car and walked toward the house. The driver watched me as I walked past him, tipping his hat with a cool expression on his face. His eyes were small and sharp. He got back in the car and started it up.

Frank Webb called to me, "You won't be able to hide from him, he'll find you somehow."

I didn't answer him. I went on into the house. From the front window, I watched the big Lincoln back down the driveway and into the road, then drive away. There were beads of sweat on my forehead and I felt strangely lightheaded, tingling with fear.

I turned around and Meredith was standing there with two drinks in her hands. "Come and sit down," she said.

I took a drink and followed her to the couch, but I didn't sit. Neither did she. The drink she'd given me was a straight scotch, at least a double. "Skol," she said, and we each downed our drinks. The room had a chill in it, but a fire was roaring in the iron stove.

Meredith said, "Can you tell me at least this much?" She held her finger from her thumb about a quarter of an inch.

"I can't," I said. "Just believe me, it's bad. I've got to go away for a little while."

"More of the same trouble?"

"Yeah."

She stared at me and for a moment a smile came to her lips like maybe she thought I was joking, but then the smile faded.

"When are you leaving?"

"As soon as I finish this drink."

"How long will you be gone?"

"I don't know."

"A few days? A week? A month?"

"I don't know."

"You *will* be coming back?"

124

"Yes."

She went over to the serving bar, rolling her glass in her hand, looking worried as hell, and poured us both another drink. "You must have a lot to pack," she said.

"I'm leaving right from here. I won't be going back to my place."

She handed me my glass. "Dear God." She walked back and forth across the room with her hands jammed into the back pockets of her jeans, her heels clicking on the bare wood floor, her jaw tight.

"I have to be going," I said.

"I don't suppose you'll let me know where you're going."

"No."

She came over to me and kissed me suddenly, throwing her arms around me. "I just found you and I'm not letting you go."

I managed to put my drink down, then pushed her away as gently as I could. "No, Meredith, I've got to go. Minutes may be important."

She kissed me. She tasted sweet, but I managed to push her away again. I said, "Damn it now, Meredith, you don't understand. The man's a maniac."

"You don't understand," she said, "I'm a maniac." She took me by the arm and led me to the bedroom and started taking my shirt off.

"No Meredith . . ."

I kept pushing her away, but she had my belt and was undoing it and she kept kissing me on the mouth and neck and then I felt myself suddenly wanting her and we were kissing and I wanted her, wanted her bad.

"Make love to me hard," she said. "Hard and fast, come on. One last time."

We were unbuttoning each other's clothes and kissing and

she brought her arms around me and pulled me to her, her breasts pressing against my chest. I could feel her heart thundering within her. "Love me," she said, "never stop loving me, love me hard."

"This is crazy, I . . ."

"Shut up and take me, take me now and fast." Her fingers dug into my back. We kissed, pressing our lips and bodies together and she moved under me and the darkness of the room closed around me and the fear and the specter of Gray Wolf dissolved as she drew me into her.

She murmured: "Harder, come on!"

She moved under me as we slammed together, and again, and again, and we seemed to explode together.

Then we lay side by side, sweating in the darkness.

"I may pay for this moment with my life," I said.

"Was it worth it?"

"Absolutely."

She kissed me on the mouth. I rolled out of bed and started dressing, feeling like the rawest rookie on earth.

"Wait a minute," she said. "I'll go with you."

"No, absolutely not."

"You'll need someone to teach you to shoot pool."

I tied my boots. "Thanks for the offer, Meredith, but no thanks. I don't want you involved in this in any way. When I walk through that door, forget you ever saw me. Tomorrow, I want you to spread it all over town that I left suddenly with an old man in a big Lincoln without ever saying good-bye. Let everyone know you're good and mad at me, okay?"

She shook her head. "No, it isn't okay," she said. "I'm going with you and that's that."

"No you aren't. It's totally and absolutely out of the question."

I went into the john and took a leak. When I came out she was gone. I called upstairs. No answer. I heard footsteps on the stairs, turned around, and saw her coming in the front door.

"Thought I heard a car," she said. "Just wanted to take a look."

"You thought you heard a car, so you went out there? Are you out of your mind? He'd cut you down like a blade of grass."

"I want to pack a few things," she said. "It'll only take me three minutes."

"I said you weren't coming," I said.

"I refuse to discuss it," she said. She went into the bedroom. I followed her as far as the doorway. "Meredith. Listen to me. I like you a lot."

"Like?" she said. "I had an inkling it was more than that."

"It can't be, Meredith. I'm sorry if you thought it was more than that. A man in my business, well, that's all he's entitled to. Women just don't fit in."

"Oh, we don't fit in."

"That's right."

"Use them up like Kleenex, that it?"

"Yeah, like Kleenex."

"Nice piece of ass, right? Feel 'em, fuck 'em, forget 'em, that it?"

"Right," I said. I turned and headed down the steps. I got in the Bronco and turned the key. It cranked over but it wouldn't start. A momentary panic flooded over me. But then it hit me that she'd tampered with the car when she'd gone outside.

I lit up a cigarette and sat there for a few moments until she came out of the house carrying a small suitcase. She came over to the Bronco and threw the suitcase in the back, then went around and opened the hood. I couldn't see what she was doing under there, probably putting the distributor cap back on.

Then she got in the car. I didn't move. She didn't move. She said, "Just tell me you don't love me and I'll get out." I looked at her. "I don't love you."

She sat there in the darkness not moving for a long moment. Then she reached over and turned the key. The Bronco started up. She slid over next to me, took hold of my arm, and said, "Just drive."

We took a back road over to Round Lake, where it meets Route 30, then we headed south toward Speculator. I took this way in case they had the main road south staked out.

It was snowing a light, wet snow mixed with rain; the road was slick. There wasn't much traffic. I kept the Bronco in four-wheel drive, staying under fifty.

Meredith hadn't said anything in a long while. She was sitting very still and rigid, and I thought she was probably scared. As for me, the further we got from Amber, the more I was afraid for her. Yet at the same time I wanted nothing more in the world than to have her with me. She stirred something in me, something I thought had been long cold dead. Before I met her, I was a man with a big hole in his center. Now it was filled to the golden brim, filled with something warm and alive.

What if Gray Wolf caught up with us and she was hit in a cross fire? The thought made me shiver. I turned to her and motioned for her to sit by me. She slid over and I put my arm around her and she rested her head against my shoulder. My throat felt dry.

"I know what you're thinking," she said. "And the answer is *no*."

"You don't know what I'm thinking."

"You're thinking of sending me back."

"I wasn't thinking that exactly, but it is a good idea."

"I'm not going back, and I won't discuss it."

"It needs discussing."

She turned toward the window.

We were going through a series of twists and turns. Barren, spindly trees grew right down to the road.

We came out on a straight stretch and I said: "Listen, Meredith. Please. Just listen and see if this doesn't make sense. The man who wants me dead is himself being hunted. A huge number of people are looking for him. Sooner or later—very likely sooner—he's going to be found and he'll be arrested and put away for life." I thought "arrested" sounded better than "taken care of." Of course the Exchange never arrested anyone; if they wanted you off the street, they just had you taken care of and no one ever heard from you again.

"In the meanwhile," I continued, "I'm going to be dodging him. He's a very determined man and very smart. It's just possible that he will be able to find me, and when he does there may be, well, trouble."

She didn't say anything. She slid over closer to the door and just sat there looking straight ahead.

"Don't you see," I said, "I just don't want to see you hurt."

I took the Bronco around some more curves. I was going a little too fast and the tire caught the side of the road, giving us a few bumps. We were lower in altitude now, and the wet snow had

130

turned to a fine, misting rain. I came out of the curves and there was a big deer with huge antlers along the side of the road staring at me; he turned suddenly and leapt back into the woods.

Just below was a white farmhouse. A sign read: Albany 45 Miles. Drive Carefully.

"You could take a bus back to Amber in the morning," I said. "I'll join you as soon as this bad business is over."

"Pull over," she said. "Let's talk."

"I'd rather keep moving."

"I'd rather we get a few things straight."

I pulled over onto a wide shoulder, killed the engine, and turned off the lights. She sat there looking straight ahead, not saying anything.

"Well?" I said.

"I'm not a fool," she said.

"I never said you were. I just think maybe it'd be better if I sent you back. The man who wants me dead would know I wouldn't have told you anything, so he won't bother you."

"Did I say I wanted to go back?" Her voice sounded reedy. "I'm afraid," she said. "Terribly afraid. From the moment I decided to go with you, I've been afraid. But I'm not afraid of what you think I'm afraid of."

"What, then?"

She took a deep breath. "I'm afraid you'll abandon me, you'll think, for my own good."

"I don't want to see you hurt."

"Hear this," she said. "My great-grandmother came west in 1874 with my great-grandfather. He wanted to open a store in Arizona. A drygoods store. Cloth. Pots and pans. Make a fortune, he said. Adventure is what he really wanted."

"But this is different."

"Shut up. They went by wagon train in one of those big Conestoga jobs pulled by oxen. They were twice attacked by Indians. Once by Apaches. Do you know how fierce the Apaches were? My great-grandmother loaded the guns and my great-grandfather shot them. She was six months pregnant at the time. She took an arrow in her butt, but she survived; they both survived. They set up a store in Waterloo in the high country. There they fought off Comancheros. Hey, buddy, what I'm trying to tell you is that I come from tough goddamn stock." She rolled down the window and breathed in some air.

"I never thought you weren't tough."

"My father was a rodeo rider. My mother rode trick bareback when she was a kid. I once stole a car when I was sixteen—on a dare. I've got guts. I come from a long line of gutsy bastards."

I lit a cigarette and opened the window to blow the smoke out.

She said, "Am I going to wake up one morning and find you gone? I want to know. Tell me now."

I took a deep drag on the cigarette. "Jesus Christ," I said.

"You just might fly away, is that what you're saying?"

"Yeah," I said, "I guess it is what I'm saying."

"I appreciate your honesty," she said. Cold as hell.

I was on fire inside. I wanted to grab hold of her and hold on to her and swear that forever and ever I would never let her go. But the truth was that if Gray Wolf got onto me, I might make a run for it to lead him away from her. And I couldn't deny it. I'd lied and flimflammed women all my life, but I wasn't going to lie and flimflam this one.

"It would never be for another woman," I said.

She turned to me in the darkness. "Don't you think I know that?"

132

She was shaking like hell. "I'm like my great-grandmother," she said. "I always told myself that if I ever found that one great love of my life, I would know it, and I would commit myself to that man and stay with him and stick with him no matter what. And as soon as I saw you, that very first day when I glanced over my shoulder when I was riding my bike, I said, 'There he is.' Just like that. I knew. I don't know how I knew, I just knew. And the more I know you, the more I feel I was right. I just feel that I belong with you, even if we're attacked by Apaches or whatever. I'm willing to pay a price to be with you, no matter what the price is."

I looked over at her and in the darkness I could sense her intensity. Like two magnets, one negative, one positive, that get close to each other and zap!—they come together and you can never get the sons a bitches apart.

"My great-grandfather could have left my great-grandmother in Boston," she said. "He wanted her to stay, but she wouldn't let him go without her. She wanted to be with her man no matter what. She wasn't afraid to die. I'm not afraid to die. But damn it, I don't want to be left behind. And I don't want to be thinking every day when I get up, is this the day he's going away? I don't want to live like that. I want you to take me with you no matter where, no matter what." She took a couple of deep breaths. "If we go on," she said, "we stay together no matter how many Apaches attack. Agreed?"

I looked out into the darkness for a moment, feeling like retching.

"Well?" she said.

A tingle of fear flowed over my back, but I said: "Agreed."

She slid back over and kissed me and I put my arms around her and held her tight and kissed her and kissed her and held her for a long time and I kept saying over and over that I would never abandon her.

We drove around Albany a while looking for just the right place to leave the Bronco. It wasn't raining in Albany. It was a quiet night, cold and damp, with just a few patches of snow on the ground. There weren't many people on the street. We headed into the industrial section between Interstate 787 and the Hudson. The river looked calm and black, dotted with chunks of ice. Lots of abandoned factories up and down the shore. Who needs factories when all the goddamn jobs have been moved to Japan, Taiwan, Korea, Singapore, Mexico?

I found a dead-end street that ran along a closed-up warehouse. Old mattresses and junk had been dumped there, along with a couple of cars sitting on their hubs, doors missing, windows smashed.

"This ought to do it," I said. I parked the Bronco and we got out. A stiff wind gusted across the river, chilling us. I handed Meredith her bag and took the papers out of the glove box. I closed the glove box up and looked for something to throw through the window. A piece of pine board lay in the gutter; that was good enough.

"What are you doing?"

"We're just going to leave it here. In a couple of days it'll be stripped, plates, everything. It won't appear on any records and won't be traced until they tow it away. By then it will be just a pile of rust. Stand back, cover your eyes." I bashed in the windshield. It stuck together like a big sheet of plastic. Then I hit the passenger door's window. It shattered into a million bits.

"Let me," she said. I handed her the board and she bashed out the other windows, then put a big dent in the hood. She tossed the board back on the pile of junk. "Sure is fun being on the lam," she said.

We started walking away, bundling up against the chill.

"Something I don't understand," she said after a moment. "How could one man find one vehicle in this great big huge country?"

"He's well connected to people who can get cops—even federal cops—to look for us. No problem at all."

We walked a couple of blocks and caught a bus downtown and got off near the Vagabond Motel. I had Meredith go in and rent the room, making sure she kept her scarf over her hair. I told her to keep her head down and not to talk much. The Vagabond was a dump that local streetwalkers brought their johns to, sometimes making a lot of noise in the hall. The carpet in our room was threadbare and the toilet gurgled, but the bed was comfortable and the room was warm and clean. Meredith cuddled up by my side, put her arm around me, and went to sleep.

I lay there in the darkness telling myself the most pleasing of lies: *everything was going to work out okay.*

The next morning I got up at half past seven and went for a little jog. It was clear and crisp. I got back about a quarter after eight with a couple of French crullers and some coffee I bought at a take-out doughnut place across the street from the Vagabond. Meredith was in the shower. I did some calisthenics and watched "Good Morning Albany" on the tube. We ate cross-legged on the bed facing each other. She had on a robe with a towel wrapped around her head. I liked watching her eat. She was meticulous. She picked the crumbs off the spread with her fingers. Between small bites and small sips she kept smiling at me smiling at her. I felt like a goddamn giddy bridegroom.

135

After breakfast I took a shower even though I didn't have any clean clothes to change into. It was twenty to ten. I took the bag the crullers came in and she took her suitcase and we walked six blocks to the Merchants' Commercial Bank on Central Avenue. The store windows were decorated with witches, ghosts, pumpkins. It was the day before Halloween.

We had to wait five minutes for them to open the door. The Merchants' Commercial Bank was housed in one of those bank buildings with a lot of marble pillars and one hundred-odd years of steadfast integrity holding up the roof. An old geezer in a baggy blue suit checked my name against the signature four times before he finally admitted us to the safe-deposit vault.

I gave the old geezer my key and he unlocked the box and carried it out of the vault to a private room the size of a closet. He said he'd be outside if we needed him.

The box was stuffed with money wrapped in bands: twenties, fifties, hundred-dollar bills. I stuffed half the money in the cruller bag and the other half in Meredith's suitcase, three or four thousand. Then I gave her a wad of bills to shove in her pocket. In the safe-deposit box there were also a small Heckler and Koch .45 automatic model 94 and four clips. I liked the Heckler and Koch better than Langston's Steyer 9mm. The Heckler and Koch model 94 carries eight rounds and has a delayed roller-lock system to cut down on the recoil. It didn't carry as many bullets as the Steyer, but it had more knockdown power and I was used to it. I checked the magazine; it was loaded. I stuffed it and the clips into my pocket. Meredith didn't wince at the sight of the gun.

On the way out, she said: "Awful lot of money."

"Ill-gotten gains," I said.

We left the bank and walked down the street to a small square with a bench overlooking a statue of a Revolutionary War soldier covered with pigeon shit. The streets were busy, full of business types trudging along carrying a heavy load of brief-cases, their faces frozen by routine.

"Okay," I said. "Here's the plan. First I want you to call your boss back in Amber and tell him your mother is ill and you have to rush to her bedside."

"She's in Hawaii."

"Do the people you were working with know that?"

She nodded. "I'm sure I must have mentioned it."

"Okay, Hawaii it is. I want you to go across the street, get into a cab, and take it to the airport. Get the first plane out to New York. Then book a flight to Hawaii."

She looked at me, and I could see she was working up a protest.

"Listen," I said. "Here's what you do. Go see your mom. Call your director from Hawaii at a time you know he won't be there, leave a message for him to call you back. When he calls, tell him you won't be coming back to work. Gossip gets around Amber pretty fast and the man that's after me will hear it, and he'll buy it. He knows I'd never go underground with a woman. He won't bother going to Hawaii to check you out, because he'd know I would never tell anyone anything. Okay?"

"So far."

"Buy a ticket to L.A. When you get to L.A., I want you to go to the ladies' room, put a dark rinse in your hair, buy a ticket on United Airlines for New York, Newark. Do what you can without being obvious to make sure you're not being followed. It's not likely, but it's possible. If you are being followed, go where it's crowded and keep making turns. Go to the cops if you can't shake them, tell them it's some guy who exposed himself; that'll take them off you for sure. I'll meet every flight from L.A. the day after the day after tomorrow. Wednesday. If I'm not there when you get off the plane, take the airport bus to Manhattan and go to the Wilder Hotel on East 42nd Street at First Avenue and register under the name of—let's see—"

"Jane Bond. 008." She grinned.

"All right, Jane Bond."

"I don't want to be away from you for three days, Tom. Is this trip really necessary?"

"It's necessary. It'll buy us time."

"Where'll we settle finally? Or do we just keep moving?"

"I have a plan. I'll tell you when I see you."

"I trust you," she said, kissing me on the cheek.

"Get going now," I said.

"All right."

I watched her get into a cab and we waved to each other. I watched the cab go up the street and disappear around the corner, then found a phone booth and called Bob Carpano, the Brooklyn gangster who owed me a favor. I'd once saved his brother from getting executed in a drug raid down in Colombia— the Exchange was settling its difference with the Mendoza Cartel and Bob Carpano's brother just happened to be there to set up a deal and I got him out of the way. At the time Bob said he owed me a service.

I told him I needed a safe house for a few weeks. He said he had the perfect place. He asked no questions.

First thing I did was go back to the bank and get into my second safe-deposit box. The old geezer who took care of the boxes didn't seem to know I'd just been there fifteen minutes before. He checked my signature against the card, then led me to the vault again. This was a small box, and inside was a large envelope. I removed the envelope and handed the old geezer back the box.

I went back out in the street, walked a couple of blocks to a drugstore, bought a pair of scissors, a package of disposable razor blades, some shaving cream, a toothbrush, toothpaste, a little hair dye, and a pair of dark glasses. In the envelope I'd gotten out of the safe-deposit box I had five fake IDs including passports. I took out one in the name of Henry William Clark and mailed the others to my post-office drop in Manhattan.

Then I took a city bus to neighboring Schenectady. There I bought a Ford Pinto out of a newspaper ad for $500. The gap-toothed housewife I bought it from swore she'd never driven it over forty-five and had polished it every other day. It had

111,000 miles on it and the seats were ratty and the rocker panels were rusted through, but it ran.

I drove west on Route 5 twenty miles and rented a roadside cabin. Here I cut my hair short and dyed it black. Made me look like an old guy trying to look younger and failing. That afternoon I drove into Syracuse and found a St. Vincent de Paul store and bought a sackful of clothes: work shirts, dress shirts, slacks, jeans, a couple of sport jackets. The whole thing ran $89. I looked rather rumpled, which is just the way I wanted to look. I bought some underclothes and socks at Sears.

I spent the next day playing the old game of hiding the peanut under the shell. Gray Wolf and I knew a guy name of Armatige who lived in Philly. I called him and told him I needed a good passport and would be down there to pick it up in a couple of days. I had no intention of seeing Armatige, because Armatige could be bought for a nickel. Next I phoned a black guy in Houston name of Witherspoon who was also in the phony ID business and made an appointment for the following day.

Of course I had no intention of seeing him either. I was just making smoke.

Then I called Frank Webb. A man answered. He said Mr. Webb was on an extended vacation and hung up.

Early in the evening I took the Amtrak Lakeshore Limited to Chicago, so anyone who might get onto me would see I was heading west. Then the next morning I caught a plane for Washington, D.C., using the name Henry William Clark.

A weather front had moved in and was lashing the capital with a freezing rain. Not many cars on the street in the early evening. No pedestrians out. A few kids in costume going trick-or-treating. I took the airporter from Dulles and checked into a small, shabby hotel on Virginia Street. The room was $60 and about big enough for a sparrow if it didn't flap its wings. A single-sized bed, a TV, a small desk, a wastebasket were all there was in the room. It smelled of Lysol.

At a quarter after seven I came out of the hotel and caught a cab and took it to 14th and H Street, near the Greyhound bus terminal. I paid the cabdriver and crossed the street. The freezing rain felt like BB-shot on my head. I kept my hands in my pockets and my right hand on my gun. The sidewalk was slippery as hell.

I walked up 14th Street. Kids roamed the streets in costume with bags of candy.

Mercy Convalescent Hospital was on the corner. That's where I was headed. Gray Wolf's Aunt Phyllis was a patient there. A guy in a faded army jacket was out in front sprinkling salt on the stairs. I didn't go in. Instead, I went down the block, crossed over the street, and went up the other side. I wanted to have a look around, just to be on the safe side.

At the next intersection, parked at the corner, was a Thunderbird with two guys in it. I walked right past them. The guy behind the wheel was Langston, the clown who tried to recruit me to kill Gray Wolf. I couldn't make out the guy with him, but it was probably his trainee, the blond guy, Vanders.

I didn't know if Langston recognized me; I really didn't give a damn. Spotting him, though, was a comfort. At least Gray Wolf wasn't around. If he were, he'd have taken those two out. What a couple of donkeys, sitting there in the open, I thought.

In the apartment building in front of me, all but one of the windows were lit up. The one that wasn't was on the third floor. That room had the best view of the street. Maybe the two donkeys weren't such donkeys after all. Maybe there was somebody up there with a night vision scope fixed to a sniper's rifle.

141

Gray Wolf and I had visited his Aunt Phyllis the year before. He told me then that no one knew about her, the only family he had. Gray Wolf said he and I were friends, so he wanted me to meet the old gal. She was checking out and he wanted to stop by and say so long. Only she hadn't checked out as quickly as her doctors had forecast. So much for the science of medicine.

I went into the convalescent hospital. Just inside the door to the left there was a waiting room. It looked like a hotel lobby, with stuffed chairs and couches spread around on a thick red carpet. But it smelled like a hospital: flowers, cleaning solvents, sickness, death. There were only two people in the waiting room: a man and a woman whispering to each other by the window. The woman was wiping away some tears; the man was comforting her. Nobody at the information desk. I took the elevator to the fourth floor, all the time keeping my hand on my Heckler and Koch.

A maintenance man was running a polishing machine. Nearby, an old guy in a blue robe showing his bony chest sat in a wheelchair watching him. He had an intense look on his face as if the floor scrubber was the most fascinating thing he'd ever seen. The old guy never even turned my way. You live long enough on this planet, this is the payoff. You get to sit around in a blue robe watching a guy machine the floors of a hospital.

I went down the hall to the nurse's station. The nurse looked up at me. She was a slender young woman with stringy blond hair. She had pale, thin lips, and seemed not too friendly.

"Ms. Fairweather," I said. "Phyllis Fairweather."

"Ms. Fairweather is very ill," she said.

"I called from Chicago this morning, talked to a Dr. Steven Prescot."

"Dr. Steven *Prescop*, with a *P*," she corrected. She showed me her wide, yellow teeth in the approximation of a smile.

"All right, with a *P*. Now can I see the patient?"

"I'll have to check." She sorted through some papers on a large brown clipboard. "Mr. Clark?"

"That's me."

"This way," she said. She led me down the hall to a door. I went into the room softly. The old lady was sitting by the window in a high-back wicker wheelchair and at first I thought she might be asleep. She had a heavy wool shawl over her narrow shoulders even though it was quite warm in the room. The disease had wasted her considerably in the year since I'd seen her. Her cheeks were sunken and her arms were like sticks. The bluish skin seemed loose, translucent. I walked over to her and she looked up at me with pinkish, hollow eyes. A flicker of recognition registered. She frowned.

"You do remember me, don't you?" I said.

She nodded slowly and her head seemed to shudder on her thin neck. She gave off a putrid odor, like death had already claimed part of her.

"I have not seen him," she said. Her voice was raspy, but surprisingly strong.

"He's back in the States," I said. "He may try to get in touch with you."

She leaned back and looked at me. "People are looking for him," she said. "They had identity papers that said they were with the government. They said he's gone over, is that true?"

"I don't know," I said. "I've been out of it for a year."

"Out of it? How can you get out of it? You can't get out of it. Nobody can. Not until you're dead." She closed her eyes and opened them again. "Did they tell you he's gone over?"

"Yes."

She turned toward the window. Outside there was a lot of traffic on the street, kids going by in small groups in costume. But she didn't seem to be watching anything in particular. She

143

shook her head, profoundly saddened. She had been a player, Gray Wolf had told me; she'd worked for the OSS in World War II. She ran Operation Rainbow, where inexperienced dumbos were dropped into occupied France with misinformation crammed into their heads so the Germans could pry it out after they were captured. Condemned spies they were called. None of them ever came back.

"He may come to see you," I said.

"He knows better than that. They're waiting for him out there. He won't come."

"He might take it as a challenge."

She gave me a grin. "They called you Coldiron, didn't they? I heard you were damn good. Theodore said you were the only one he thought was in his league."

Theodore was Gray Wolf's real name. I never heard anyone call him Theodore except the old lady.

"No one was ever quite in his league," I said.

"Ah, it's all a different game now anyways. Glasnost. The fucking Russians lost their guts. With them out of the way, there's great opportunity in the game now. The Third World will be our playground."

"Where can I get in touch with Theodore? Do you know?"

She scowled. She shook her head. "My sister's boy. Always a wild kid. We were so pleased when he went with the Exchange. They showed him how to channel that wildness. We never figured him to roll over, why would he do something like that?"

"I don't know," I said.

"Must be for the money. He never could hold onto it once he had it, but he sure did have a great fondness for it." She coughed up some phlegm and spit it into a bowl in her lap. "You know what it is, this game we spend our life playing? Playing God, that's the attraction. Choosing who lives and who dies. There's

144

nothing quite like it on the face of the earth. Killing, I mean. It's what we were born to do."

She looked up at me with a strange glint in her eyes, and for a moment she resembled the painting Meredith made on the backdrop for the play. Then she laughed, making a horrible cackling sound in her throat. She straightened up and took a couple of deep breaths. "Changing sides is a terrible business," she said. "They will fucking kill you for that. They will kill your friends sometimes, too."

Then she looked at me with her mouth agape. "That's why you're here, isn't it? You want a lead on him so you can do him? Good. He went over, he should have to pay the price, nephew of mine, or not."

"I'm not after him. I want to tell him that I'm not coming for him. No matter what, I'm out of it. I've found a woman I want to be with and I'm going away with her. There's no reason for him to follow."

Her eyes widened. "If they want you to kill Theodore, it's your duty!"

She grabbed my arm with her skeletal fingers and held on with amazing strength. "Go and get him and kill him. You're a player and he's gone over. He must die!"

I tried to peel her fingers off, but they were like steel clamps and I couldn't budge them.

She shrieked: "Kill him! Kill him! Kill him!"

Suddenly the nurse was in the room. "What's going on here?" She shot an angry glance at me. The old crone let go of my arm, coughed and spit into her bowl, then took a breath and turned toward the window, waving me off with her bony hand. The nurse straightened her shawl. "There, there," she said. Then she turned to me and said, "I think Ms. Fairweather needs to rest now."

145

On my way out I found Langston waiting in the lobby.

"Have a nice visit?" he asked me, flashing a grin. He had his hand in his coat; I doubt he was just keeping it warm.

"Fuck you, Langston."

He laughed.

On the way up the street I met a kid coming the other way wearing a death's mask and a black robe.

I stopped. My hand closed on my automatic.

He was big enough to be a man. His face glowed under his black hood, eerie as hell. I watched his eyes, they focused on me with a strange intensity and I was ready to pull my gun on him.

But suddenly he gave me a wave and a laugh and said, "Good evening, sir. Happy Halloween." He had the squeaky voice of an adolescent kid.

I said nothing. He moved on by.

The following day I spent sitting in a green Naugahyde-and-chrome chair in a lounge at the Newark airport waiting for Meredith. I wore jeans and a knit cap pulled down over my ears and a black leather car coat. I read newspapers, smoked cigarettes, and drank evil-tasting coffee.

I met every United Airlines flight coming in from L.A. and there's one about every half hour. And with each my expectation that I'd see her climbed higher, but she wasn't on any of them, and when the last passenger would get off, a hollow feeling would come over me. As the day wore on I began thinking maybe she'd talked things over with her mother and her mother might have pointed out how totally insane it was to go off with a man who was obviously into some very shady dealings.

By ten o'clock that night I was on the edge of despair, vacillating between hope and an impulse to get stinking drunk. Every half hour or so I called the Wilder Hotel in Manhattan to see if "Jane Bond" had checked in. She hadn't. And, no, she hadn't called to cancel her reservation. And no, no one else had been asking about her.

The next-to-the-last plane that Wednesday was at 11:10. Flight 807. I watched the passengers disembark while sitting at a nearby lounge. First a bunch of business types got off, then a couple of Catholic priests, then an Asian couple wearing Hawaiian shirts with cameras dangling from their necks. Behind them was an old lady in a wheelchair and, behind her, a fat man with a briefcase. The fat man was rubbing a spot off his tie.

And then there she was.

She was wearing a short gray coat, a yellow scarf around her head, and a pair of jeans and running shoes. Her hair was chestnut brown. She looked worried and scared. She carried a gray flight bag, one of those nylon bags with a shoulder strap. She didn't look around, she didn't even hesitate, like she wasn't expecting to meet anyone anyway; she just headed for the baggage-handling area, eyes straight ahead.

Goddamn I was glad to see her, even though for the moment I'd have to keep my distance. There was something in the way she hurried away that told me that maybe she'd been followed. And so I just stayed put and watched her disappear down the corridor. I turned back toward the door where the passengers were coming out of the plane and that's when I noticed the little man walking off the ramp. He had curly black hair, an anemic complexion, slumped shoulders, a shuffling gait. Viktor Dukas.

The pig hadn't changed much since the last time I saw him. He was wearing his hair shorter, cut close to his scalp, and he'd put on a little weight around the gut. But it was Viktor all right, the guy who used to run errands for Gray Wolf down in the Caribbean.

There was something about having that slime even in the same airport with Meredith that nauseated me. I got up out of my seat slowly, picking up a newspaper, and started following him. A prickly feeling went up my back, that same feeling I always got when the Exchange sent me to make someone go away permanently.

I followed Viktor down an escalator and through a mob of people waiting at the carousel. He was standing behind Meredith. He kept looking around the room, looking for me, no doubt. He knew my tendencies, which were to hang back, so he wasn't looking in close. But I was breaking my tendencies, so I was close enough to smell his stink. I held the newspaper in front of me like I was reading it, so when he turned, all I had to do was lift it a little to stay hidden.

Meredith grabbed a gray nylon suitcase off the carousel and walked away, glancing once back over her shoulder in Viktor's direction. He averted his face. He stayed that way for a moment and I thought maybe he'd pick up his luggage, but I guess it wasn't on the turnstile, because he turned suddenly and started after Meredith, with me right behind him. If he'd been working in a team, this would have been the time to pass off the surveillance to someone else. But he didn't, so I figured it was just Viktor, and now I had him.

He followed Meredith down a corridor. He hung back fifty feet. Here there weren't so many people and he should have hung back a little further, but Viktor Dukas never was that talented. The Exchange used him because he came cheap and he did what he was told. I caught up with him and pressed my finger in his back like it was a gun.

"Hello, Viktor, how's life?"

He stumbled a step or two, but kept walking, only slower. "Coldiron, my old friend." Fear rang in his voice. Meredith disappeared through an archway, heading in the direction of the cab stand in front of the terminal.

"I've been looking for you, Coldiron," Viktor said. "I've been following your girlfriend. Shouldn't we catch up to her and you can introduce me?"

"Some other time."

"What's the matter, my friend, you are not angry with old Viktor, are you?"

"That big black thing you killed in my kitchen wasn't a rat, Viktor, it was my dog."

He cleared his throat. "I did it so that you would know the seriousness of things. Out of friendship, I did it."

I jabbed my finger in harder and said, "Let's move along."

He kept moving ahead of me. His shoulders slumped like those of a man going to the gallows.

We came to some escalators going up to the mezzanine. "Up we go, Viktor."

"What can you do with all these people around?"

"I can kill you and be ten miles from here before they figure out you didn't die of indigestion."

His dark eyes narrowed. He glanced at the escalator. He wasn't going anywhere with me. He turned around to face me, looking down at my empty hand. "You won't kill me," he said.

"An eye for an eye. You killed my dog."

He ran his finger around the inside of his collar. "But a human being is worth more than a dog."

"Not in your case."

He smiled grimly at what he thought was my little joke. He kept his eyes on my face for a long moment and then a hiss escaped his lips. "What do you want from me?" he said. His voice fell into a lower register. He looked around at the people going by, but no one was paying the least attention to us.

"Why is Gray Wolf hunting me?" I said.

He shrugged. "He thinks you are his enemy because you

150

are good and he fears you. In his mind he has made you into a monster. He is not the same man he once was. He used to be serious on the job, but when away from the job, he was joking always. Now he no longer jokes. He is sad, you know, all the time. His mind is going. He thinks you are coming after him. He cannot sleep, thinking of it. "

"But I'm *not* coming after him, damn it!"

He shrugged as if to say he could do nothing about that.

"What are your orders?"

"To find you. "

"And then what?"

"To report. Viktor would do nothing to you, you know that in your heart, Coldiron. "

"How do you get hold of him?"

"I wire messages to a private spook; he passes them on."

"What private spook?"

"Toad. "

Sylvester Rohm. They called him Toad because he looked like one. He ran a phony security service as a consultant to big business and government. What he really did was supply high-tech espionage equipment and trained technicians; he was running a private CIA, only he never did any of the dirty work himself.

"Okay, Viktor. You listen carefully to what I'm going to tell you. I don't want you to forget it. "

"I'm listening. Viktor Dukas is totally trustworthy."

"If I ever see you anywhere near Meredith again, or I hear you've been asking about her, or looking for her, or are even in the same city as she's in by design or by chance, I will kill you in the most excruciatingly painful manner possible. Do you understand that?"

He looked at me and his big eyes blinked. He swallowed. "I understand," he said.

151

"There's one more thing."

"What, my friend?"

"You have to pay for the dog."

"What do you mean? How much?"

"You have to pay with your arm. Give me your arm, I'm going to break it."

Fear flickered across his eyes. "No," he said. He drew back.

"If you run and I have to run after you, I will break both of your arms."

His lips drew tight across his teeth. He squinted, his pupils turning to dots. "Do not do this to me. I was only doing what I was told. I must do what I am told, like anyone else."

"Your arm, Viktor, your right arm."

"Not the right one, please." His eyes teared over. His lips trembled and I could see he was looking around for help, but there wasn't a cop anywhere around, just travelers going about their business. "Don't do this thing," he whined. "Please."

"Your right arm, Viktor. Now. Give."

"Not the right one, I am right-handed."

"The right one—or both—it's up to you."

He slowly moved his trembling right arm away from his body. Sweat formed on his forehead. His lower lip curled in. He stared at me and after a moment he moved his arm toward me. I grabbed it above his wrist; it trembled violently.

"His name was Prince," I said. With that, I folded his wrist swiftly under; his body bent forward and I swung around to the side, bringing his arm up behind him. He folded over forward with a groan, dropping to his knees. I jerked his arm straight up and then I pivoted and swung my knee against his elbow from the opposite direction, breaking his elbow with a loud crack. He let out a yell. I let him go and backed away from him.

152

He dropped to the floor, moaning. A swarm of people had just picked up their luggage and had entered the corridor. They stopped, frozen with astonishment. Viktor looked at them pitifully, holding his arm and hissing through his teeth. I turned and hurried away. Somebody yelled, "Police! Police!" But no one came after me.

I turned the corner and went out the door and sprinted across the street to the parking garage. I took another exit out of the garage and caught a cab.

I leaned back and caught my breath. I was sweating, but I felt good. I felt I'd evened things up just a little. If I felt bad about anything at that moment, it was that I didn't break both his arms. A piece of shit like Viktor Dukas didn't deserve any mercy.

That's the way you think when you're playing the game, and whether I knew it or not at the time, I was playing.

On the way to the Wilder Hotel I had the cab stop at a liquor store
and called Gray Wolf's contact, Sylvester Rohm, in Washington.
I got a recording machine that said I'd reached the offices of O. O.
Cummings Security Services.

"This is Mr. Coldiron," I said. "I want to leave a message for
Mr. Graywolf. It's important we have a meeting on neutral
ground. I'll call again tomorrow." I bought a bottle of blackberry
brandy and got back in the cab.

The cab took me to East 42nd Street and Second Avenue. It
was one o'clock in the morning and was cold and damp when I got
out of the cab. The Wilder Hotel was a block away. A young
couple on the corner were arguing about something. She was
stamping her feet; he acted relaxed, hands in his pockets, shaking his head. An old guy walked past, pulled along by a little gray
dog. Nobody else around. A cocktail lounge at the corner called
The Rainbow had a sign blinking: Lowenbrau.

Everything looked as it ought to, but when you're playing you don't take chances. I crossed the street to a bank of pay phones and called the desk clerk at the hotel, who told me that Jane Bond had just checked in. I asked if anyone else had been looking for her and he said no one had. So I asked for her room number. Eight-ten, he said. She answered on the first ring.

"Jane, this is Ed." Since she'd know my voice, the name I used didn't matter.

"Nice to hear from you, Eddie."

"How about having a drink with me tonight?"

"Sure," she said.

"The Rainbow's right across the street."

"Fine. When?"

"Soon as you can get there."

"Give me five minutes."

She hung up. I pulled back into the shadows and waited. Five minutes went by. She came out of the hotel dressed as she had been at the airport. She walked up to the corner and waited for the light, then crossed the street and went into The Rainbow. I waited another five minutes. No one followed her in. I walked to the corner and couldn't see anyone hanging around in a parked car. I went back to the phones and called information and got the number of The Rainbow and called the bartender and told him to tell the woman who just came in that Ed phoned and said he'd be a few minutes late.

Then I went into the hotel, took the elevator to the eighth floor, and went to room 810 and jimmied the lock with my jackknife. I turned on the light. She hadn't hung up anything or put anything away in the drawers. I picked up her gray nylon bags and carried them down the back stairs to the street. I walked a block and got a cab and had the cabbie put the luggage in the trunk. I told him to drive to The Rainbow, go in and ask for Jane Bond, then bring her back here. "Say that Eddie sent you. Can you handle that okay?"

"Might be able," he said.

I gave him three twenties.

He looked at the bills, then he looked at me. "This ain't got nothin' to do with drugs?"

"No drugs. Her father doesn't love me as much as I love her. He's got private detectives on us."

He grinned. "I do it, man."

He got in his cab and made a U-turn. I crossed the street and stood near a subway entrance with my hand in the pocket where I had my Heckler and Koch automatic, safety off. Five minutes went by. Nothing much happening on the street. A few cabs went by. A cop car. A big truck. The wind gusted every once in a while, cold as hell.

Then my cab came back and stopped across the street where it had stopped before. Nobody followed it as far as I could see. A rusted-out car came by slowly, dragging its muffler. It kept on going.

I could see Meredith sitting in the back of the cab looking all around for me. The cabbie got out and looked around. I jogged across the street and hopped in. Meredith threw her arms around me and held me tightly without saying anything. The little door in the Plexiglass divider between the front and back seats was open and I heard the cabbie say, "Ain't love something else?"

We took the cab to Times Square.

Once we were alone, she said:

"I hardly recognized you!"

Her chestnut brown hair made her look more serious. I ran my hand through it.

She said, "It's only a rinse. It won't last."

"It better not."

We walked a few blocks and doubled back, going in one door of a bar and out the other. Then we caught another cab up to West 99th and Riverside Drive across from Riverside Park. I kept looking out the back window. The traffic was light, and I was pretty sure we weren't being followed. Even so, I told the cabbie to go around the block before he left us off.

I had a key to the front door that Bob Carpano had sent to the mail drop the night before—along with a letter detailing the protection mechanisms and the escape routes out of the place. Inside, a lanky Puerto Rican security guard sat behind a desk reading a book. *Principles of World Economics.* He looked up. "May I help you?"

"I'm a guest. Thirteen A."

"Ah, yes. Mr. Able. Welcome." He glanced at Meredith.

I said, "This is Mrs. Able."

The guard tipped his cap.

Meredith and I took the elevator. We kissed all the way going up. On the thirteenth floor there were four apartments. The door to our apartment looked like wood on the outside, but it was only a thin veneer; the door itself was made of two-inch-thick armor plate. A six-inch naval gun might blow a hole in it, but anything smaller would bounce off.

Whoever decorated the place, I guess, liked things functional, not fancy. Leather-covered chairs, solid wood tables, brass lamps, earth tones, and nothing on the walls. The windows had been covered with plastic covers. We could see out, but no one could see in. Two of the three bedrooms were piled high with boxes of canned food and toilet paper, soap, cleaning supplies—everything two people would need to last a year without ever going out.

Meredith looked at everything with a detached air. I could tell she didn't think much of the place.

"How long will we be staying?"

"A few days."

"I guess I can stand it."

Beyond the kitchen was a sort of solarium with high walls. Here there was a platform mechanism like a fireman's ladder laid flat that would reach twelve feet to the apartment building next door. Bob Carpano's instructions said that once you crossed to the building next door you pulled a lever to send the thing crashing into the alley to cut off the pursuit. In the bottom of the broom closet was a trap door, and under it, a ladder leading to the apartment below.

I poured us a couple of brandies. We drank them sitting at the kitchen table. Then, while Meredith got ready for bed, I went out for a walk. I walked around several blocks holding onto the gun in my pocket and looking for stakeout teams. I didn't see any. I didn't see anything suspicious at all.

The next morning Meredith said she wanted to go out and buy some clothes and things. "Girl stuff," she said. I told her I didn't like the idea, but she said she had to buy some unmentionables.

"I can't stay cooped up in here all the time," she said. "I'm not an indoor cat."

"Okay," I said. "Better get some more hair color."

We went out about noon in a sleeting rain and took a cab downtown. I left her off at Macy's and told her I'd pick her up in an hour and a half. I went to a bar and had a beer and called Sylvester Rohm in Washington. I got the same recorded message. O. O. Cummings Security Services.

"This is Mr. Coldiron," I said. "I'll call back in an hour."

I had another couple more beers and tried Rohm's number again. Same message. I got a cab and went back to Macy's and picked up Meredith.

When we got back to our apartment building, the guard told us someone was nosing around. Meredith tensed.

"Who?" I asked.

"A guy, big, dark. Looked like he might have been a cabbie. He described a guy, could have been you, but he didn't know your name."

"What'd you tell him?"

"Nobody around here like that."

"Good."

"Don't think he'll be back."

I spent the rest of the day sitting in a small alcove around the corner from the guard station in the lobby waiting for the man to return. He didn't. I figured he'd been looking for someone else that just happened to look like me.

Meredith dyed her hair jet black that night. I laughed at the way she looked. I called her Vampira. She smiled, but I don't think she thought it was that funny. She was edgy.

The next day we went out early and took a packed subway down to Greenwich Village and while she sipped a cappuccino, I tried Sylvester Rohm one more time.

This time a woman answered: "O. O. Cummings. Your security is our security."

"Mr. Rohm, please."

"I'm sorry, Mr. Rohm is out of town and can't be reached."

"When will he be back?"

"Mr. Rohm's plans are at this time indefinite."

"Where is he?"

"He's on an extended business trip."

"This is Mr. Coldiron. I left two messages for Mr. Graywolf; do you know if he's gotten them?"

"We did receive your messages and they were passed on."

"Do you know that he's received them in person?"

"I'm sorry, sir, we do not give out that kind of information."

"Did Mr. Graywolf leave me a message?"

"No, sir."

I hung up.

When I got back, Meredith said, "What's going on?"

"Nothing."

"You look upset."

"We better get out of here."

"I haven't finished my coffee. It's delicious."

"They may have traced the call. It's all very complicated. We just shouldn't sit around here, that's all."

We went uptown on the subway, less crowded, but the brakes howled like a wounded lion. We got off at West 96th and Broadway.

As we were walking back to the apartment, she said, "I'd like to know what's going on." She had tension in her voice. Fear. She was trying to cover it up, but it was there.

"Nothing to worry about. The man who was following you at the airport told me I should call a man named Sylvester Rohm if I wanted to get a message to the man who's after me."

"I see."

"And when I leave these messages, the call could be traced. Rohm is working for the man who's after me, so I have to be extra careful."

"Don't you have to stay on the line a long time to trace a call?"

"These days it can be done in a second."

"You're certainly clever when it comes to this sort of thing. What are you going to do now?"

"I'm going to get in touch with a woman I know by the name of Wanda Void."

"What an unusual name."

"She's an unusual gal."

Wanda was in her midfifties, short, plump, and stoical. The morning of our meeting, she wore a brown skirt and brown suit jacket and a white shirt with plain brown tie. Wanda Void was the pseudonym she used when she was a KGB assassin in the Brezhnev days. At the UN mission where she worked presently, she was known as Ludmilla Arkoff.

She stared at me blankly across the white tablecloth. We were at the Hunan Palace on East 77th Street, in a back booth. Soft Chinese gongs played over hidden speakers, very soothing.

"You want me to what?" she said.

"Set up a meeting between me and Gray Wolf. On your territory, with your people to insure that neither of us gets frisky."

She kept staring.

The waiter poured tea and drifted away. It was eleven in the morning and we were the only customers in the place. She opened a menu. "No wonder I'm fat, I eat whether I'm hungry or not. It comes from growing up poor."

"You were far from poor. Your father was a factory manager in Tashkent. You had maids, for Christ's sake."

She blinked at me. "How you know this?"

"I read your K file at the Exchange."

"Amazing."

She went back to reading the menu.

"Gray Wolf is doing contract jobs on your side now," I said.

"What else it say about me in your K file?"

"That you've liquidated sixteen people."

"Amazing." She looked up from her menu and blinked at me again. "I'm having Kung Pao Chicken, what you having?"

"Just the tea. Will you set up the meeting with me and Gray Wolf?"

She put the menu aside. "You're after Gray Wolf. I hear you're getting quarter of million for this one wet job, is that right?" She gave me a wink. "You capitalists are so wicked."

"That's just the point, Wanda, I'm *not* after Gray Wolf. I think if I can talk to him face to face, I can convince him of that."

"We know better."

She flagged the waiter. He came over to our table, pad ready. "Kung Pao Chicken and fried wonton," she said. "Give me some of that sizzling rice soup. That's all. My friend's not eating." She waved the waiter away.

"Wanda," I said, trying to keep a cap on my anger. "Why the hell would I want you to set up a safe meeting if I wanted to kill him? It wouldn't make sense."

"What do you bet that my beloved country is as capitalist as yours in forty, fifty years? Only we do it better. We leave you in our dust."

"I don't give a shit if you do. Are you listening to me?"

"You really don't want to do Gray Wolf?"

"No."

She scratched her head. "I don't understand this. Why should I help you?"

"We've done each other favors before."

"Little favors. Nothing substantial. The whereabouts of British defector, minutes to some meeting or other. Things that don't matter. It's just good business to do small favors for colleagues on the other side once in a while, you get lot of return goods that way. But this, this is beyond small favor. Especially since you're no longer in game and have gone to live with squirrels in the Adirondacks." She grinned. "We have files, too."

"I'll pay you twenty thousand dollars."

"Twenty thousand . . ." She picked up her chopsticks and clicked them together. "Consider it done."

"I'll call you tomorrow." I got up from the table. "Enjoy your lunch."

"When do I get my money?"

"I'll bring it to the appointment."

"Not good enough. I need advance." She handed me a card with a box number at a private rent-a-box place on Second Avenue written on it. "Send it here. Five thousand dollars. By this afternoon."

"It'll be there."

I arranged to have fifty thousand telexed from my bank in the Bahamas. I sent five thousand to Wanda's drop box. Then I rented a VCR and a bagful of films.

Meredith loved Robert Redford. And Woody Allen. And the goddamn Three Stooges. So I rented some of each.

She watched them with me that night and we laughed together, but I had the impression she was pretending to have a good time for my benefit. The next morning I called Wanda and she said she had no good news for me.

I rented some more movies that day. Meredith and I watched them from just after six in the evening to nearly midnight.

The next day when I called Wanda, she said Moscow central was out of touch with the subject and asked me to try her again the next day. I rented some more movies. When I returned to the apartment, Meredith had a strange look in her eyes and for a moment I thought she might be fighting back tears. I had no idea what might be bothering her, and at the moment I said nothing. She seemed to recover herself and went into the kitchen to put something in the microwave.

The next morning Meredith and I went for a walk. It had snowed overnight and the city looked clean. People were out shoveling sidewalks and sprinkling salt on them. She was withdrawn. I asked her what was wrong, but she wouldn't tell me.

When I called Wanda that morning she said she had a lead on our subject and would know Friday morning for sure. It was Tuesday. She said I should not call her until then.

Meredith seemed to grow more and more quiet the next few days. She went into the second bedroom and painted all day and half the night. Finally, at dinner on Thursday night, I said, "You've got to learn to trust me."

"I do trust you."

"Then you've got to tell me what's bothering you."

"Nothing's bothering me." She got up from the table and went into the bedroom where she was doing her painting. She didn't come out until after midnight. She went straight to bed.

The next day, Friday, while I was taking a shower, she went out without telling me where she was going or when she'd be back. I went into the bedroom to dress and that's when I noticed her boots were missing. She'd left them by the radiator to dry the day before and now they were gone. I called the security guard downstairs: "Able, 13A, did my wife just go out?"

"Yes, Mr. Able," he said.

"Did she say anything?"

"Not to me."

I hung up and paced around a bit, then I got dressed and had a cup of coffee. After a while I got on some boots, took my gun, and went outside. It was snowing heavily. Wet snow. I walked to Broadway and checked in the supermarket, then went up and down the blocks looking in the little shops. The liquor store, the dry cleaners, the florist, the video rental place. Not a sign of Meredith.

I stopped at a pay phone and called Wanda.

"Gray Wolf is in New York."

"Have you spoken to him?"

"Not yet, but I hope to contact him soon. Call me in three hours' time."

When I got back to the apartment, Meredith was sitting in the living room staring at the wall.

"You going to tell me what's going on?" I asked. Light coming through the plastic shields on the windows turned the room a bluish color. I closed the blinds. I sat in the chair opposite her in the darkened room and lit a cigarette.

She said, "I have to know what this is all about."

"What what is all about?"

"Who's trying to kill you and why. We're hiding out here like a couple of Bonnie and Clydes and I really don't know what it's all about."

"We go out."

"Like hell we do! We stay away from restaurants, theaters, nightclubs. We're living like hermits. I'm entitled to know what's going on. Why we're doing this. Maybe then I'll know better what the future holds."

"It may be all over soon. We'll rent some more movies."

165

"You don't seem to be listening to what I've said."

She got up and went out the front door.

After a while I went out and took a bus uptown to a bookstore near Columbia University and called Wanda. She said she was meeting with Gray Wolf to work out the details and I should be ready for a meeting at noon on Sunday in Central Park. She wanted to meet me for lunch on Saturday to discuss the details and collect another ten thousand.

"Agreed," I said.

Meredith came in late that night smelling of scotch whiskey. She crawled into bed with her clothes on and went to sleep.

In the morning I got up, exercised, showered, shaved, and got dressed. I cooked and ate some ham and eggs and was sitting at the table drinking coffee and reading the *Times* before I heard a peep out of her.

She came out of the bedroom and went directly into the bathroom. I heard her retch, then she took a shower for half an hour and came out in her yellow terrycloth bathrobe with a towel wrapped around her head. She looked gray. She sat opposite me at the table in the kitchen and rested her chin on her palm.

I poured her a cup of coffee. She dumped some sugar and cream into the cup, gave it a stir, and started sipping it. Her eyes were red and full of suffering.

I offered to fix her ham and eggs.

"I'd rather not, thank you all the same."

"I've got some good news," I said. "Our troubles may be

over. Tomorrow I'm going to have a powwow with the man who's after me. I'm sure I can convince him I'm no threat. We can go back to Amber and just be normal people."

Her face brightened a little, but just a little. I'm not sure she believed me.

"And when we do go back to Amber, will you still be the mystery man?"

"I'm no mystery man."

She got up and paced back and forth in the narrow kitchen, holding her cup. "I guess," she said after a moment, "you're going to keep on being the mystery man."

"You're the mystery," I said. "Ever since we've been in New York, you've been acting more and more strangely."

She put the cup down on the counter and took the towel off her head and draped it over her chair. Then she sat down, facing toward the window that looked out on the river. She ran her hands through her wet hair and said, "You're the only man I ever really truly loved."

"That's nice to hear."

"Do you love me?"

"I don't have to say it, do I?"

"If you do, why won't you tell me the horrible secret?"

"Can't."

"Do you think I'll run away? I want to share whatever it is that you have to share, the good, the bad, everything. That's what loving is about. Two people sharing a life. I want you to share your life with me."

"Silence is an old habit of mine," I said.

She sighed. "What we have going here is good, Tom, and when two people live like we're living they have to do it completely together. I have to know. I told myself at first I didn't have to know, that the feelings I had for you were so strong they could overcome everything, but they can't. It's like part of you isn't here. Part of you is off someplace in a cave that I can never enter."

"I guess I was worried it might sicken you and you would leave. It's not pleasant."

"What's not pleasant?"

"My past. The people I've been living with and dealing with. The things I've done."

She touched my shoulder. "I can live with whatever it is. I can love you no matter what you've done. What I can't live with is the great silence. You don't owe anything to anybody but me. And I don't owe anything to anyone but you. Is it so much to ask just to know who it is we're hiding from?"

"It's very complicated."

"You think I'm too dumb to understand it?"

"Not at all."

"Then tell me."

I felt a catch in my throat. I'd never told anyone anything about the Exchange. Not even my father when he was alive, and he would have been wildly enthusiastic. I looked at her. A strange sensation came over me. I could see the pain in her eyes. I could feel her wanting all of me, the past, the future, the now. The Exchange was past. Everything was past. She was now and the future and so what the hell difference did it make?

"You see, there's this quasi-government outfit I used to work for that wants me to track down a man for them. The man's name is Theodore Fairweather, his cryptonym is Gray Wolf. We worked together for years. I know his tendencies. I know how he thinks, how he feels, what's in his soul. They think that would give me the edge."

Her expression didn't change, but her eyes softened. "And you refused to go after him?"

169

"Yes."

She sat back down and poured some coffee in her cup, then dumped sugar in it. "Go on," she said.

In twenty years of being a player I'd never told a civilian anything. Not one word. Not one damn syllable. And here I was spilling it all. I felt both horribly guilty and greatly relieved at the same time.

Meredith reached across the table and touched my hand. "Go on, please."

"Okay," I said. "Well, somehow, some way, I guess Gray Wolf was told I'd taken the assignment to go after him and he wants to kill me first."

"I see now why you want to meet with him. I'm so glad you told me this." She got up and paced around the kitchen for a few moments, thinking, then she went into the bedroom where she did her painting and closed the door. I guessed she wanted some time to digest it all.

That evening she said, "I want to go to a play."

"Not wise," I said.

"Not Broadway or Off-Broadway or even Off-Off Broadway. A class of fledgling actors at Columbia are doing *Hamlet*. Real amateur stuff. You can stay home if you think it's too risky."

"I suppose it's not all that risky. Okay, to be or not to be, we go to *Hamlet*."

She smiled. It was nice to see her look happy.

The play was held in a classroom. The radiators rattled, but emitted no heat, so we had to keep our coats on. The actors dropped every third line or so and the guy playing old Polonius was maybe eighteen and his white beard kept falling off his chin. The audience was not more than fifty people, mostly friends and relatives of the actors, and was respectful, but not too enthusiastic. In the last act, Hamlet's mother sat down on her throne and it collapsed, sending her into a backward somersault. She just kept rattling on lines as if that was the way Shakespeare had intended it to be played. One other person and I laughed out loud, but we were quickly hushed by the rest of the audience.

Afterward, Meredith and I went to a restaurant and had a hot chocolate and rehashed the play. She remembered every gaffe and goof, it seemed to me, and she chuckled and laughed as she retold it, as if I hadn't been there and seen it for myself.

". . . and then Hamlet turned the wrong way and couldn't find his way off stage—and Ophelia gave her last speech two scenes too early and caught herself and said 'oops, whoa, what a scene . . .' " And she kept laughing, her eyes sparkling.

We decided to walk home. It was a clear night and briskly cold. We walked down Riverside Drive, along the park, which is a little risky given the chance of muggers, but I liked to look out across the river at the lights of New Jersey and the water.

For the first couple of blocks she talked about the play and other plays she'd been to that were even worse. And then she was quiet for a while, walking along next to me holding my arm with her head down, lost in thought. We continued on for four or five blocks without saying anything. I was feeling good. Feeling hopeful. Feeling free. Feeling now that I had this woman and we were going to have a life together, I could forget the goddamn Exchange once and for all.

Finally, she said: "What if you meet with this man and he doesn't believe you?"

"What do you mean?"

She shrugged. "I mean do we stay on the run?"

"I guess we do."

"There isn't any other way?"

"I'm doing the best I can."

"I don't want to stay on the run. I want to be with you, but I'm not really built for this kind of life."

"I don't know any other way of handling it."

"What if you paid someone else to kill him?"

"The Exchange already sent four men to try that."

"I see. We're condemned, then, to live like this the rest of our lives."

"He'll fall eventually."

"Eventually could be a long time."

"We'll find a safe place to hide."

"I trust you," she said. "I know you'll do the right thing— for us."

I had the feeling she was trying to tell me something, but she wasn't quite ready to come out and say it directly. I wondered if she wanted me to kill Gray Wolf, but I was afraid to ask. If that's what she did want, I didn't know what my answer would be.

The next morning I left early for my meeting with Wanda Void. I walked through Central Park. It was a damp, overcast day. The snow was still on the ground from the day before, but it was melting. A lot of kids were out sledding and making snowmen and I thought about that great day up near Amber when Meredith and I had the snowball fight.

For the first time since Langston and Vanders had come to visit that morning, I was feeling optimistic. Gray Wolf was in the city and Wanda Void was in contact with him. I knew her well enough to know that she wouldn't sell me out to him. If she ever betrayed anyone for a buck, she was finished. Once she had taken your money, she would keep her word. That's how she'd managed to become both a high-level agent of the KGB, and one of the richest women in the Soviet Union.

I walked over to East 77th, bustling with Saturday morning shoppers. Thanksgiving was a week away and I guess people were getting ready for it. As I approached the Hunan Palace I spotted a crowd gathered around the door, cop cars and an ambulance in the street. I pushed my way through the crowd. The cops had a rope barrier up.

"What happened?" I asked one of the cops.

"Some Russian woman, a diplomat, looks like she got herself mugged. She must'a fought him, because he rammed a switchblade right through her throat."

I stepped back. The neck was Gray Wolf's favorite spot to stick someone. Once you cut the carotid artery, you know it's cut by the gush of blood and you're sure of your kill.

I backed up through the crowd, looking around. Suddenly I felt exposed. I ran across the street and up the block, crossed Third Avenue, and kept on running.

When I got back to the apartment, Meredith wasn't there. I paced around and kept telling myself she had to be safe, had to be. Gray Wolf probably thought Wanda Void was setting him up to be killed and so he got to her first. Players often go mad after they go over. It must have happened to him. That made him even more terrible.

Then again, maybe he had wanted her to turn on me, and she wouldn't, and that's why he did her. He would have had to be mad to do that, too. If you're in the business, you need people like Wanda Void. If you kill them, no one will want to do business with you on either side of the street.

Whatever the reason he did it really didn't matter. What did matter was that I now saw that coming to some sort of accord with Gray Wolf was not going to be possible. I was going to have to go deep underground and not come up until Gray Wolf was put away once and for all.

I started packing—just what would fit in two easily portable bags. Everything else I'd donate to my host. When I finished, I started packing Meredith's things. That's when the phone rang.

"A man's following me." It was Meredith. She sounded alarmed, but in control.

"Where are you?"

"Plato's Drugs near 96th and Broadway. He's standing in a doorway across the street."

"Describe him."

"Forty, forty-five. Heavyset. Salt-and-pepper hair. He's wearing a yellow jacket with a sheepskin collar."

"He working alone?"

"Christ, how would I know?"

"Take it easy, it's all going to work out. Did you see anyone else who might be working with him?"

"No."

"Where'd he get onto you?"

"I went to an art exhibition this morning at the Museum of Modern Art. I didn't see him before I got there."

"When did you first see him?"

"When I came out. I couldn't get a cab, so I took the subway. When I changed to the express, he changed too. God, I'm scared. Tell me what to do."

"Walk down Broadway to 96th, then go over to West End Avenue. Turn right and keep going until 101st, then walk back over to Broadway and get a cab. I'll take care of the guy who's on you. If no one follows the cab, go to a subway stop and take the subway home. If anybody follows the cab, go downtown and head into a crowd, lose them there."

"How you going to take care of him?"

"Best you don't know."

A pause. "I love you."

"I love you, too."

She hung up.

I got on a pair of boots and a coat, grabbed my gun and some extra clips, and was out the door in thirty seconds. On the way down in the elevator, I laced up my boots. I was feeling angry and afraid for Meredith, but my head was clear. The guard at the door was the young Puerto Rican. He was reading his economics book. "Stay sharp," I told him.

"Always sharp, Mr. Able," he said.

I went through the double door and into the entryway. I had my hand in my pocket, clasped tight onto the gun. I eased my way along the entryway and took a look out into the street. It had started raining. No one around but the building superintendent trying to patch a piece of broken masonry on the front of his building. I crossed the street and headed up the block, turning around every few feet to see if anyone was watching me. Nobody was, as far as I could tell. A shadow moved in a window in my building, but I was pretty sure it was a nutty old woman I'd seen at that window before.

I hurried along 99th to West End Avenue, crossed back over the street, and kept moving. Traffic was minimal. I crossed the street and ducked into the doorway of an apartment building. The wind whipped the rain, making it tough to see more than half a block. My hands got cold quickly. I didn't bring gloves. You can't use a gun well if you've got gloves on. I kept checking the street. Meredith would be along any minute. I waited, stomping my feet and rubbing my hands together to keep warm. Finally I spotted her coming toward me, bent forward into the wind.

I slipped back into the doorway and let her pass. Then I eased my way out to the edge and stole a glance down the street. No one following her that I could tell. No suspicious cars. No guy in a yellow jacket, either. I gave it another couple of minutes. Nobody passed by.

He must have been following her from the other side of the street, I figured. I ran across the street, the wind blowing the rain hard against my face. I couldn't see anyone on the sidewalk in either direction. I jogged up the block in the direction Meredith had gone. A couple of telephone workers were fixing some wires, and I met a lot of people getting off a bus, but I didn't see the guy in the yellow jacket.

Maybe he'd been picked up in a car and somehow they'd gotten ahead of Meredith and she was walking right toward them. I dashed back across the street and hurried up the block. I crossed West 100th Street on the run. I hit a slick spot and went down, got up, and kept on running. A few people around, but no man in a yellow jacket, no Meredith. I turned right on West 101st and headed toward Broadway.

Here the wind wasn't as strong and I could see all the way to Broadway. She wasn't there. My heart pounded. I'd handled it completely wrong. I should have had her wait in the drugstore. She'd have been safe there. But I had to set it up so I'd know how many there were, and now they had her.

They wouldn't hurt her until they had me. At least I didn't think they would. That gave me a chance.

At Broadway, there were more people, and the traffic, mostly buses and cabs, clogged the streets. No Meredith. I caught a cab and told the cabbie to go up Broadway, then at West 110th Street I had him turn around and go back. I kept a lookout for Meredith, but didn't see her. Then I spotted a guy in a yellow jacket. I told the cabbie to follow him, but when we got closer I could see he was a young guy, tall. So I gave the cabbie my address and had him take me back to the apartment. When I stopped in front of the place he said, "You okay, pal?"

I told him to mind his own fucking business.

The wind was gusting cold from the river. I went up the front

steps and into the entryway, taking it slow and easy. That's when I
saw a hole in the plate glass door about the size of a fist. I backed
away quickly and checked the street. There was no one coming
up behind me. I went through the entryway and took a look
inside. The Puerto Rican security guard was sitting there, only
he was leaning back in his seat as if he were watching something
on the ceiling.

Reaching in through the hole in the glass, I opened the door
and stepped into the vestibule. Nobody around except the guard,
and he wasn't anybody anymore. His eyes were glassed over and
there was a black bullet hole in the middle of his forehead and
the back of his head had leaked brains all over the chair and the
wall. Exploding bullet. Small caliber. With a silencer, it
wouldn't have made as much noise as a hiccup.

I drew back along the wall and made my way to the elevator.
I couldn't see anyone around, or hear anyone, or smell anyone. I
noticed the elevator indicator said the elevator was coming down
from the thirteenth floor, my floor. I waited, holding tight to the
gun in my pocket. The elevator stopped and the door opened. A
woman in her sixties got off. She was carrying one of those little
dogs that everyone but old ladies hate.

"There's some trouble in the lobby, Ma'am," I said. "I don't
think you want to go out right now."

"Oh dear," she said. "New York is just going to pieces."

I got on the elevator and pushed the button for the twelfth
floor—one floor below mine. The dog trembled in the woman's
arm, and she trembled too. They got off on the sixth floor.

On twelve, I checked the hallway. No one around. I put the
gun in my pocket and knocked on 12A. An eye appeared in the
peephole.

"It's me, Able," I said, out of breath.

A woman of about forty with alcoholic eyes opened the door.

"I've got to use my ladder," I said.

"There's no trouble, is there?" she asked.

"Just forgot my key."

She let me in. I went to the back closet and slowly made my way up the ladder, breathing deep, slow breaths, my gun out. I pushed open the trap door into the darkened broom closet above, being as quiet as I could. I let the hatch back down and stood up and put my ear to the door. Somebody was moving around, but no one was talking. I crouched down and looked through the keyhole, but couldn't see anything.

I held my gun up, then I reached down and put my hand on the doorknob, twisting it slowly. When I had it turned all the way, I took a breath and kicked it open, springing out with my gun in front of me.

Meredith was there; she turned, startled, and dropped the cup she was drinking from. I took a look down the hall, then out in back to the snow-covered deck.

"Nobody here but me," she said, trembling. I put my arms around her.

"Did you see him?" she said. She meant the guard. "Did you see his eyes? His head, the way it was torn open like that?"

"We better go."

We finished packing her things, then she followed me out and down the back stairs all the way to the ground floor without saying a word.

I drove on through the night in a rented Chevy. Meredith kept pressed to the door, looking straight ahead, sipping blackberry brandy from her silver flask.

Like a frightened child, she kept repeating what happened. "I was just walking down the street . . . I don't know how he spotted me. I saw nothing when I came out of the building . . . is it possible that he'd been hanging around all the time we were there? Why'd they shoot the security guard? I never even knew his name . . . he was always pleasant, a student at Hunter College . . ."

I wanted to reassure her somehow, but I didn't know what to say. I had no idea how we'd been found. It would have taken a huge manhunt to have done it, even knowing we were in New York. Which probably meant Gray Wolf somehow had control of somebody high up in some goddamn investigative branch of the government, somebody who could have ordered up a million manhours of work to look for me. And if Gray Wolf had tapped into the FBI or the CIA, Meredith and I were in a hell of a lot of trouble.

After a few hours, Meredith climbed into the back seat to stretch out and get some sleep. I asked her how she was doing, and she said all right, but she didn't sound all right. She sounded scared. I drove on.

When you're running with someone, the wisest thing to do is split up. That's basic tradecraft. Two together are a lot easier to spot. But I didn't want to split up. I wanted Meredith with me. I wanted to protect her. That, anyway, is what I told myself.

She took over driving just after midnight and I tried to sleep. I dozed on and off. She had a talk show on; an expert in auto repair was the first guest, then a minister who said he'd met Jesus Christ and he was gay.

Just before dawn we stopped at a Motel 6 outside Lexington, Kentucky, and I registered under the name of Philip O'Hara, because the car was registered to Philip O'Hara and I had a complete set of ID in that name, including credit cards.

We slept till about noon and walked to a pancake house down the road. It was a brilliantly sunny day, but chilly. There was only a light dusting of snow on the hard, frozen ground. It was hilly, wooded, horse-farm country. Meredith's face was milk-white in the sunlight. She was quiet, twirling a strand of hair and folding it back around her ear.

After breakfast we went back to the motel to shower and change. Leaving the motel, she said:

"Which way are we heading?"

"West."

She nodded absently. I drove for a few hours without either of us saying much. The traffic was light and we stayed under sixty. Finally she said:

"Are we just going to keep traveling west until we hit China?"

A hardness I'd never heard before had crept into her voice.

"No," I said.

"Just where are we going?"

"The Rocky Mountains. Great cross-country skiing. We'll get a cabin, you'll like it."

"How long do we stay?"

"I don't know."

"We'll have to keep moving, won't we?"

"Until I can make some arrangements to get someplace where we can never be found. Latin America, maybe."

"And when we get there, then what?"

"Then we'll have a good time."

"Will we be able to settle down, make a home, have friends? Go to a play or a show when we want to?"

"Sure."

She fell silent for a moment. Then: "You have no right to do this, you know."

"Right to do what?"

"Make all these plans without including me."

"I told you when you first signed up for this trip we might have to keep moving."

"That you did."

"You're making it sound like I was naively headed for a big damn adventure or something."

"I didn't say that."

"You implied it."

I glanced over at her; she was staring at me, her mouth tight. "We better talk. Please stop someplace."

She never liked to discuss things in a car. She liked to pace around when she was upset. We stopped at a rest stop and found a deserted cluster of picnic tables. She wasn't wearing a coat, so she kept pacing and rubbing her arms to keep warm.

"You wanted to talk," I said.

"We're facing an impossible situation," she said. She stared off at some snow-covered hills in the distance. "When that man followed me yesterday I was scared."

"I was scared for you."

"Let me finish. It's a terrifying feeling to be hunted. What if he wanted to kidnap me to get to you? Isn't that possible?"

"Sure it's possible, but unlikely."

"Why?"

"Because he'd have to go through so much trouble to kidnap you, he might as well just shoot me. Besides, with most Exchange people, it wouldn't work. Before I met you, it wouldn't have worked with me."

"You mean you'd just let them kill me?"

"I was a bad apple."

She turned to me and leaned against the rock wall that separated the picnic area from the grassy walking area beyond. She had a vacant, scared look in her eyes.

"It's going to be all right," I said. "He won't find us again. He got lucky."

"He could get lucky again."

"But he won't."

"How do you know he won't?"

"I'll be more careful."

"That's not good enough." She rubbed her arms some more and paced up and down.

"He must have traced me through the safe house," I said. "You were right about that. I must have fouled it up somehow."

"You don't know that, though, do you?"

"No, I don't. How else could he have found me?"

"I can't guess. But that's just what I'm getting at. As I said before, I can't stand being hunted. I can't stand the idea of us hiding out for maybe the next twenty years. Especially not since there's a way out."

"I'm not going after him."

She stood in front of me. Gooseflesh stood out on her arms. "Even for us?"

"No."

She nodded, her jaw set firm. "You've made your choice, Tom, and now I've got to make mine." Her voice faltered. "I'm not going to be on the run with you."

My gut squeezed tight, but I didn't say anything.

"I mean it," she said.

"All right," I said. "I'll take you wherever you want to go. Name it."

"The nearest airport. We can't be fugitives," she said. "It's no way to live. We have to face that first of all."

"You don't understand, Meredith."

"Then make me understand."

"I'm no longer a player. A player is on the edge at all times. Being on the edge sharpens him. He's ready to kill or be killed. He feeds on fear, his and others'. A player lives by a set of rules no ordinary person could live by. Once you turn your back on it, you change. I've changed. I just couldn't be a player again."

"You could be one for a week or a month. Long enough to deal with this man. Then we can be together."

"No, Meredith. We can find someplace to hide where he can't find us. Someplace where we can be happy."

"While we wait for this guy to come and kill you? Not me. I'm not built for a life like that." She said it like it was forced, like inside some part of her didn't want to say it.

She walked back to the car and got in the passenger's seat. I got in behind the wheel, then took a map out of the glove box and studied it for a few minutes.

We were on the Blue Grass Parkway, a few miles from where

it intersects Interstate 65 above Mammoth Caves. "The closest airport is Louisville," I said.

"Okay," she said. "Fine."

I drove to I-65 and turned north. A tractor trailer had overturned up ahead and the traffic crawled along for a while at about ten miles an hour.

"A player is cursed," I said. "It's like being a professional soldier. Killing becomes a way of life. Blood lust, something like that. A player is given a license to do what all men would do were it not for civilization. A player is given permission to give vent to his baser instincts. You get a kind of charge out of it. You get hooked on it. You can't stop."

"Yet you did stop."

"On account of a poor slob named Benevides. A goddamn clerk. The CIA had him on the dole and they found out he was selling to someone else too and they wanted to know who. We took him to a shack to work him over, get him to tell us who he was dealing with."

"I don't want to hear about it."

I shot her an angry glance. "I'm trying to tell you why I'm not a player! All I want is to love you and take care of you and be with you for the rest of my natural life. I don't want to kill Gray Wolf. I don't want to kill anyone. I want only what every human being on the face of the earth has a right to expect out of life."

"But how can you expect to have the same things other people have?"

I looked at her. We were even with the tractor trailer. It had flipped over on its side and cans of motor oil were all over the road. The traffic sped up.

"Damn," I said.

"What?"

"Just damn. How can you say that I haven't the right to expect the same things out of life as other people?"

"Because you have a past. You make decisions about how you're going to live your life and you can't take them back."

"You can't? Well, I sure as hell am going to try."

She had tears in her eyes. "If you won't do it because the Exchange wants you to and you won't do it because he's after you, then do it for me."

I looked out over the farmland flying past her just outside the window. I looked at the clouds, checked the mirrors, watched a guy in a red Porsche go by.

We were both quiet for a while. We were heading into Louisville. I turned off the Interstate and headed toward the airport. She pulled one leg up under her and put on a pair of sunglasses. A swirl of dust whisked across the road in front of us.

"Where will you go?" I asked.

"I have friends in Mexico. A friend of my father's, a Mr. Sanders. He robbed a lot of money from his company about forty years ago. He hid himself in Mexico. I used to go there as a kid, it's like a second home to me. I'll stay there until you tell me this man who is after you is finished. I wouldn't want him using me to get to you. No one can find me there, believe me. No one can find this place, not even the Mexicans. The government mapmakers were bribed to leave his valley off their maps."

"All right, fine. Go there. But what about us?"

"Yes, what about us? How much could you really care for me, that's what I'm wondering."

I didn't say anything to that. I couldn't go after Gray Wolf, not for her, not for anyone. I pulled into the main drive to the terminal and parked at the curb.

"Well," she said, "I guess this is it."

"Guess it is."

186

She looked at me. Tears streamed down her face. "You must think I'm a monster," she said. Her voice cracked.

"I don't think you're a monster."

She opened the door but she didn't get out. "What's the worst thing that ever happened to you?" she asked.

"I've had a lot of worst things happen to me."

"I mean really the worst."

"I don't know. I try not to think of such things."

She closed the door again and covered her face with her hands. She started sobbing. I rubbed my hand over her back.

I said, "Why did you ask that?"

She turned to me. Her face looked puffy now. "Because," she said, "this is the worst moment of my life."

I reached over and took her hand.

She turned toward me. "I don't want to see anyone killed," she said, her voice choking. "I just don't want to be on the run, always looking over my shoulder. What happened in New York horrified me. I wish I were stronger. Forgive me, Tom."

"I forgive you," I said.

She got a couple of Kleenexes out of the glove box and wiped her face. Then she said: "Come to Mexico with me. You'll be safe. You could at least come for a little while. I swear to you, I won't say another word about killing anyone. I've got to go there, to feel safe at least for a little while." She pleaded with her brown eyes for a long moment. "Well, Tom, what do you say?"

A player never lets anyone pick where he goes or what he does. Not when he's on the run.

"Please," she said. "For me. For us."

I knew better, but found myself nodding yes.

Meredith and I split up. Traveling separately, we'd be harder to spot.

I took a plane to San Diego, California, posing as O'Hara, then took a bus to the border and walked into Tijuana. The weather was warm, pleasant. I caught a dilapidated bus full of Mexican farm workers and their kids to get the train, the Ferrocarril del Pacifico, at Mexicali. I bought a second-class ticket to Mazatlán. The train goes down the west coast of the Mexican mainland, along the Gulf of California, down through the hot, arid country, through Hermosillo and Guaymas and Ciudad Obregón.

The train was crowded and was probably forty or fifty years old, the old style, with high ceilings and narrow armrests. The train was clean and well maintained, and the drinks were cheap. I passed the time talking to an aging hippie who was on his way back to his commune down in Yucatán. He said he raised chickens and smoked pot and thought if you passed your life on this planet any other way you were a jerk. He said he used to drop acid, trying to find God. He thought everyone was trying to find God in their own way, and the only time you can be happy on this planet is when you quit trying to find God. He said he'd found Mexico; he didn't need God.

I thought he was an idiot.

I dozed through the night and off and on the next day. Out the windows I glimpsed farms and deserts and barren mountains and, to the west, the blue sea dotted with sportfishing boats. The Sea of Cortés is supposed to have the greatest sportfishing in the world.

On the second day, as we headed south, the vegetation started getting more lush, more tropical, and the sport boats on the sea became thicker.

On the third day, we arrived in Mazatlán, which is lush and green and a tourist trap with broad white beaches and lots of neon and gringos in Bermuda shorts sitting under sun umbrellas drinking tall drinks with fruit in them. I registered in a glitzy tourist hotel, La Posada, under the name of Mike Doss. I spent two days drinking in the hotel bar, watching the fat tourists sun themselves by the pool, all the time making sure that none of them were watching me.

Satisfied I wasn't being tailed, I left my Mike Doss identity behind and took a bus northeast, toward Durango. I traveled as R. G. McPherson, wearing worn sneakers and faded blue jeans and carrying my clothes in a rucksack I bought at a secondhand store in the old quarter of Mazatlán.

Meredith was to fly to Colorado and then buy a car and drive to Albuquerque. From there, she was to take a plane to Mexico City, purchase some used clothes, and take the train to Guadalajara as a Mexican. From Guadalajara she was to take the bus north to meet with me.

189

I took a tourist bus to Laguna del Llano. The bus was air-conditioned and pleasant, and full of tourists. I was feeling safe and happy at first, but gradually a dark and ominous feeling came over me, and as we climbed on a narrow, curving road over the mountains, the feeling grew stronger and stronger—the feeling that Meredith wasn't going to be there to meet me. I knew it was irrational. After all, I was going where she wanted to go, yet I couldn't shake the feeling. It settled into me the way dampness settles into you in rainy climates and colors your every movement.

Meredith had acted so strangely in New York, and then she had pressed so hard to get me to go after Gray Wolf. I figured it was the pressure. Civilians have a tough time with those kinds of pressures. What if she decided to say the hell with it? It would be the smart thing for her to do.

The deeper into the country I went, the more I was sure she would have wised up.

At Guatimape I caught another bus. It was packed with Mexicans. One passenger had two live chickens in a cage and another had a live goat. The bus stank of sweat, cigarette smoke, and diesel fumes. We headed north, into the high country. The road was narrow, but paved, and we made good time.

What I was going to do if she took a walk on me, I didn't know. Go crazy, maybe.

We came down off a mountain and onto a hot dusty plain.

The driver left me off at a crossroads. A small, closed-up fruit stand sat on the corner, a shutter banging in the wind. To the east were low, grassy hills, and, beyond, some rocky rust-colored cliffs covered with Joshua trees and lupine. To the west was a ridge of tall mountains, a couple of them snowcapped.

I waited an hour in the noon sun. Another bus came, an old yellow one, loaded down with passengers. I climbed aboard and sat in the entry-well. The bus groaned up over the hills on a dirt road, twisting through the mountains. As we climbed, there were more trees and we crossed some gushing streams. Here and there we passed a cluster of dilapidated tin-roofed huts that made up a sort of village; occasionally we passed a large house with a satellite TV dish. From time to time there were small herds of sheep and goats or a few scrawny cows.

Every few miles more passengers got off. We went through a high river valley and came down the other side and into a small town.

"El Yoro, senor," the driver said. I'd told him that's where I wanted to get off.

I looked ahead through the dusty windshield. It wasn't much of a town. At the lower end was a Pemex gas station and, next to it, a whitewashed café. The street curved upward along a ridge. At the top of a hill was the *zocalo*, the town square. Across from the square was a two-story hotel, a row of shops, and a stone church with a single steeple. The buildings were brick and weatherbeaten wood. Mexicans in jeans and colored shirts sat around on steps drinking beer and talking. A few women with dark, Indian features were carrying sacks and walking with kids. Chickens and dogs in the street, everywhere. There were no more than a half dozen cars and trucks in the town. No sidewalks.

The bus came to a stop in front of the town hall. A few people were waiting for passengers. I looked around, but didn't see Meredith. For a moment, I was gripped by a strange fear that she wouldn't come. Then I turned and saw her coming toward me. She was wearing black, head to toe, with a black scarf over her head. Her skin was darker and I couldn't see a freckle. She approached me, tiptoeing and head bowed, and said:

"Senor, estoy para a acompanarle a la casa de los monjes."

191

She was there to take me to the monastery. She took my bag. I could see she loved playacting; her eyes twinkled.

She took me to an ancient black station wagon that had been smashed in the rear; the damage had rusted through. She deposited my bag in the back and opened the right side rear door for me with a little bow.

"A su servicio, senor." At your service.

I got in. She closed the door, went around to the other side, and got in. She started the car, which ran smoothly, and we headed east, up into the mountains along a dusty, rut-filled road. Through the outskirts of town we passed some small adobe houses with kids running around. Dirt lawns. Some of the houses had TV antennas on top; a few had cars parked in front. Mostly old Chevys and Fords, a couple of pickups. Everything was covered with red dust.

"I'm glad to see you," I said. "You don't know how glad."

"Did not las senoritas of Durango take good care of you?"

"Of course."

She laughed. I climbed into the front seat and kissed her. I was as happy as I'd ever been in my life.

The road out of town followed a creek bed, which was gushing with snow melt. A guy on a swayback horse waved to us. Mexico's a friendly place, when you get off the beaten track. The pace is so slow a glacier could overtake some of these towns before anyone would notice. I was already feeling relaxed, and so was Meredith. She reached over to the glove box and popped it open and there was her flask. We passed it back and forth as we wound our way up into the hills, Mexican music playing on the radio.

We passed a couple of shacks just before the tree line. Kids playing around. After that the road became two parallel dirt paths full of rocks.

"Where the hell are we going?" I asked.

"Paradise," she said. "You'll see."

We wound around the mountain, generally following the creek, climbing higher and higher. I had the window open. The air was clear and clean and cool. In front of us was a large, snow-capped mountain shrouded in clouds.

"The locals call her La Madre del Diablo. I call her Mom. She belches a little smoke now and again, but otherwise she's a dear."

"Let's not make her mad," I said.

We kept going for an hour or so; as small side roads peeled off, the road became more rutted and bumpy. Occasionally we passed by a pickup truck coming the other way filled with hay or firewood, and now and then we passed a hiker. We crossed over a pass and started down the western slope, covered with pines.

It warmed a little and the air was heavily scented with flowers. It was like the high country of California. Below us was a valley, laid out in squares, crisscrossed with dirt roads. We turned off here on what seemed to be little more than a logging road, which traversed the side of the mountain. We went over a couple of rickety bridges. Meredith pulled off the road and turned off the engine. Then she slid across the seat and kissed me. Supple, warm, nice.

She reached over and opened the door. "Got to show you something," she said.

She took my hand and led me down a path that led to a sort of cliff. We went around the cliff and there was a pool made by a wooden dam with a waterfall crashing into it. The trees and high grass grew right down to it on the far side, but on our side it was mostly granite slabs.

"Very nice," I said.

"I used to swim here as a kid," she said. "The water coming

down from above is cold, but the pool is heated by an underground hot spring, so it's always warm and cold. Exhilarating. Come on."

She pulled off her clothes. Her freckled skin glowed in the afternoon sun, in sharp contrast to the dark makeup on her face and arms. She turned and made three long strides; her body was sleek like an animal's in the sun. She dove cleanly into the blue-green water and came up waving to me.

I stripped quickly and made my way down a huge rock and slipped into the water. The water was warm as a bath in spots and cold as ice in others. I swam down into the water looking for her, and popped up to see her climbing up the rock wall beside the waterfall.

"Hey, watch it!" I called after her.

She just waved and smiled. She was thirty feet up there, maybe more. Suddenly, she turned and stood with her head back, back curved, breasts thrust out, narrow waist drawn in, hands to her sides. She sprang into the air like an eagle soaring from its nest, arching into the pool, cutting the water like a knife.

I saw her yellow, shimmering outline gliding through the blue water toward me. She came up a few feet away from me, her wet hair parted in the middle. She wiped her face with her hands. "Well," she said, "Pretty good dive, wasn't it?"

"I'm awed."

"Care to try it?"

"I'd care to try you," I said, throwing my arms around her.

We kissed and held each other and rolled in the water, we swam and kissed some more, and found each other under the cold waterfall, then in a hot stream pouring out from someplace deep in the earth.

There was only the water, the rocks, the waterfall, and Meredith, and the rest of the damn world seemed to evaporate.

She took my hand and led me up through the trees to a small open space on a warm rock, where the soft breeze coming down from the mountain warmed us. The brown makeup had come off and her freckles showed. We kissed each other long and deeply, and I ran my hand over her firm yet supple body and she smelled clean and new and alive, and she made me feel clean and new. When she was ready she rolled over on top of me and put my mouth to her nipple and with her gentle movement we came both at the same time, as if the mountain itself under us had released some of its power.

I was in a dream and nothing else mattered. There was no Benevides and no Gray Wolf. I had no past. It had floated away on the wind.

Late in the day, when the air turned cooler and the shadows were long, we dressed and went back to the car. We sat in the front seat and ate some *chorizo*—hot Mexican sausage—with hard-crusted bread Meredith had brought along. We split a small bottle of red wine. We were relaxed and happy and we didn't say much.

Then we drove along the dirt path for a half hour more and turned onto a wide strip of graded road that ran down the side of a hill into a deep canyon. We passed the last of the wine back and forth and settled into a languid quiet as we listened to soft Mexican music on the radio. She told me stories of where she rode horses and hiked and climbed when she was a kid and came here every summer and it made me feel nostalgic and full of warm feelings for the place even though I'd never been there.

Evening was upon us. Just as she switched the headlights on, we came around a bend in the road. A heavy iron gate blocked the way. A sign on the gate said LA ENTRADA ES PROHIBIDA. Entrance prohibited. A little ways up the hill was a man carrying

196

a rifle with a telescopic sight. Meredith waved to him; he waved back.

She handed me a key and I got out and opened the gate. She drove through, and I closed the gate and locked it. We drove another half mile through a thickly wooded area and over a small hill, and there before us was a wide strip of pasture cut out of the woods, with dozens of grazing horses, and beyond was a large ranch house, already fading into the darkness of the night, but inside lights were coming on, and there were more lights along the paved driveway that led up to the house, so that it created the feeling of coming out of a wilderness into Disneyland.

We pulled up in front of the great house and a young Mexican in a blue blazer and tie came out. "Qué gusto a verte otra vez, senora," he said. "Bienvenidos!" Enchanted to see you again. Welcome. She introduced him to me as Hector, the overseer. He explained that Senor and Senora Sanders were away on urgent business, but that all had been prepared for our visit and we were to make ourselves totally at home. He then showed us to a small cabin built along the creek. We could smell the horses and the hay.

The cabin needed paint, but it was newly scrubbed and had indoor plumbing. There was a hot plate and a small refrigerator, a table and a couple of chairs, and a large brass bed with a down mattress. Nothing on the walls or floor, plain white curtains on the windows.

We carried our luggage in and from that moment on we thought of that place as our home. The dream was good. And in the days and weeks that followed, the dream became ever better.

We ate our meals in the big house, seated at a massive oak table. The servants knew Meredith, and all seemed happy to see her. I was introduced as James Thomas, her husband-to-be, and

everyone congratulated me. The servants were efficient and polite, and seemed genuinely pleased to make us feel at home. For
breakfast we'd have eggs and bacon with toast or pancakes or
French toast, always with large mugs of French roast coffee.
Lunches were burritos or enchiladas or tostadas, all hot as hell.
Supper would sometimes be more American, with roast duck or
lamb or beef and gravy, or thick steaks.

Senor Sanders, Meredith said, had a lot of spies in El Yoro
and anyone who arrived who was the least suspicious would be
reported. Anyone who came near the hacienda was investigated
immediately. There were always men patroling the boundaries of
the ranch. All strangers were told to go away. No one would
bother us.

After a few days, I started to relax. The beautiful red color
returned to Meredith's hair, made golden in the sun. Her skin
turned bronze, the freckles got larger and darker and she looked
stunning.

In the mornings we went horseback riding on magnificent
animals. We rode English style, which I could do, but I had no
hope of keeping up with Meredith. She was a natural horse-
woman, and loved to ride at full gallop, her long red hair streaming out behind, the horse pounding away beneath her. She'd ride
through the woods on narrow trails, jumping over logs and
fences, thundering through glades and pastures.

In the afternoons we went for long walks around the ranch,
feeding the horses carrots or apples, petting them. She knew
most of their names. In the late afternoons we'd read or nap, or go
fishing in the crisp clear stream. Whatever we caught, and it was
mostly little silvery fish that wiggled like mad, we'd apologize in
English and Spanish, then throw it back.

We had long talks, sitting on the banks of the stream. Now
that I was talking about myself, she wanted to know all about me,

where I came from, the girls I dated in high school, and before that, what had happened in Hungary. I told her everything. I told her my name had been Toth in Hungary, but my father had changed it to Croft after coming to the States. I told her how my mother had run into the street when the Russian tanks were coming and joined her neighbors on Baross Utca and threw bottles and bricks at the tanks, and how she fell in the melee, and how the crawler treads of a tank chewed her up as the horrified neighbors held me back. I told her how my father lived day and night for the liberation of Hungary, and turned me into a soldier by the time I was fourteen, a soldier in the worldwide war against Communism. Fighting was to be my life. But later, I told her, who we were fighting and why we were fighting got all mixed up. After a while, I was obeying orders of men who had no commitment to anything but body counts.

Like a good Nazi, I kept obeying orders long after the orders stopped making sense. Benevides, I told her, finally woke me up.

It felt good to be telling this to someone, someone who really cared to listen. I felt like I'd had a spear stuck in me for all these years and she was pulling it out.

I wanted to know all about Meredith, too: what were her favorite desserts, her favorite color, what her mother was like, everything. She said when she was in kindergarten the teacher asked her what she wanted to be when she grew up. She remembered saying, "I don't want to be anything different from what I am now—an artist."

She said she thought of an artist as being someone who could create something that people could look at, and that would make some of the people who looked at it come away having seen something in a new way. And from then on, they would be somehow changed. Expanded. That's what real art is, she said: it has the ability to transform the human spirit.

199

I remembered the piece she'd painted for the theater group back in Amber. That was what she was talking about. It could haunt you.

Sometimes she'd make pencil sketches as we talked, sketches of birds and trees and me, but there was always something strange and foreboding about everything she'd draw. A picture of a bird would have a hawk circling over it. A fish would have a hook in its mouth, or another fish stalking it. Frightening. Always, somewhere in her work, death lurked.

I asked her about it, but she said she didn't know why. Maybe a past life was intruding on her present one. But I don't think she really believed in past lives.

We'd often go to bed early and make love on the feather mattress slowly, with a quiet burning intensity, and then sleep with the window open. And sometimes late at night I'd wake up and she'd be walking the floor and I knew there was something deeply troubling her, but when I'd ask her, she'd say it was nothing, and she'd rush back to bed and throw her arms around me and say everything was okay.

Days ran into one another invisibly. After a while I hardly thought about Gray Wolf. I felt completely safe. Completely free. We both cut down the drinking. We were tanned and becoming more fit. Her freckles were as red as strawberries.

She began what she called my training as an artist. She said she wanted me to see the world aesthetically. Which was sort of like teaching an elephant to crochet. But I was game. I started noticing colors and sniffing the flowers. I didn't say so, but flowers don't smell all that good to me. Most of them are sickeningly sweet. We spent half an hour watching a calf suckle at his mother's teat, which Meredith thought was wonderful. It didn't do much for me.

This is Zen, she said.

Zen is seeing the beauty in the everyday. Feeling it, touching it, letting it work its magic on you. *Truth is beauty; beauty, truth.* Keats the poet said that, she said.

But the only beauty I had eyes for was Meredith. She was my truth. I had been longing for her without knowing it, and now that I had her, I was never going to let her go.

Christmas came and went. There was a fiesta with dancing and singing and the breaking of a piñata. We went with some of the hands to church in El Yoro. The children were given small gifts and candies, and there was a large nativity scene in the living room of the ranch house and the whole house was covered with lights and I thought this is the way life is supposed to be.

Senor Sanders and his wife came home on New Year's. He was heavyset and jovial, and so was his wife, and they seemed to love Meredith like a daughter, and treated me like an honored guest.

One day in mid-January, one of the hands found evidence that someone had been camping on ranch property, way up in the hills. Senor Sanders and I and a couple of his men rode up there in a jeep. We found the campsite, but whoever had been there had gone.

Two days later one of the hands came back from patroling the fence and said someone had shot at him. Whoever it was got away in a Land Rover.

I told Meredith we had better leave.

"It might not have anything to do with you," she said.

"We're not safe here," I said. "Once Gray Wolf gets onto you and your family, he'll get onto Sanders. We don't want to create problems for these people."

201

"All right. Where'll we go?"

"I've got friends in Costa Rica. We'll be safe there until I can find someplace more permanent. Someplace in the Andes, maybe, where the German Nazis hid after the war and were never found."

It was decided that we'd have a farewell fiesta.

There was an immediate buzz of activity, cleaning and hanging up white, green, and red ribbons for decoration, and putting a string of Chinese lanterns around the front porch of the great house.

Meredith barely touched her dinner that night and when we returned to our cabin she said she'd like to go right to sleep. The next morning she said she didn't want any breakfast, but that I should go ahead. She said she didn't feel well. I didn't want to press her, so I walked over to the main house and had some coffee and a roll.

We skipped the horseback ride that morning and took a walk along the trail that ran by the creek up to a high pasture where a few fat black-and-white milk cows were kept for the benefit of the servants' children. They munched contentedly away on the tall grass in the morning sun.

At the end of the pasture was an old barn, half falling down. It was quiet, no clouds in the sky.

"I want to spend the rest of my life with you," she said.

"That makes us even," I said.

She bit a nail, then brushed her hair back. She kept looking up toward the mountain with this sort of frightened look on her face as if she expected the mountain would suddenly erupt.

"I don't know how to say what I want to say so it will come out right," she said.

"Just say it."

"I want to ask you again. The man who's after you, I want you to kill him."

"I've already explained—"

"No, listen. I'm asking you out of love. The love I have for you. I can't have peace until he's dead. Please, please, do it. For me. If for no other reason. Do it for me. I'll never ask you to do anything again as long as we live. I'll make you happy. I'll go with you anywhere you want to go. I'm begging you, please do it."

I shook my head.

"I can't believe you're afraid."

"I am afraid."

"Is that why you won't do it?"

"It's part of it."

"Is there nothing I could do or say—doesn't our love mean enough?"

"It means everything."

"Then why won't you do it? I want to understand. You admit you've killed dozens if not hundreds of men."

"Besides everything else—me being an ex-player and all that—Gray Wolf was my friend. I have had in my lifetime one friend. One. One real, true honest-to-God friend who I thought wouldn't sell me out for the price of a cheap bottle of booze."

"I want him dead. I don't want to worry about him for one more hour."

"I can't do it. It's just not right to kill a friend. That's what playing the game does to you. It makes you think right's wrong and wrong's right. You want an example? We infected a guy with an experimental plague because he sold the CIA some bogus data. He turned green and bumpy like a frog before he died. What do you call people that turn human beings into frogs? You call them monsters. I was a monster, but I'm not a monster any-

203

more. And not being a monster, I just can't go out and kill a friend."

She was looking at me, sadness in her eyes. "I won't ask you again," she said.

We started walking back to the ranch house. She was quiet for a while, staring down toward the ground. Then she looked at me and said, "Tomorrow I'm going into El Yoro to have a new dress made for the fiesta."

We rode over to town the next morning in the old station wagon.
Meredith wore a peasant skirt and blouse with a large gold Aztec
medallion hanging from her neck. She said she was given the
medallion by her father and it was supposed to bring her luck.
She was all smiles that morning, but behind the smiles I sensed
something deeply troubling her. She kept turning her head away
from me, and when she held my hand, it was moist and her grip
was tight.

I thought if I waited she'd tell me about it without my
asking.

A stable hand, Juan Rodriguez, drove us. He was a happy-
go-lucky sort of fellow in his sixties who liked to play a guitar and
sing. Everyone liked him. Every time he saw me around the
ranch, he'd say, "How you like Mexico now, senor, eh?" I'd
always tell him it's getting better and better.

As the three of us drove through the mountains the sky
darkened and it looked like rain was certain. Juan said, "We

should hurry back." I knew he was worried about the road washing out.

We parked the car on a grassy hill just outside town. I took my gun out from under the seat of the station wagon. I hadn't been carrying it at the ranch, but here in town I figured it was good to be on the safe side. Meredith ran ahead, anxious to get to the dressmaker. She said she'd meet me at the cantina.

Juan headed for the church, where he said he had to buy some blessed candles for his wife. He said she was crazy with religion.

I crossed the *zocalo*, the square, passed the bandstand and the statue of Victor Hernandez, a local hero in the revolution, and went to the cantina for a beer. The cantina was in a crumbling adobe building. The furnishings were made of gnarled wood, and there were pictures on the wall of Pancho Villa and Victor Hernandez on their horses. A white-haired American was sitting by himself on the porch drinking tequila. I'd heard of him; he'd been a movie actor in Hollywood and became sick of it. He was now in his seventies and seemed to have no interest in anything other than tequila. He asked me to join him.

"Weather front moving in," he said. "Winter storm."

"Guess so." The beer was warm.

He rubbed some lime on his hand, sprinkled it with salt, and threw down half a glass of tequila and licked his hand.

"I guess those fellas that was looking for you found you," he said.

"What fellas?" I asked.

"A couple of gringos. They had a picture of you." He downed the rest of his drink.

A jolt of fear shot through me.

"Where are they now?" I asked, keeping my fear in check.

The old man shrugged.

I went out the back door of the cantina and down an alley to the hotel, already planning how we were going to get out of town. The old station wagon couldn't outrun anything. There was a small airport south of El Yoro, with a grass field and one or two planes that might come in handy. The mayor had a jeep I could steal. I kept my hand in my jacket on my gun. I went in the back door of the hotel, and down a dark hallway to the hotel lobby. The clerk was reading a newspaper.

"Two men were looking for me. Who?"

"Mr. Thompson and Mr. Gray," the clerk said. "I told them nada, senor. I say I never in my life heard about you."

I handed him a wad of money.

"What did these men look like?"

"A tall blond gringo, *muy alto*, and a shorter dark man, had his arm in a cast and mucho curly hair. *Griego*. Greek. Something like that."

The short one would be Viktor Dukas; the other, Gray Wolf, I figured. "Where are they now?" I asked.

The clerk scratched his head. "Looking for you."

I had but one idea, and that was to get the hell out of there. I went out the back door and down a back street, then came up an alley and looked up and down the main street. Only Mexicans on the street. I crossed over to the dress shop and burst in. No Meredith. I tried the dressing rooms.

"Qué es la problema, senor?" the dressmaker said, alarmed.

"Where's the redheaded woman?" I asked in Spanish.

"Senora Kellerman?"

"Sí."

"Acaba de salir."

"Dónde?"

She shrugged. She didn't know where she went.

I went back out on the street. A sprinkle had started. I

spotted Juan Rodriguez, our driver, across the street running for the cantina.

"Juan! Where's Meredith?"

"She send me to look for you, senor. She say someone looking for you. She say she go get the car, meet us at the gasoline station."

"Come on."

I led him down an alley to a back street. I figured I'd have a lot less chance of being spotted.

Suddenly: a low-pitched phooomp came from up the hill. An explosion. It came from where we had parked the station wagon. I felt sick.

Juan and I turned around and headed back toward the hill, running. I could see smoke and then the orange flames pouring out of the black station wagon; it looked like little more than a lump of scrap, twisting in the flame, and as I came closer I could see a body at the wheel completely engulfed in flames, and I could see the Aztec medallion around her neck, and then her whole body burst in a gush of yellow flame and disappeared below the level of the dashboard.

I stood paralyzed and mute, barely conscious of the people around me.

Juan Rodriguez turned me away. "Nothing can be done for her."

I staggered down the hill a few steps. The rain came harder. The old *guardia*, the town cop, was running toward us, making the sign of the cross on his chest, his pistol flapping against his side. "Oh, senor, was anyone in that thing?"

Most everyone in town was on their way to look at the burning car. I ran back to the hotel. The clerk stood behind the counter. He froze with fear when he saw my gun.

"Where are they?" I said.

"The two men? They have gone, senor. Senor Martinez was just here looking for the *guardia*. Mr. Martinez owns the little airport for our town. The two men, he said, took a plane, and have cut the wires on the other planes so they cannot fly. We have called the authorities in Jalapa, whatever airport they land, we will catch them."

I went down the hill and walked into some trees where I cursed and cried and swore blood oaths into the wind. Gray Wolf had always liked bombs. He was trying for me, but something must have gone wrong. He would have used a remote device, but maybe he hadn't planned to stick around and wait for me to get back to the car.

Or he had killed Meredith as a bizarre kind of challenge, like killing Prince. Or perhaps, like Viktor Dukas said, Gray Wolf had lost his mind.

After dark, after prayers were said in the church, I dug the grave myself while the people from the ranch stood by and prayed and cried. It rained as I dug, and my muscles ached, my hands blistered and bled, but I dug the grave deep, and with each shovelful of the hard clay I swore another oath of vengeance against Gray Wolf.

The women of the village put the charred body in a wooden box and lowered it into the ground while a priest mumbled words and sprinkled holy water that mixed with the rain.

Then Juan Rodriguez drove me to the airport at Jalapa, where I chartered a plane and called Frank Webb and told him what had happened. Frank Webb said he'd have someone meet me in San Antonio as soon as I could get there.

I flew north in a four-seater, an old twin-engine job, just me and the pilot. We arrived in San Antonio, Texas, at nine o'clock in the morning. I cleared customs and went through a doorway and into a long hallway and found Bill Vanders, Langston's young assistant, waiting for me. He was wearing a light tan suit and looked immaculate. He greeted me with a friendly smile, like we were real old pals.

"May I express my condolences, Mr. Croft," he said. "I'm very sorry."

"Have they got a line on Gray Wolf yet?"

"No, sir, but Viktor Dukas flew to Grenada late last night. We're watching all the docks and airports and have a dozen good men looking for him."

"What happened to Gray Wolf?"

"By the time we picked up Viktor's trail in Mazatlán, he and Gray Wolf had already separated—please follow me, sir. Our plane for Miami leaves in twenty minutes."

We flew a commercial jet to Miami. Along the way Vanders read some kind of manual and kept making notes. In Miami, he made a report to his superiors by phone. They told him they had Viktor Dukas and were holding him for me to interrogate. We took off from Miami at eight that night and got to St. George's Island, Grenada, after midnight. We flew into the huge Point Salines airport the Soviets and Cubans built before Reagan invaded and took it away from them.

On our approach, the island was a dot on the black ocean. I could make out white sand beaches and city lights, and vast areas of darkness I figured were either jungles or plantation. The moon was low on the horizon.

We changed to a four-seater Cessna and flew to a cigar-shaped island nearby. A private airstrip had been hacked out of the jungle. The pilot, a young daredevil, dove straight down, then leveled out and came to a bumpy landing. I opened the door and stepped out into the humid jungle. It was hot. Frogs croaked. Insects buzzed.

A young black man waited with a jeep. Vanders and I climbed in while the pilot waited with the plane.

"Where'd they get Viktor, you got any idea?" I asked the driver.

"No, sir, they tell me nothin'."

"What's his physical condition?"

"Has a cast on his arm, but otherwise looks healthy enough."

That was good. I wanted him healthy. Good and healthy.

Vanders said, "They said he won't say anything about Gray Wolf to anyone except you."

"Yeah, how come?"

"He says he wants to deal. He wants to live."

"A man who cares about living should never be a player."

211

Vanders chuckled like I'd made a joke. Only I wasn't joking.

We pulled off onto a dirt road and drove for half a mile or so. The jungle growth came down to both sides of the road and brushed the jeep. It smelled of nutmeg. A quarter of a mile or so off the main road we came to a large, brick, Victorian house. Portions of the porch had collapsed. The shutters were falling off. The jungle grew right up to it. I got out of the car. A bird screeched in the darkness.

"May I speak to you for a moment?" Vanders asked.

"Go ahead."

"I just wanted to say I understand why you were so, ah, so *unpleasant* when Mr. Langston and I visited you."

"You do, do you?"

"Yes, sir. You had every right to be left alone if that's what you wanted."

"Okay, Vanders." I gave him a pat on the arm.

He walked up the front steps of the house. I followed along. Inside, the place smelled like mildew and decay. It was lit by candles put around in saucers and jars. Mold grew everywhere, on the windows, on the floor. Dust lay thick on the furniture. Langston, wearing a white suit, came out of the kitchen with a beer in his hand.

"Hello, Croft. How the hell are you?" He took a swig of beer. "Too bad about your lady friend."

"Where's Viktor?"

"Not so fast. We've got to make sure you understand the ground rules."

"Sure, Langston, anything you say."

"He's ours, Croft. All ours. That's means you can look, you can talk, but you can't touch. We want him alive so he can tell us all about what he's been up to since he left us."

"Sure. What the fuck you think I'm going to do with all you guys around?"

"He gives you what you want, we want you to guarantee his safety. He spills what you want, you let him go. Forever."

"Sure, what the fuck do I care about a piece of shit like Viktor Dukas?"

"I want your word on that."

"You've got it."

"Okay then." He turned and spoke to someone in the next room: "Bring him in."

Langston picked up his beer and took a few swallows. It was warm and stuffy in the house. I guess he figured by not offering me any beer, he was showing what a heavyweight he was.

"You know whose house this used to be?" Langston asked.

"No," I said.

"A retired British admiral. When the Brits had Grenada, before independence. Used to bring his broads up here. We found some whips and shit in the attic. Leather. Guess he had a real good time."

"Why should I—or you—give a shit?"

Langston scowled. "You know something, Croft? I'd have never in a million fucking years let you come here, it was up to me."

"Can't you hurry those guys up?"

"They're coming, they're coming. What the hell's your hurry? You find Gray Wolf, you know what? He's going to burn you right down to the ground. That's what I think."

"That a fact?"

Suddenly Viktor Dukas appeared in the doorway, two muscle guys shoving him forward. His clothes were torn, his right eye bruised. He hung his head like he was really so damn sorry for being a bad boy. He wouldn't look at me, the cowardly little bastard. I never understood how Gray Wolf could stand having him around, except that he always did anything Gray Wolf told him to do. And anything included *anything*.

He coughed and fanned away the dust.

They pushed him past me into the living room, where they sat him down in an overstuffed chair, raising a cloud of dust. His right arm was in a cast in a tan-colored sling. Langston sent the two muscle guys away. Vanders stood in the doorway with his jacket open, showing off a gun in his belt. A shaft of light from a flashlight fell on Viktor; he turned his head away.

Langston said, "Okay, we're all here, Viktor. You can start talking now."

Viktor moved his head, but he didn't look at me. "We must have deal first," he said.

"Always the deal, eh, Viktor?" I said. "Didn't you hear me when we met in New York?"

"It's not a fault of mine," he said. "How can I, Viktor Dukas, a day laborer, say no to a man like our friend?"

"Where can I find him, Viktor, that's all I want to know."

He looked at me now for the first time. "I will tell you, Coldiron. Out of friendship. Didn't I tell you everything when we met in New York? Out of friendship?"

"Yes, Viktor, you did. Now tell me the rest of it." I kept my voice nice and even, smooth.

"You and I, we were friends, were we not?" Viktor asked.

"Just tell me where to find him, and I'll let you live."

"And you will not break my arms or my legs?"

"Our friend is all I want."

"You swear to this. You swear in front of witnesses?"

"I gave you my word, Viktor."

"Swear. Say that you swear. No man in this business do I trust, but you, my friend. Swear to it, I would believe you. Gray

214

Wolf made me go to Mexico. He made me. I didn't want to go. Please, swear an oath."

"I swear."

"I don't know if I believe you."

"I said I swear, that's enough nonsense. Where, Viktor? Tell me where I can find him and you will live to be an old, old man."

He looked up at me with unbelieving eyes, full of uncertainty and fear.

"Croft cannot hurt you, Viktor," Langston said. "He's not armed and we guarantee your safety."

That brought a thin smile to Viktor's lips. Outside, a bullfrog struck a deep note. Then another. Viktor shivered as if it were a bad omen.

"We're waiting," Langston said.

Viktor licked his lips. "Gray Wolf will kill me if he finds out that I told on him."

"And we'll kill you if you don't," Langston said.

"The story of my life, lose on the left, lose on the right." He looked at Langston like he wanted pity. He didn't get any. Then he turned to me and said, "Do you remember Lintz, the Kraut death merchant?"

"I remember," I said.

"Lintz has bought himself a mansion in Indonesia—on Lombok, the big island near Bali. Gray Wolf will be there until the tenth. He's meeting with some very important Iranians, they have work for him. Go quickly, he won't be there long."

"There you have it," Langston said to me.

"What work do these Iranians want?" I asked.

Viktor shrugged. "I only know he is there." He wiped some sweat off his brow with the back of his hand.

I turned to Langston. "Let me have a few minutes with him,

215

there are some other questions I want to ask him. Questions that have nothing to do with the Exchange."

"No," Langston said. "Not permitted. Anything he's got to say, we want to hear it."

"I was promised if I told you where he was, that was all I had to say," Viktor said. He rubbed his hand on his cast.

"Relax, Viktor," I said. "I'm not going to ask you anything to tax your mind. Get him a beer, would you?"

Langston nodded to Vanders, who headed for the kitchen. "Get us all one," Langston called after him.

"I don't know anything worth knowing," Viktor Dukas said. "I do what I'm told, that's all I know."

"I know, Viktor," I said. I stood by the window and looked out through the grime. There were car headlights lighting up the yard. There was once a shallow pool of some sort in the side yard, but it was now completely overgrown with tangles.

"I want to know about Mexico, Viktor." I said. I said it softly.

"What is there to know?"

"I want to know first how you knew I was there."

"I don't know how he knew. He just knew."

"You came by plane to Jalapa?"

"Yes, then we rented a small plane. Gray Wolf flew it from there. To ride with him was a terrible scary thing. He liked to fly low, almost on the ground. Under bridges—a dangerous man."

"When you got to El Yoro you asked around about me."

"Yes."

"He didn't know I was at the Sanders' ranch?"

"No, I think not."

"Okay, then what?"

"And we found out you were on the ranch high in the mountains."

216

"How did you find that out?"

"I don't know. Gray Wolf found it out. He paid someone a lot of money. A clerk at the hotel, I think. And then he found out you were coming because your woman wanted a dress for a party."

"He knew that?"

"Yes."

"How did he know that, Viktor?"

"I don't know."

"How could you not know, you were with him."

"Not all the time. He went out after breakfast. He said he wanted to have a drink at the cantina. I don't even know if it was open yet, but I never argued with him. You know how he treated me. No respect. When he came back I was still eating. He said to me, 'Coldiron is coming. We will do it today.' "

"And did you know what he meant?"

"Yes. He meant to kill you."

"He knew the car?"

"Yes."

"How did he know?" I turned around and was looking at him now. He shrugged. "I don't know anything. He came back from wherever he went and he said, "We will do it today." That's all he said. So he told me to pack our bags. That is what I do for Gray Wolf. Pack bags. Run errands. He say I should pack the bags. I pack the bags—even with a broken arm. He didn't care what discomfort I had to endure."

"And then what happened?"

Langston said, "Is there any point to this?"

"Relax," I said. "Go on, Viktor, what happened next?"

"Then he had me take the car and get it filled with gas. I did that. Then I met him back at the hotel. The sky was getting dark with clouds. That worried him. He went someplace and made a phone call, I think."

217

"To who?"

"I don't know."

"Go on."

"He knew you'd be parking your car outside of town, I guess, because we went up there and waited about fifteen minutes. We were in the trees beyond the hill. We saw you get out of the car with the woman and the Mexican driver."

"Did Gray Wolf have a gun with him? I mean a gun you could use reliably at a distance?"

"Sure."

"Why didn't he just drop me there?"

Viktor shrugged. "Perhaps he didn't think he could make a clean shot. He's afraid of you, I think. That is true. That's why he wanted to use the bomb."

"Bullshit, I never knew him to be afraid of anyone."

"Just you. I have never seen him nervous before, but at the sound of your name, he gets jumpy. After we left the Exchange, he was never himself. He was crazylike. Remember Stan Thompson? He went over, and the next year he climbed out on a ledge of his hotel in Moscow, naked, and jumped into a fountain. Being hunted by your former compatriots does something to your mind."

"I still don't believe Gray Wolf's afraid of me."

"Maybe he was afraid if he shot you, we would not be able to get away. The airport would be closed—he wanted to be far away when the bomb went off."

"Okay, Viktor. Then what happened?"

He wiped his face with his sleeve. His face looked like someone had thrown a bucket of water at him. "He—he wired the bomb into the car."

"He had you pack the bags, but he wired the bomb himself?"

"Yes."

Vanders came back with the beer and passed it around. I didn't have any. My mouth felt dry as sand, but I didn't want beer.

"I think, Viktor, that you planted that bomb," I said.

"No, I swear. He did it. He never let me do something like that, especially not with a broken arm—the arm that you yourself broke. Gray Wolf is a careful man, you know that."

"Okay, Viktor, what happened next?"

He took down half the beer and wiped his mouth with the back of his hand. "You know what happened."

"I want to hear it from you." I was standing in front of him, three or four feet away, looking down on him. I had my hands in my pockets. "Tell it all, Viktor."

He looked up at me, his eyes dancing with fear. He wiped his mouth again with his sleeve.

"Tell me the rest, Viktor."

"All right. After he finished wiring in the bomb, we saw your woman coming back up the hill to the car."

"You saw she was alone?"

"Yes."

"And Gray Wolf saw her too?"

"Yes. But what could we do? Run out there and shout, 'Don't get in that car!' I could do nothing like that. I would not have lived one minute, not with Gray Wolf standing right beside me. He was in a hurry to get to the plane and besides . . . well, never mind. It happened. It's finished. There, I've told you the whole truth. We got into our car and raced to the airport. We were already in the plane when we heard the explosion."

"So you just let her die?"

He didn't answer.

"I asked you a question, Viktor."

"You know what happened. You were there."

I sprang on him and had him by the neck, lifting him out of the chair.

I screamed: "So you just let her die!"

He swung at me with the beer bottle, smashing it against my head, but I didn't let go. Vanders leapt on me, pulling my arm back. I flung Viktor forward, dropping him over the chair, then I turned and hit Vanders in the mouth, staggering him. His knees buckled, but he didn't fall.

"Halt!" Langston shouted.

I turned and saw he had his gun out. I hit Vanders again, spun him around, and pushed him into Langston, shoving him back into a wall. Vanders went down. I grabbed Langston's gun hand, twisted it, and sent the gun flying. Then I hit him in his soft gut and he folded like a newspaper, groaned, and dropped to the floor. He scrambled toward the door.

Vanders got up on his knees, staring at me. I put up my hand to signal him not to move. He didn't. Then I turned back to Viktor Dukas, who was just getting to his feet.

"Please . . ." he said. "There was nothing I could do. Nothing. Nothing no one could do. Gray Wolf would have shot me dead if I did anything. Gray Wolf said, 'We got a hen instead of the rooster.' He laughed about it."

I grabbed his shirt and pulled him to me.

"Did you laugh, too?"

I grabbed him by the collar now, bending him forward in front of me so that his head was below the level of my waist.

"You promised not to hurt me!"

I brought my knee up on his forehead and my right fist downward at the same time, snapping his neck with a loud crack.

He dropped to the floor, his legs flopping around crazily in a cloud of dust, his head at an acute angle. Then he vomited, cried out, and the last of his breath hissed out of his mouth.

Langston was back with his two muscle boys. "Oh, shit," he said. He clenched his teeth and glared at me. "I'm going to see you pay dear for this," he said. "Wait until the Director gets my report. He doesn't like it when other people break his toys."

"Viktor wasn't his, he was mine. If the Director wants to talk to me about it, I'll be in Indonesia."

She called herself Nagal; she had large black eyes and long, jet-black hair that reached to her belt. She was wearing a sari, diaphanous, flowing, silken, and had small blue flowers in her hair. Nagal was slender, about thirty, and had beautiful golden skin. She seemed strong and fragile at the same time and reminded me of Meredith. It was something in her eyes, something unknowable.

She met me at the small airport at a quarter past one in the morning. The corners of the roof of the single terminal building at Lombok were turned up, in the Balinese style. Nagal guided me through customs. None of my bags were checked. I guess the inspectors had been bought by the Exchange.

The first thing Nagal told me was that Gray Wolf had been spotted at Herr Lintz's mansion. I felt a surge of excitement, but she said it would not be easy to get to him and she would show me why.

We drove down the two-lane highway lined with tall palms.

The place seemed deserted. Lombok is one of the world's true backwaters. The few buildings I could spot were square, white-washed jobs: an occasional temple with its tiered roof, a mosque. Lombok is multicultural and multiethnic, with Balinese, Chinese, Arabs, Malaysians. We drove into Cakranegara, one of the four principal towns which sort of run together along a road going inland from the coast. The brochure given to me on the plane said it was the former royal capital. It looked to me like it had fallen on hard times.

Nagal drove me to an apartment in a four-story building. The apartment was large, but sparsely furnished with cheap rattan. There was an inside circular stairway leading to the floor above. She took me upstairs and into the master bedroom, which faced north. Here were two stakeout men, both young, both dark. I took them to be Arabs. One was asleep on a cot; the other was looking through a telescope. He said something to Nagal in Indonesian.

Nagal nodded and said to me: "There's been no one in or out since I left. Would you like to see?"

I took a look through the light-collecting telescope. It was focused on a large stone building with small windows. The building had wood trim and shutters—the Dutch influence—and Balinese turned-up roof corners. Behind it was a hill, thick with foliage. I could see no guards, but a high fence surrounded the grounds, with a huge wrought-iron gate across a drive that went up to the front of the house.

"Looks formidable," I said.

"Herr Lintz has friends in the government who offer him sanctuary. A powerful local politician is married to Herr Lintz's sister. Herr Lintz also has many friends with the police."

"What kind of security?" I asked.

"Come downstairs, we'd better talk."

She handed me a glass of Japanese scotch that tasted almost like the real thing. The windows were open and a cool breeze caressed the curtains. I sat down on the couch and she sat opposite me, her legs folded up under her.

"Are you acquainted with Herr Lintz?" she asked.

"I met him once," I said. "I remember him as a man who loved to eat roast beef and drink red wine. He had a coarse laugh and dog hairs on his expensive blue suit. That's about all I remember about him except that he had an insatiable greed."

"He is trying now to become the number-one private arms dealer in the world and was once a good friend of the Exchange, but no longer. We contacted him some months ago to help us track down Gray Wolf, but he ignored our request and now harbors him. We feel he must be taught a lesson."

"I see."

"We do have an inside man in Herr Lintz's employ," she said. "A Javanese cook. He gets a list each day that tells him the meals to prepare for the next day, so he knows who is coming and going. We should know the day before Gray Wolf is to leave and then we will be ready and waiting."

I said, "Gray Wolf has a habit of doing the unexpected. Has Herr Lintz got any more guests?"

"Some Iranians and two Europeans. One Iranian is an arms dealer. One of the Europeans is a Corsican politician. We don't know who the other European is at the moment, but we're working on it."

"I would like to get a closer look at that house."

"You look very tired, perhaps you should rest."

"Until Gray Wolf is dead, I can't rest."

"Sleep at least until dawn. In the dark there is not much to

see, and with no one about we will only draw attention to ourselves if we go near the house."

"All right," I said.

Nagal showed me to a bedroom upstairs across the hall from
the master bedroom where the stakeout men worked. It had its
own bathroom. I showered first, then got into a too-soft bed
crowded with large, sweet-scented pillows. After a while a heavy
rain started and beat strong against the windows.

Before drifting off to sleep I thought of the rain on the roof of
the small cabin in Mexico, and I ached terribly for Meredith. I
burned for her.

When I awoke a few hours later I heard the song from the
minarets calling the faithful of Islam to morning prayer. It had
stopped raining. I would kill Gray Wolf this day, I thought.

I got up and put on a robe and went down into the living
room. Nagal was there cleaning a small automatic. She wore a
dark sweatshirt and black pants. She had braided her hair and
wound it tightly to her head and she looked younger than she had
a few hours before. Almost like a teenager.

"You slept well, sir?" she asked, getting to her feet.

"Tom. Call me Tom."

"Tom."

"Yes, I slept well. Are we ready to go?"

"You had better eat, you will need your strength."

She served me a spicy rice and vegetable dish with hot
black coffee. While I ate, she kept cleaning the gun, sitting on
the floor by the coffee table.

"I want you to tell me everything you know about Lintz,"
I said.

225

"All right." She removed some files from a briefcase. "I had to get special permission to take this from the center." She put on a pair of heavy-framed glasses, which weren't very becoming, and looked over some papers in a thick file.

"He is fifty-five years old," she said. "A German with a Swiss passport. He's six feet tall, portly, is not married, and has no close relatives. His mistress, Dawn Anderson, lives with him most of the time. Lintz was educated at the Prussian military academy in East Germany; he defected in 1959. He is a breeder of prize-winning Afghan hounds. He prefers heavy German food, strong coffee, and has a great appetite for sweets. Doesn't smoke, drink, or take drugs, as far as we know. Mostly he deals in small arms, but sometimes supplies transport services to drug runners on a quid-pro-quo basis. He is ruthless, cruel, and has been known to change loyalties quickly—if the money's right. He likes having many guests, but spends most of his time alone in his study where he reads and listens to classical music, especially operas."

"Tell me about the security arrangements."

She nodded and looked through her file again. After a moment she looked up and said, "He has a state-of-the-art security system, one of the best in this part of the world. That's all I can tell you."

"Who installed it?"

"He had a German company come in and do the job. We're not sure who they were."

"What's the routine at the house?"

She sifted through some papers and read them over. "Lintz comes out twice weekly for a luncheon at his club. Sometimes he meets with public officials. He is always well guarded. His mistress plays golf occasionally and goes scuba diving with a scuba diving club."

"She guarded?"

"At all times. Two men. Herr Lintz's cars are all bullet-proofed, of course."

"Okay, go on."

. "There are grocery deliveries twice weekly, and other services at unscheduled intervals. Plumbers, electricians, and so on. Every single vehicle in or out is thoroughly searched twice. Every person is searched. Absolutely everyone. Even his mistress."

"Anyone else in or out on a regular basis?"

"Two security men take Herr Lintz's two prize Afghans out every day at nine in the morning for a run."

"Where do they go?"

"There's a park about a mile from the house. A lot of people exercise their dogs there."

"With such a large lawn, isn't that strange?"

"He has flowers and things growing there the dogs disturb."

"Anything else?"

"Herr Lintz is a Go player. He holds regular tournaments at the Hilton Hotel in Bali, twenty to forty people. He stays at the hotel then."

"When's his next tournament?"

"June."

I got up and walked to the window and looked out on the city. Lintz's house was just a dot on the hill way off in the distance.

"When Gray Wolf leaves, how will he go?"

"Most guests go directly to the airport. Depending on the importance of the guest, they will have two or three escort vehicles of security men."

"When Gray Wolf arrived, was he escorted?"

"Yes. Three vehicles."

227

The town shimmered in the morning sun, mostly white-washed blocklike buildings. I could see a few tall buildings, a river beyond, and the tops of the tiered roofs of a large temple. I closed the drapes.

I said, "Besides the airport, how else could he get off the island?"

"A private landing field twenty miles up the coast. And by boat of course."

"Gray Wolf sails and can pilot a plane."

"I will have some of our people make inquiries and find out if he has been seen at any harbors. We have both airports watched, of course."

"This man you have planted inside, the cook, is there any way he can find out which way Gray Wolf will be coming out?"

"I'm afraid not."

"Okay, Nagal, let's see . . . We can't go in and get him. We can't know for sure when he's coming out. We won't know what route he's taking or where he's going when he does come out."

"All we know is he most probably will go to the airport."

"Gray Wolf never did anything 'most probably' in his god-damn life."

"The only thing we can do is wait and watch, and when he comes out, you can try to take him. We have a very good sniper's rifle with exploding rounds that ought to penetrate the bulletproof glass."

"What the hell kind of an operation is this? He *might* come out the main door, but he *might* not. He *might* go to the airport, but he *might* not. An exploding bullet that *might* penetrate the glass. We've got to know. You've got to control your target factors, haven't they at least taught you that?"

Her mouth was tight. "It's the best we can do at this time. If you don't want to try him en route, you can intercept him at the airport."

"Where there are security people and police by the score."

"No one said it was going to be easy, but it looks like your best option. I don't like it, and I don't blame you for not liking it, but that's the best we can do."

"I want to see the route to the airport."

"Let's first wait and see what comes out in the garbage."

"Pardon?"

She smiled. "Our inside man sends his messages out in the garbage, which is picked up every morning at nine. We usually hear by ten."

"Christ. Waiting for the goddamn garbage."

I went back to my room and did a little workout. An hour later there was a soft knock on the door and I said to come in. It was Nagal. She had a pot of coffee.

"We have sent two men to see if Gray Wolf has docked a boat anywhere on the island. These are good men, smugglers, who know these waters."

"Good."

"So, you see, we are hard at work doing everything we can." She poured me some coffee. "Would you now like me to rub your back? It is good for tension."

"No thanks, I like to be tense."

She smiled at my little joke. "May we talk?" she asked.

"Sure."

She sat on a chair, on the front edge, and clasped her hands on her knees. She had long, graceful fingers.

"I just wanted you to know we're on the same side."

"I know we are," I said.

She smiled nervously and brushed her shining black hair

out of her eyes. "They told me what happened in Mexico. I want to say something to you and I don't know how you'll take it," she said.

"Just say it and we'll find out."

"Well, among my people, for centuries they have had a strong belief that there is not any such thing as death. The soul, that which makes you you, does not die. It goes someplace else and it lives. Many people all over the world believe that, perhaps in a different way. I believe it." She waited a moment; maybe she wanted me to say something. I didn't. Then she said, "I think your grief is like a fire that will burn you up. I'm sorry if you think it is improper for me to speak of such things with you. I want to help you put out the fire."

"I'll put out the fire when Gray Wolf is in the ground."

She nodded and started to get up, then halted like she wanted to say something, but she changed her mind. She went to the door. "The garbage man called. Gray Wolf is staying at least one more day."

The rain stopped as suddenly as it had begun.

Nagal and I took a ride up and down the road Gray Wolf would most likely take on his way to the airport. We carried the sniper's rifle and exploding bullets in the trunk and the car was equipped with a two-way radio, so if Gray Wolf were to come out of Lintz's house we could be alerted and make an attempt. We didn't go near the house itself. I didn't want my picture taken by any hidden cameras.

Below the house, the twisted streets were narrow and the houses had walls around them that ran along the streets. There were few places with good cover, and fewer yet where there were good escape routes. Not that that was my main concern.

We figured we could lay some charges along a bridge across the Ancar River once he was on the main road, or use an antitank rocket, which Nagal said she could get for me. She said she could get a few men to give covering fire, but none of that Rambo stuff appealed too much to me. First of all, if I blew up a bunch of cars with people in them, how would I know for sure I got Gray Wolf?

No, sir. I wanted to see his face when I put a bullet into him.

We drove around the hill and approached the house from behind. There was a large, sparsely populated, wooded area back of the house. A road ran by the house, then turned and went up the hill. I asked Nagal where the road led. She showed me on the map. It made a loop and connected with a main road on the other side of the hill.

She said she had men watching the back of the house as well, but she didn't think it was a good escape route because there was a tunnel to go through on the way down the hill and Gray Wolf would be smart enough to avoid being trapped in the tunnel.

I got out of the car and walked into the woods. There were hiking trails. That's how he'd leave, I thought, if there were trouble in the house. By motorcycle, through the woods. It would take dozens of men to cover every trail. He could get around the tunnel. He'd only be vulnerable the moment he left Lintz's house. After that he'd have good cover and a dozen possibilities.

It would be worth the risk if we knew for sure he would come out the back way. But there was no way to know for sure.

I figured it might be better to do the job at the other end— the airport.

Nagal had arranged for me to get a phony air-conditioner repairman's uniform and forged a picture ID with my face darkened, cleanshaven, my hair dyed black. I spent the afternoon walking around the airport with a utility belt full of hand tools strapped to my waist and a small automatic under my shirt. There were no more than two or three large planes and half a dozen small ones around at any one time. If Gray Wolf left by the

232

airport, he would have to pass through customs, whether he was taking a scheduled flight or a private jet.

It was no good. Too open. Too many cops around. Too much security. Besides, there was no guarantee he'd come this way. Too much of a gamble. Nagal figured the way to get him was before he came into the airport, to wait in front in a car and shoot him as he went in through the door.

I didn't like it. We weren't that certain he'd be coming to the airport, or if he did, that I'd get a good shot at him. But then I figured that with the limited intelligence and manpower we had, we'd have to go with it. We went back to the apartment and waited for some word from the surveillance units that he was leaving. Two more people arrived; no one left. We had an early supper of fish and rice. I paced around, had a few drinks. Nagal and I played gin. She won. About midnight I went to bed.

I awoke from a fitful sleep at five in the morning. I laid there for a long time, thinking about Gray Wolf and I remembered the first time we went on tour together.

After Vietnam I didn't see him for a while. I spent a year learning tradecraft in Georgia, then I went for advanced guerrilla operations training in the jungles of Panama. After that I went on tour twice, once in Central America, and once, briefly, in Canada. Next, I was sent to Lebanon, where the civil war had been going on for a few months and things were messy. I was told I'd get my operational orders when I got there.

I arrived on a Friday night in early May 1975, on a commercial airline. Coming in for a landing, I could see the snow-covered mountains to the east. The city of Beirut below was lustrous in the moonlight; the power was out and only a few buildings had lights. Most of the city was still intact, but various factions were holding sway in different sections: the army, the

Christian militias, various PLO factions, Marxist groups, criminal gangs.

When I arrived, the airport was in the hands of the Phalangists, the Christian-dominated ruling party that still had at least partial control of the government. Roving bands of gunmen and snipers were causing a lot of trouble. On the way into the city, I saw several burned-out vehicles and looted stores, a few buildings turned to rubble, but I heard no shooting. A few army patrols stood at intersections in armored personnel carriers.

Downtown Beirut, which was full of modern high-rises and looked very European, seemed untouched. I could see why they called the place the Paris of the Middle East. Beyond the downtown section was the hotel section, near the beach. Here the streetlights were working and the hotels were well lit, the streets were full of cabs.

I walked into the Holiday Inn lobby and spotted Lieutenant Fairweather headed toward me. I'd heard he'd joined the Exchange and had taken the code name Gray Wolf and he was on the way to making himself a legend.

He'd changed since I'd seen him last. He no longer seemed like a college kid. He was still heavily muscled, and still had a ready smile. Only now he had a cunning look in his eyes that hadn't been there before. He was wearing a blue sport jacket and jeans, his shirt unbuttoned.

"Hey, Croft, nice to see you."

I remembered Colonel Willows and the Saigon sewer rats, and I really didn't want to have anything to do with him. A lot of the people I had to work with were real cowboys, barely under discipline, and I took him to be one of them.

"What's the project?" I asked.

"Swatting a few flies, Croft, swatting a few flies. An evening's fun and games and you'll be in London tomorrow having a cold Guinness."

We went up to a fifth-floor suite, where three guys were waiting for us. One, I knew. Berengeir, called the Frenchman. A gun for hire. Good, reliable, well schooled. Fought in Algeria with the French Foreign Legion. He was short, stocky, sullen. He nodded to me and went back to cleaning an Uzi machine pistol at a small table.

The other two were, I guessed, Americans. One tall, young, nervous looking. The other was maybe fifty, had some hard fat around the middle like an old boxer. He must have taken a bullet or some shrapnel because the whole left side of his face was scarred.

"I guess you know the Frenchman," Gray Wolf said. "This is Cutter and Dubney."

Cutter was the tall, nervous one; Dubney, the one with the scar.

"What kept you?" Dubney said to me.

"Flight was late leaving Heathrow."

He lit a cigar, all the time glaring at me, I guess to let me know he didn't approve of flights being late.

"What's the job?" I asked.

"A rabid PLO splinter group called Fire of Allah grabbed a CIA deputy chief of station the night before last. They took him to a command center just east of the city. We're going to get him back."

"Sounds good," I said.

Dubney asked if there were any questions. I wanted to know how good the intelligence was and he assured me it was Class A, that they knew for sure where he was being held. I asked how many men we were going up against and he said no more than a dozen—and we'd have the element of surprise on our side.

"Easy money," Gray Wolf said.

The Frenchman didn't look too happy. He didn't like it, you could tell by the squint in his eyes. But he didn't say anything. The Fire of Allah were holding a deputy station chief, they had to know they'd have company.

Dubney showed us some maps, giving the location of the command center, the routes in and out, and a floor plan of the inside, which was a maze of small rooms and hallways. They didn't know in which room they were holding our man, and they weren't sure where the guards would be posted.

Gray Wolf and I were to go up on the roof and down a skylight, Dubney was going to attack from the rear as a diversion and the Frenchman and Cutter were going in the front. We were each given whistles to use if we found the deputy chief. We were given his photo so there'd be no mistake. Our orders were to take him along if he was able to keep up. If not, we were to kill him.

We left the hotel at midnight. Dubney, the Frenchman, and Cutter went in a black Peugeot, I went with Gray Wolf in an old Mercedes. We had forged papers saying we were part of a United Nations survey team, in case a military patrol stopped us. We weren't armed, there was nothing in the car that would have tipped them off.

"What's the matter, Coldiron, you don't look too happy," Gray Wolf said.

I said, "Curly, Larry, and Moe must have planned this operation."

Gray Wolf laughed. "They plan all the mission profiles for the Exchange. But don't worry, it'll work out. The guys we're up against aren't exactly crack troops. When we open up on them, they'll fold and run. I've dealt with these camel jockeys before."

I said, "I've learned never to count on the opposition folding."

We drove through darkened streets, past rows of tall, modern apartment buildings. We passed a checkpoint manned by Moslem militia men. They took only a cursory look at our papers and accepted the hundred-dollar bill Gray Wolf gave them. We drove on, heading into West Beirut, into the Shiite section.

"I've got a question for you," I said. "How come you never thanked me for saving your life?"

He laughed, but didn't give me an answer.

We pulled into an alley surrounded by decrepit apartment buildings. Dubney, the Frenchman, and Cutter were waiting for us. The place smelled of cooking oil and urine. Here, a small delivery van was waiting. An Arab got out from the back and handed us our weapons and black jumpsuits to put on over our clothes. Dubney handed him a stack of bills that he slipped inside his robe without counting.

I could hear artillery fire someplace in the distance. It sounded like distant thunder. There were muzzle flashes in the suburbs to the east. Dubney indicated with a nod that Gray Wolf and I were to take off.

Gray Wolf and I drove half a block and parked our car behind the building. We were to execute our exfiltration on foot, get to the car, leave our gear, and drive back to the hotel.

I followed Gray Wolf, we jogged down the alley and made a dash across a street. This whole section of the city was dark, we didn't see a single other vehicle. We stayed low, keeping close to the houses. In the second block we ducked down another alley. At the end of the alley was a fire escape. I slung my assault rifle over my shoulder, and Gray Wolf gave me a boost up. I lowered my rifle for him, and he climbed up it, as quick and graceful as a trapeze artist.

237

We crossed over the top of the houses. A warm breeze blew off the desert. Our senses were alive. Gray Wolf moved silently, quickly, and I was right behind him. I'd expected sentries on the roof, but there weren't any. The rooftops were deserted. It was possible that they thought their location was secret and placing sentries outside would have drawn attention to them. The other possibility was that they were inviting us in. Not that it mattered, we were going in in any case.

Gray Wolf found the skylight we were supposed to go through. It was dark beyond the frosted window. I put my ear against the glass and heard voices. I nodded to Gray Wolf to let him know there were people in there. He pulled his finger like a trigger.

I was edgy. I didn't like it. This all looked too easy. There should have been sentries on the roof.

Suddenly there was a terrible explosion and the whole building rocked. Dubney's diversion. We could hear automatic weapons firing in the street below. That would be the assault on the front door. Gray Wolf smashed down on the glass of the skylight with the butt of his assault rifle. We dropped into the darkened room, and made our way down darkened hallways. We checked the first couple of rooms we came to, then went down a flight of stairs. The place smelled faintly like the sweat of men. The firing below was intense, both outside in the street and inside the house.

We checked out the next floor down, it was as empty as the upper floor. One room had enough bedding strewed on the floor for perhaps a dozen men. The door at the end of a twisted hallway opened onto another stairway leading down to the second level. This was well lit. Below was an open area with tables and chairs and maps on the walls. A briefing room of some sort. Gray Wolf motioned for me to follow him. I shook my head. He looked at me quizzically.

I gestured that I wanted to check the upper floors again to make sure the opposition wasn't sealing us off. He pointed to his watch and started down the stairs. If it was a trap, this would be the perfect spot. If the opposition were behind us, we'd be caught in the open. I shook my head. He took a few steps without me. The fire down on the first floor was increasing in intensity. It sounded like a .50-caliber machine gun had opened up. Then I knew for sure they had been waiting for us. I grabbed Gray Wolf's arm and tried to drag him back upstairs, but he jerked himself away and glided down the stairs, fanning the area with his assault rifle. I covered him.

That's when I heard someone above me. The trap was closing. To warn Gray Wolf, I took a few steps forward and opened fire on a closed door, it disintegrated in a shower of splinters. Two men fell into the open room.

The other doors opened, and gun barrels appeared, spewing fire. Gray Wolf dove over the banister and took cover behind a filing cabinet. I sprayed some covering fire, and he sprinted for a window and smashed his way out. I saw him drop down off the edge.

I turned and headed back upstairs, shooting in front of me, dodging, firing behind me to keep the pursuit back. They were waiting for me on the third floor. I was on the stairway; there were a couple of men above and more below. I could hear voices now, shouting excitedly in Arabic. I guess they'd finished their business with the rest of our team, and now they planned to have me for dessert. I slammed another clip into my rifle, started firing blindly and charged forward. I made it up another flight of stairs, driving the opposition backward by laying down nearly continuous bursts.

I was at the corner that led to the room with the skylight. Down the hall I could detect movement. They'd thrown up some sort of barricade for a firing line. I was trapped. There were dozens of men below me, and more ahead of me, and I knew the rooms to the left and right had no windows.

Somebody said, "Throw down gun!"

"No thanks, pal!"

If they got their hands on me, I'd be their entertainment for a week. I changed clips again. I figured the guys down the hall ahead of me were waiting for me to attack, but maybe the larger bunch below wouldn't be expecting it if I attacked them. I remembered what they had taught me in the Special Forces: if you're going to be killed, take as many as you can with you.

On three, I thought. *One, two*—

That's when fire broke out above me on the roof and I heard a couple of guys cry out. Somebody was attacking them from behind. I turned and fired at the guys behind me, then ran forward.

Somebody shouted: "Okay, Coldiron!"

Gray Wolf.

We went out the skylight and over the roof and made it back to the car all in one piece. He'd been clipped by a bullet in the thigh and had been cut by the glass, and I'd been cut in the neck by a wood splinter, but besides that we were okay. He told me the Frenchman and Cutter were dead, and they got Dubney alive. He had no idea what had happened to the deputy chief of station.

We drove a couple of blocks and pulled into a driveway and parked behind a burned-out building. He put a bandage on his leg and we had a drink of strong liquor and a smoke. We were feeling a sort of high, a high that comes from being alive and more or less in one piece.

The feeling quickly passed. We had failed in our mission and lost two men and that didn't set well with either of us.

After a few minutes he turned to me and said, "Now I've thanked you for saving my life."

"You're welcome," I said.

He took another few swallows of the strong liquor we were drinking. "You know something, Boy Scout, you tell yourself you're in this for the flag and all that horseshit, but you know what? You're just like me. You cut across a little corner of hell and it gives you a charge."

I said nothing to that. We were both quiet for a moment, then he said, "I'm going back."

"For what?"

"I don't like getting my ass kicked. You coming with me?"

It was against everything I'd ever been taught, but I found myself saying yes. We scrounged around the rubble and found some empty bottles, then we went back to where we'd left the Mercedes and drained its gas tank and made some Molotov cocktails. "A little fire for the Fire of Allah," Gray Wolf said.

When we got back to the safe house, the opposition's celebration was in full swing. We started the building on fire, front and back, and then waited on the roof for them to come out the skylight. The fight didn't last long, the fire got to their munitions in a few minutes and blew the building apart. We managed to get off the roof a second or two before it collapsed.

Starting that night, Gray Wolf and Coldiron were a team, on and off, for the next dozen years.

Laying there in that bed in Lombok, it seemed like we'd gone down a long crooked road to this place; this place where I was going to kill him.

The garbage man brought word from the cook that Gray Wolf was still on the meal schedule. That son of a bitch was in there just

241

waiting for me to come and get him. Daring me to come and get him, and there was no way to do it. I felt like I was wrapped tight in a tourniquet and someone was twisting it tighter by the hour.

The rest of the day I paced and smoked cigarettes. It rained heavily all day. I could not sleep that night. I got up and went into the living room, where a stakeout man was sitting and watching through the night scope and smoking a long, black, perfumed cigarette. The room was lit by a low-amp red light, so everything was dim. The other stakeout man was asleep on the cot. Soft, atonal guitar music played on the radio.

"Any action?" I asked the stakeout man who was looking through the scope.

"A man in a van came and left a package at two and he went away."

"Who took the package in?"

"I did not see him. The door opened a few inches only. No one came out."

"Where's Nagal?" I asked.

"She took a few hours off to be with her man, I think. She said she thought you would sleep until morning."

I made some coffee and sat for a while looking out on the dark city. There was no moon. The sun would be up in two hours. Another day of the same thing. Watching. Waiting. Watching. Waiting. I was sick to death of it.

"I need a car," I said.

"There are keys on a hook by the door. The Toyota."

I took my holster gun and put it in my belt, put on a jacket, took the sniper rifle, and went downstairs. Outside, it smelled like a florist's shop. I got in the red Toyota and drove through the crooked streets, crossing over the river and up the other side of the valley. I drove all the way up to Lintz's place and stopped at the huge wrought-iron gate. Beyond, I could see tire cutters imbedded in the driveway.

If they photographed me, so much the better, I thought. Maybe if Gray Wolf knew for sure I was out there he'd sweat just a little, then maybe he'd make a move. Maybe even the wrong move.

Funny, but up close the house seemed larger than I'd expected, and more formidable. No one around, but I could see the red lights of the security cameras and Doberman pinschers roaming freely in the grassy area between the gate and the walls. I realized that was why they took the Afghans to the park to run them. To keep the watch dogs and the show dogs apart.

I turned the car around and drove down the twisting road, back to the apartment. I went upstairs, taking the sniper rifle with me in the case. The same stakeout man was at the telescope, still smoking. He nodded absently to me. His partner was awake and reading the Koran.

I had a drink of Japanese scotch and sat at the kitchen table in the dark, smoking an American cigarette. A reddish dawn was forming on the eastern horizon; it made the hill opposite and Lintz's house turn first pink, then red.

I heard a car drive up, and a few minutes later Nagal came in and spoke to the stakeout men. Then she came into the kitchen.

"It is bad for you, this waiting," she said.

"Yes, it's bad."

She poured herself a drink of bottled water and sat down at the table. "Everything looks beautiful at this time of day."

I said nothing. She turned to me in the dim light and said, "If I ever had a man love me as much as you loved her, I . . . I don't know how to say it, but it would be wonderful."

"I'd rather not talk about it."

She touched my hand. I pulled it away. I turned and looked out the window. A moment later she got up and went into the other room. I stared out the window for a while until it was fully light. Nagal came back and made a breakfast for us and the two stakeout men. It was a simple meal of toast and coffee, with hard-boiled eggs and dried fish and vegetables. Some of it hot as a Tijuana taco.

After breakfast I went back to the window and looked through the telescope. I sat and watched for a couple of hours and gave the stakeout men a break. A motorcyclist came and went, leaving a letter in the mailbox. An hour later, the milkman came. He went in the gate and a moment later disappeared within the great house, its massive door swallowing him up like a giant dinosaur. Ten minutes later the dinosaur's mouth opened and he came out again.

Nagal poured me some more coffee. I dumped brandy in it. I kept watching. At half past nine the dinosaur door opened again. That would be Lintz in his Rolls, I figured. But it wasn't. It was a Peugeot with the two security men and the dogs. The Rolls was right behind them. The wrought-iron gate slid open and both vehicles came out and headed down the hill. They continued through the first two intersections, then both headed for the park.

I got up and said I was going out for a while. Nagal said she'd go with me. I grabbed the sniper's rifle and we went downstairs and got in her Datsun Z and took off. I drove.

"Where we going?" she asked.

"The park. Lintz went with the dogs this morning."

"Is this significant?"

"Maybe it is and maybe it isn't."

I drove down to the park and circled the central area. Some kids were playing soccer at the far end of the field, a long way off.

The Peugeot and the Rolls were parked on the far side and Lintz was watching a security man run the dogs. I watched Lintz for a while through the binoculars. After a while he started throwing a stick and the two dogs would glide over the lawn and one would get it, then both of them would tear back toward Lintz and he'd throw it again. Lintz had the look of a man in rapture.

After a while he started looking at his watch and I knew it wouldn't be long and he'd be heading to the office.

I turned to Nagal and said, "I'm going to take those dogs."

She just looked at me.

"He can have them back. All he has to do is have me as a guest in his house for ten minutes."

She smiled. "It might work," she said.

We drove around the sprawling park to the far side and stopped the car on the road at the point nearest to where Lintz was playing with his dogs. Lintz threw a ball and the dogs raced after it, dogs and owner having a great time.

A few cars came by, and motorcycles, then a bus. In the distance I could see the towering Pura Meru pagoda, shimmering in the morning sun. Beyond was Mount Rinjani, rising out of lush green hills, ten thousand feet high.

I asked Nagal if she was armed. She nodded. I looked into her eyes to see if I could detect any fear. Her eyes were bright and sharp. Eager. She was a player, all right.

I took out the small-caliber automatic I was carrying and pumped a shell into the chamber and put it in my overcoat pocket.

"We won't kill the security men unless we have to," I said.

"We won't have to," she said. "I am very good, you'll see."

We got out of the car. A white stone path wound its way through some shrubs down to the grassy field. We hurried along the path and when we came into the clearing we slowed down. I had on a long coat and a hat with a wide brim. I pulled the hat down over my eyes and turned up the coat collar. Nagal held my arm and I walked with a limp, stooped over, to give the appearance of a young nurse helping a cripple.

I could see Lintz heading back to his car with his driver, and the two security men returning to their car with the dogs. But Lintz could not resist one more turn with the ball. He told his men to release the dogs and he flung the ball as far as he could and the two dogs tore off after it.

The newly mowed grass, still wet with rain, smelled strong and fresh. Two women in colorful dresses were walking along the path on the far side of the park.

I crossed the road and sat on a bench opposite Lintz's car and Nagal walked across the grass and watched the dogs bring the ball back to Lintz, whose round face glowed with pleasure. He patted the dogs on the head and rubbed them, and gave them each a treat out of his pocket. Then he turned them over to the two security men. They clipped leashes on the dogs and headed off for their car, parked close to Nagal, who was standing on the path smiling at them.

As they neared Nagal they slowed down and let her pet the dogs and I knew they suspected nothing. The dogs wagged their tails happily.

Lintz and his driver were coming my way. The driver was Chinese, about forty, muscular and intense, and I knew he was more than just a driver. His black uniform fit tightly to his hard frame and there was a small bulge under each arm. He walked ahead of Lintz, his narrow eyes darting back and forth, alert to danger.

I could see beyond them that Nagal had a gun on the two security men already.

247

Lintz's fleshy face was red, sweaty from playing with the dogs. He dabbed his face with a handkerchief.

"Hello, Mr. Lintz," I said. He and his driver both stopped. Lintz said, "Have we met, sir?" And then he looked closer and his face suddenly went white. I guess he recognized me.

"My partner has your dogs," I said. "If you ever want to see them alive again, you will do as I say."

He glanced over his shoulder in time to see Nagal getting in the car with the dogs. He went rigid. The veins on his neck stood out. The chauffeur, too, was rigid as stone. Red spots formed on his cheeks. He looked to his boss and waited for orders to attack.

"What is this?" Lintz asked. "A dog-napping?" He laughed humorlessly, then peered at me. "You're Tom Croft, aren't you?" And then he figured out what I wanted. His face looked pained and he puckered his lips and rubbed his fleshy hands together. "They've sent you to hush Gray Wolf?"

"You will do exactly as I tell you and neither you, nor your dogs, nor your hired help will be bothered."

Lintz wiped off the side of his nose with his finger. "Perhaps you've not heard, Mr. Croft, but your employer and myself are involved in many joint ventures."

"I have some personal business, Mr. Lintz. It involves neither you nor the Exchange."

"My man here is very well armed," he said, his voice rising in pitch. "Suppose I tell him to shoot you in the kneecaps if my animals are not returned at once!"

"My colleague will kill your dogs in two hours' time, unless I tell her otherwise. You will do well not to waste time making threats."

"Shoot him!" Lintz commanded. I jerked my gun out of my pocket. The driver had just gotten his hand in his coat. He froze, then slowly raised his hands. I told him to turn around. I hit him with the gun at the base of his skull and put him out.

Lintz stared at me, trembling—more with rage than fear.

"Now," I said, "all you have to do is take me to your house and get me in the door. The worst that'll happen is you'll get some red smears on your walls."

He swallowed, but said nothing.

"This way," I said.

We walked back up the hill to the car. My heart was beating fast. Usually I'm as cool as frost on the job, but not this time. My tongue felt like a rock in my mouth.

Lintz stopped and turned toward me. His eyes were downcast.

"I'm sorry," he said, "but I cannot go with you."

"Not only the dogs get it, my friend. You get it."

"Do whatever you're going to do, Mr. Croft. I can't give him up. For one thing, you might miss him. If I betray him and you don't kill him, he will kill me and everyone in the world I love. You would not. I know you. You might kill me, but it would end there. And if you did kill him, I could not live with myself. I am a man of almost no principles, but I do have some. If you are in my house, you are under my protection and I will not betray you."

I pointed the gun in his face. He shut his eyes. We stood there for a long moment; neither of us moved.

"Go ahead and shoot," he said.

I lowered the gun and pointed it at his kneecap and pulled the trigger. The gun made its poof sound and his leg shot back in a splash of blood. He cried out and dropped to the ground, cursing me and squirming around.

I hurried back to the car and started up. I figured I had about fifteen minutes. His driver would come around and get

Herr Lintz to his car. They had a car phone. They'd call their cop friends and they'd call the house to alert Gray Wolf and he'd make a run for it.

I drove around the curving roads up behind Lintz's house and hid the car in a stand of trees. I got out the sniper's rifle and a two-way radio, climbed a small embankment, and came up behind Lintz's house. I was right at the top of the trail that led up through a dense thicket, which is just where I figured he'd run. Once he came out of the thicket, he would turn toward me and I'd have a frontal shot at about five yards.

I opened the case and took out the sniper's rifle and snapped it together. I inserted the exploding bullet. I looked through the sight at the house, carefully scanning the rear windows, which seemed opaque or frosted. No movement on the grounds. If they'd received the alarm, it wasn't showing.

I picked up my radio and called the surveillance unit to see if anyone had come out of the house in the last fifteen minutes.

"No, sir."

"I'm on channel four, up behind the house. Call me if anyone comes out."

"Yes, sir."

I waited five minutes, ten, fifteen. No one came or went. I could hear my heart pounding in my ear. I called the surveillance unit again.

"No one's come out the front?"

"No, sir."

Another ten minutes passed. Finally the back door opened. A man, dressed all in leather, came out. He had a helmet on with a visor. He looked around and then stepped back inside.

Gray Wolf. I was sure of it. I could tell by his swagger, his cockiness.

Sweat started down my goddamn forehead. I never sweated

on a job before. My mouth was dry. Someone else came out. A guard. He had a Doberman on a leash and carried an assault rifle. He scanned the hill with binoculars. I ducked, then looked again a moment later. The guard made a gesture and the motorcycle rider came out again, this time pushing a motorcycle. A big black job. He kick-started it and got on, gunned it a few times, then turned up the road and sped away. Damn. The guard went back in the house.

I waited a moment and was just about to head for the car when the motorcycle suddenly came back and turned up the trail. I dropped into a crouch and took aim at the spot where he'd be coming out of the thicket.

I heard the motorcycle getting louder and put the rifle to my shoulder and looked through the scope. Suddenly there he was, filling the disk of the scope, the cross hairs on his chest. I pulled the trigger, the rifle cracked, and I looked up. The motorcycle was still coming at me as the rider tumbled off the back in a halo of blood, his legs going straight up in the air.

I pulled my handgun and ran over. He was lying on his back with his arms out to his sides, one leg twisted under him. The bullet entry hole was over the breast bone right above his jacket zipper. The grass nearby was speckled with blood and bits of cloth and skin so I knew the exit hole in the back would be huge. I reached down and pulled off his helmet.

It wasn't Gray Wolf.

I went back to the car and drove to the airport. Gray Wolf knew that I always went for a head shot. He probably figured I'd nail this guy and think it was him, and before I figured out that I'd made a mistake, he would be back sipping afternoon tea with Khadafy.

I drove out to the airport as fast as I could. I called the surveillance units and told them to maintain surveillance and that if they spotted Gray Wolf to have me paged at the airport as Mr. Cripps. I didn't figure they'd spot him. I figured he'd already left. I also told them to call Nagal and let her know where I was.

I still had the air-conditioning mechanic's coveralls in the trunk. I put them on and walked through the airport, keeping my hand all the time on my gun. There were just two planes there, both of them bound for Manila. There weren't more than a few dozen passengers in the terminal. None of them could have been Gray Wolf, even if he was wearing the best disguise he'd ever worn in his life.

The coffee shop was on a raised platform in the center of the terminal building, so I sat there drinking coffee and watching the exits until dark and by that time I knew I'd missed him.

I felt empty inside. I'd had him and I'd lost him, and I might not get another chance for a while. Maybe not ever.

I called Nagal and got a busy signal. Then I tried the radio, but I wasn't in range. I drove back to the apartment building and went in the back way and up the stairs. I came down the hall and gave a knock at the door. No answer. I fumbled around for my key and opened it. I heard nothing inside. Something was wrong. I pulled my gun.

I slipped into the living room, keeping low.

One of the surveillance men was lying on the floor on his side with part of his head blown away. Behind him, blood and bullet holes were stitched across the floor. His partner lay face down on the stairs going to the second floor. He had his hand on the gun in his holster, but hadn't managed to pull it out before taking a bullet in the middle of his forehead.

I didn't move. I didn't even breathe. If the killer was still there, he would have heard me come in. I pulled back into the

252

entryway and closed the door and waited. Ten minutes, twenty, thirty. I wanted to make the killer, if he was still there, think that I'd left to call the cops. No one came down. I finally went across the room and slowly up the stairs.

Nagal was lying in the middle of the hallway on the second floor, shot half a dozen times in the chest. She had a peaceful look on her face, serene.

I took a look around. No one there. There was a message written with Nagal's lipstick on the bathroom mirror: SEE YOU LATER, COLDIRON.

I went back downstairs and poured a drink, then I called the Exchange and told them they better get their body disposal team over there. They told me that Frank Webb was waiting to see me at a hotel downtown.

Frank Webb sat on the bed in the small room, wiping sweat off his face. The overhead fan was on slow, making a clicking sound each time it went around.

"You blew it, Coldiron, you fucking blew it. We were having a little tiff with Lintz, but now, now we ain't ever gonna be able to do business with the old buzzard. Three good players down. Jesus. And you failed to get Gray Wolf. That's the worst of it. We had him bottled up in there and you let him get away."

"I'm not making any excuses for myself, Frank. I took a gamble and it didn't pay off. That's the way it goes. It's a risky business. You don't always win."

Webb sat down on the bed. He looked white. His hands shook. "I'm supposed to be retired. What the hell am I doing here?"

I didn't answer him. I didn't think he really wanted an answer.

He took out his pipe and tobacco and started to load it. A truck rumbled past under the window, blowing its horn. Someone shouted.

"I'm still going to get him, Frank," I said.

He nodded. "I know you are," he said, his voice soft. He inhaled the smoke from his pipe. "I guess we can patch things up with Lintz after a while. After all, he did harbor Gray Wolf, knowing we wanted him. The Exchange can give him a couple of big orders for some heavy ordinance, that ought to warm the cockles of his heart."

I stood up. "Have we got any leads on where Gray Wolf might have gone?"

"No. But do you remember a woman he went around with now and again? Married to Wilbur Ferris the comedian?"

"Yeah, sure, I remember her."

"She's been living with Gray Wolf, we think. She's coming back to the States, to Long Island. Her husband killed himself day before yesterday."

The next day I was in Southhampton, Long Island.

The sky was gray. I parked on the street by a tall hedgerow that was sagging with snow. Behind the hedgerow was Wilbur Ferris's house. An icy wind blew off the Atlantic a block away.

I got out of the car and walked through the front gate. The house was a massive Georgian with tall pillars along a narrow porch. A broad-shouldered young man was shoveling slush from the brick front steps. I asked him if Mrs. Ferris was in and he looked at me with watery green eyes and said yes. I guess Wilbur Ferris's suicide had him pretty shook up.

I rang the doorbell. A young maid answered. I pushed on past her and said, "Tell Mrs. Ferris that Jake Mann's here to see her." Jake Mann was the cover name I was using when I knew her.

I went into the living room and took off my coat and threw it over a chair. The living room was done in earth tones with Indian-style artwork and southwestern-style rough-hewn furniture that didn't go with the high ceilings and the huge, white-

255

marble fireplace. Cindy Ferris liked Indian things, she always said they connected her with the earth and nature. Her comedian husband thought it was a great joke, so he indulged her.

A wall of windows looked out on a tennis court and swimming pool, both now covered with snow. Wilbur Ferris did all right for himself having pies thrown in his face on TV.

The house we stayed in that summer when Gray Wolf first met Cindy Ferris was next door, on the far side of the hedge. I could see part of its roof through the bare branches of a stand of poplar trees. I sensed someone coming into the room and turned and there was Cindy standing in the archway to the front hall.

She was small, with thin bones and pale white skin. She had on a black dress and had her hair styled in soft flowing waves, and it was the first time I'd ever seen her without glasses. She looked more womanly than I remembered and the mousiness was gone, and I thought I was seeing the woman that maybe Gray Wolf saw all along.

"Hello, Jake," she said tonelessly.

"Cindy."

"Would you like some coffee?" she said. "A drink?"

"Nothing, thanks."

She entered the living room and sat on the couch. Her eyes were vacant. In mourning, maybe. I'd read someplace that every suicide is an attempt to kill two people. Make somebody pay for their wrongs. Cindy Ferris looked like she was paying dearly.

"I was sorry to hear about your husband," I said.

"Were you?"

I didn't answer her. She crossed her legs. She kept her eyes on me, cold.

"I don't know where Gary is," she said. "And if I did, I wouldn't tell you." Gary was the name she knew Gray Wolf by. Gary Strong.

"You know he tried to kill me?" I said.

"No, I didn't know. But I'm not surprised."

"He killed a woman agent in Indonesia yesterday. He was after me, I guess, and when he couldn't get me, he took her out. Nagal her name was, she was dark and pretty and she liked to cook."

"What makes you think I care who gets killed in the business? It's nothing to me."

"When was the last time you saw him?"

She shrugged. "A while ago."

"You were living with him?"

"We haven't been living together for some time."

"Where and when did you see him last?"

She shrugged again. "Here and there and everywhere. I'm not going to give you anything that will help you track him down and kill him. He told me I'd be seeing you. He told me you and the Exchange were looking for him. You'll never get him. You're not smart enough."

She raised her chin.

"Why'd you leave him?" I said.

"It's none of your business."

"Look, Cindy, it's not what you think. I'm not looking for him because of the Exchange."

"Oh?"

I told her about how I'd quit, how I'd gone to Amber and met Meredith and fell in love.

"You, in love?" She shook her head.

"Yeah, me. Stupid, wasn't it?"

"I don't believe you."

"She was younger than me," I said. "An artist. She was real, not like anyone I'd ever known. She painted beautiful pictures that could make you feel pain if she wanted to. We wanted a life,

257

Cindy, the two of us, an ordinary life having what ordinary people have."

She laughed, throwing her head back. "You? My God, Jake, if only you knew how pitiful this sounds."

"Yeah, I know. But it's true. When I got word Gary was looking for me, we ran."

"You ran? You?"

"First to New York City, and then to Mexico. He found us there. And he tried to kill me, but he missed, and . . ." My damn voice was choking.

She stared at me.

"He got her," I said. "Blew her up."

She kept staring at me, her eyes narrowed, concentrating. "You're not making this up, are you?"

"I wish to God I was making it up."

She turned her head and stared out the window for a long moment. Then she said, "Oh, God, it had to come to something like that. If only you hadn't run out on him. That's what did it, you know."

"I didn't run out on him, what the hell are you talking about?"

"After you broke it off with the Exchange, after he saw you that time in New Orleans, he came back to Switzerland where we were staying then, and he started brooding. He hated the men he had to deal with at the Exchange, and he just couldn't face them without you around."

"I know just who he meant."

"He kept calling them paper pushers and telephone soldiers. He despised them all. To him being a player wasn't like it was for you. For you it was . . . well, patriotism, I guess. A cause. For him, it was different. For him it was more of a sport, or something like that. He wanted to be a part of something, to belong. You were like his family. You and Frank Webb."

"Still, he went over."

"He had to. He couldn't take it—the stupidity. After he quit the Exchange he got a few jobs from the Arabs. But he hated working for them. Religious fanatics. Kill in the name of Allah. So he wanted to free-lance for the Exchange or the Company or the Israelis, but they wouldn't give him work. The Director put the word out that he wasn't to get any assignments. Gary was very angry about that, Jake. His family not only didn't understand him, or accept him, they had actually turned on him."

"Once you work for the Exchange, they think they own you."

"Well, they didn't own Gary. He took a trip last June, and when he came back I knew he had done something that bothered him—not because he loved his country or anything like that—but because he knew you wouldn't approve and you were like his conscience. And once he'd done it, he knew you'd be coming after him. He said they'd make you, somehow, some way, and you'd be coming."

"Goddamn it, there was no way they could have gotten me to do it! They offered me a hundred thousand dollars and I turned them down. They tried to scare me into it, saying he'd be coming for me. But I wouldn't go for it. I was out of it, I was a goddamn civilian and determined to stay a civilian."

"The Exchange sent two men to kill him in September; he killed them both. Then they sent two more in October. He killed them in front of the villa we were staying in. They'd come as health inspectors, claiming there was a rat infestation. Afterward, he said you must have briefed them on how to get to him. He was angry. He cursed himself for not killing you before."

"I didn't brief anyone."

"He had information to the contrary."

"Where'd he get this information?"

"I don't know. He had contacts in the Exchange. Anyway, after that he turned cold and began to detest me because I was part of his past and he'd turned his back on his past. One day I woke up and he was gone and that was it, no note, no nothing. I haven't heard from him since. I don't know where he went. I don't know anything that can help you. Please, Jake. Just go and leave me alone."

She got up and left the room without looking back. I waited for a few moments to see if she might return, but she didn't.

I picked up my coat and went back outside. The guy was done shoveling the stairs. He was standing there smoking a cigarette, admiring the nice clean walk.

"Looks like it's gonna get colder," he said.

"Yeah, doesn't it," I said.

Over the next few days the Exchange reported Gray Wolf being spotted in Algeria, France, Brazil, Iceland, and South Africa, but none of the sightings could be confirmed.

I decided to try to draw him to me. I checked into the Morgan Hotel on West 55th near 7th Avenue in Manhattan and made a few calls to people I knew in the business asking them to help me find Gray Wolf. I called only my supposed friends. I told them I could be reached at the Morgan. I figured one of my old friends would be sure to see a buck in it if they betrayed me to Gray Wolf.

I was playing a risky game, and I figured Gray Wolf would know the game I was playing, but wouldn't be able to resist the challenge.

The trap I set was simple. I was taking calls in room 614, but they were being relayed from down the hall in 622. If Gray Wolf came for me, that's where he'd come. I could see the door to 622 from 614 and had it rigged to sound an alarm if anyone tried

to open the door when I was sleeping. A simple ploy, but sometimes simple ploys work best.

I didn't have any other surveillance teams working the
hotel. Inexperienced or inept people can bring worse disasters
upon you than cunning enemies. But that wasn't the only reason I
wanted to work alone. I didn't want a repeat of what had happened in Indonesia. I didn't want what had happened to Nagal to
happen to anyone else.

So I waited, but Gray Wolf didn't come. He was playing it
safer than he usually did. Maybe, like Viktor Dukas said, he was
just a little scared of me. That was good. Boldness was one of his
strengths. If he was playing it safe, he'd be less formidable.

Two days went by, then three. The Exchange reported Gray
Wolf had been seen in Orlando, Florida, but again the sighting
could not be verified. Oscar Morales, who I knew long ago in
Guatemala, called, offering his help. I'd saved his wife's life, he
said. I vaguely remembered the incident. He wanted to come to
New York and back me up. I thanked him, and told him this was
something I had to do alone. He said he understood and wished
me luck, but if I needed him for anything he was ready to go at a
moment's notice.

At least it told me word was getting around.

On the fourth day I got a call from Paddy O'Neal in Dublin.
Paddy was an IRA man. A cunning, ruthless son of a bitch, but a
man who was known to be good to his word. He and I had done
some business in the past and we'd gotten along.

A few years back he'd had trouble with Gray Wolf. They'd
once been on a mission together in Northern Ireland and had
come to blows over tactics. Gray Wolf fractured Paddy's jaw.
Paddy was not a man to forgive and forget. His call came in at a
quarter after eight in the morning.

"Hello, Tom."

"What you got, Paddy?"

"I hear on the grapevine you be looking for Gray Wolf. A dirty business, old friends not getting on, I hate to be a witness to it. Despite the fact you know my feelings for the man."

"Where is he, Paddy?"

"He's got a job here tomorrow. Be at the Kilronan Inn just above Kildare on the Dublin road tonight and I'll be getting in touch."

"I'll be there—and thanks, Paddy."

"I just hope you get the job done right."

I called Frank Webb to make some hasty arrangements and two hours later I got on a plane at JFK for London with connections to Dublin.

I arrived in Dublin late that night.

It had been a rough ride aboard an aging 707, and the plane put down hard and bumpy on the runway in a rainstorm. A woman two seats away threw up in the aisle.

I was in first-class and picked up my flight bag and was out the door as soon as it opened. Coming down the gangway, I spotted Bill Vanders waiting on the other side of a window barrier. Frank Webb must have arranged to have him meet me. Vanders had darkened his hair and was wearing a yellow ski parka. He gave no indication whatever of recognizing me.

The customs man spent two seconds with my bag, then waved me on. The Exchange must have smoothed the way again.

I followed the crowd through the terminal and through a tunnel to the parking garage. Vanders was waiting for me at the end of the tunnel.

"This way, sir," Vanders said. He led me to his car, which turned out to be a cramped little Ford Escort. We got in. He drove. He handed me a 9mm Steyr GB and a couple of extra clips. Eighteen rounds each. I threw my bag in the back seat. We headed southwest toward the Lakelands in the storm. He had trouble with the left-hand shift, I guess he wasn't used to driving from the right seat.

"We had a surveillance team spot Gray Wolf at the Dublin railway station early this morning, sir, but the surveillance team lost him. He's definitely in the country."

"Good."

"Will I be going along with you, sir? I mean, as your backup."

"I'd like to first get a look at things, I'll let you know."

"Just wanted you to know I'm up for it."

I hated his kiss-ass attitude, especially since I'd beaten and humiliated him, but I knew this job was an important step up for him and he wanted to please. You could never trust a sycophant like Vanders, but he was all I had.

I could see his face in the lights of the passing cars. He had his eyes fixed in a cold mean stare, and his jaw was firm, heroic as hell. He turned to me and said, "I hope you do take me along. New men don't get much of a chance for this kind of action."

He said "action" with the kind of look on his face a kid gets when you tell him he's been picked for first string on his Little League team. The fool.

We drove along a twisting road for a couple of hours, through half a dozen small towns. The storm seemed to get worse. Vanders prattled on about how he had read all the files on Gray Wolf and knew all about him, about how he worked, what he'd done, what he was like, how he thought. I dozed on and off.

Finally he pulled off the road and I sat up. It was after three in the morning. We were parked in front of the Kilronan Inn, an old, three-story stone building with a slate roof. It stood on a bend of a lonely stretch of two-lane road, built alongside a canal. A light was on in the entryway, and there were a couple of cars parked in the lot, but other than that the place looked deserted.

Vanders flashed the lights twice and turned off the engine.

"Leave it running," I said.

"Okay." He started it again.

The front door opened and a man stepped out. I could see it was Paddy O'Neal. He waved us in. Vanders opened the door and started to get out, but seeing I wasn't moving, he sank back into the driver's seat.

"Aren't you going in, Mr. Croft?"

"Tell him to come here."

"I thought this guy was a friend of yours."

"Go tell him to come here. Pat him down and take his weapons."

He nodded and got out of the car and went up on the steps. I could tell by Vanders's hand gestures he was apologizing all over the place. He patted O'Neal down. No gun. He brought O'Neal back to the car. I could see O'Neal clearly in the headlights and he looked pretty much the same as I'd remembered him. A big, bony man with unkempt white hair, a flat face, and hard, serious eyes. He looked old and tired. He walked with a limp.

I slid over into the driver's seat to let O'Neal get into the passenger seat. I told Vanders to wait inside. Vanders nodded and backed away toward the inn.

O'Neal closed the door. "You always were a careful man, Tom."

"You don't last twenty years in this business if you aren't."

I drove to the back corner of the parking lot. The sleet was

265

turning to snow now, large, wet, flat flakes. I left the engine idling and the heater fan blowing. "What's going down?" I asked.

O'Neal rubbed his hands together. "It's a bad business, Tom. The fellas Gray Wolf's working for, the Dark Watch, they're a bad bunch of rascals, they are."

"How'd Gray Wolf get mixed up with them? How could they afford his services?"

"The Dark Watch gets a lot of money from America, besides the banks they rob. Kidnappings for ransom. I know nothing of why he took the job, if he has a personal stake in it or not."

"How'd you hear about it?"

"I got one of my men to join the Dark Watch about a year ago, he keeps me posted. The Dark Watch and my boys don't see eye-to-eye exactly on things, and so I expect some day we'll be having real trouble. So I keep an eye on them."

"When's the job going down?"

"This morning in Brent, a few kilometers up the road. It's a small village, Brent is. Sean Rohan—he's the subject—he's got a girlfriend there, lives right up over the pub on the main street. The pub's called The Dragon's Egg. Sean's staying there tonight with his girl. He'll be leaving at 6:30 in the morning or so. No later than 6:40 because he's got to be catching a plane in Dublin. He owns a Jaguar that he always parks around the corner where he thinks it's nice and safe."

"You figure Gray Wolf will put him down on the way to his car?"

"There's no other way to figure it."

"How about interference from the police?"

"Not in Brent. There's a town watchman about seventy years old. He's not armed."

I offered O'Neal a cigarette. He took it. We both lit up. In the light of the match, I could see his eyes and there was fear in them. I didn't quite know what to make of that. I'd seen this man in action and he was cool as a melon. But then I thought maybe he was getting too old for this business.

"Will you be going along with me tomorrow, Paddy?"

He rolled down his window a bit to let out some smoke. "I wish I could, Tom, but I'm no good for field work anymore. It's the arthritis, it's in my spine. I'd be no good to you."

"I understand."

I put the car in gear and drove around to the front of the inn.

"Sorry I can't be with you tomorrow," he said when he got out. "I'd really like to pump a few into the son of a bitch."

"Good night, Paddy."

I watched him walk over to his car. He moved slowly across the gravel, leaving crooked footsteps in the snow. Vanders came back to the car. I let him drive. It was ten minutes to four in the morning. We headed for Brent.

The road twisted and turned and went up and down over small hills. Stone walls ran along both sides of the road most of the way. We didn't see any other cars on the road. The snow came down mixed with rain. Vanders didn't say much along the way. He drove stiff. Fear was taking hold of him. It can do that. It can take hold of you and squeeze the guts out of you.

"Just relax and breathe easy," I told him.

"I'm fine, Mr. Croft, honest. I always get the jitters before, but once the action starts I'm fine."

"How much action have you seen?"

"Ah—not all that much, actually."

"Any?"

"Well, not really."

We were coming into Brent. A few streetlights lit the main

street dimly, and there were a few lights on here and there in a house; other than that, the town was dark.

"Slow down and drive on through," I said. He slowed to about fifteen miles an hour.

We passed by some small stone houses and a petrol station, a church, a town square with a children's playground with a stone wall around it, a restaurant, a school. I looked up and down the side streets. There was a Jaguar parked up one of the side streets, and just beyond was The Dragon's Egg.

We continued on through the town. There were shops, a town hall, and a couple dozen more houses, and that was about it, we were outside town.

We drove back through the town, up and down the side streets this time. The town had a simple layout. There was the main street and two streets parallel on either side of the main street, crossed by four other small streets and a couple of alleys. On the back streets there were a few small woodworking shops in square, stone garages, and more stone and brick houses. I told Vanders to park in one of the alleys where we couldn't be seen from a house.

I checked my watch. It was almost five.

"Well, what do you think?" Vanders asked.

"Show me the tools."

We got out of the car and went around in back and Vanders opened the trunk. I clicked on a flashlight. Inside the trunk was a mahogany box and a small red nylon bag with a shoulder strap. He opened the red bag slowly and showed me a Heckler and Koch automatic assault rifle and a few clips full of teflon slugs that could penetrate body armor.

He looked at me to see if I approved. "Can you hit anything with it?" I asked.

"I can hit anything with it."

He removed the mahogany box and opened it on the ground. Inside, laid out on green velvet, was a disassembled Marlow-Chilton single-shot sniper's rifle, with a day/night scope and four rounds of exploding ammo.

"Okay," I said. He closed the box and handed it to me.

I took the tire iron out from behind the spare. I didn't tell Vanders what I wanted it for. Then I asked him if he had any radios. They were standard equipment for an operation like this.

"Oh, yeah, hold on."

He had them crammed under the front seat. He dug them out and handed me one of them.

"I'm all set," I said. "Here's what I want you to do. Pull the car forward until you can see down the main street. Keep me informed about anyone moving about. And if you see anyone, keep your head down. I don't want him to see you."

"Where are you going to be?"

"In the church. Okay, we clear on everything?"

"I want in on it."

"I want you here."

"Believe me, I'm good. Really I am. I was the best shooter in my class."

"I'm giving you a direct order. Stay here."

"All right. Fine. Just one thing, sir . . ."

"What's that?"

"I don't mean to put a jinx on you or anything, but what do I do should the unthinkable happen?"

"And he gets me first?"

"Yes, sir."

"Then you better run like hell."

I walked across the main road and up an alley to the next street, turned right, and walked up to the cemetery behind the church. The snow was getting heavier.

I went into the graveyard toward the back of the church. It was an old stone Gothic with a round stained-glass window in back. The wind picked up suddenly and whirled the snow around me. I put the tire iron between the door and the jamb and pried it up. The lock gave with a cracking sound.

I went in and found myself in a narrow passageway. I went along the passageway to a heavy oak door and gave it a push. The door creaked and echoed in the cavern of the church. I clicked on a dim penlight and had a look around. There were tall stained-glass windows. The figure of Christ over the altar looked down on me and for some strange damn reason I thought of the painting Meredith had made for the play and I felt an awful emptiness.

My footfalls echoed in the stillness of the church.

I made my way down the side aisle and went up into the choir loft. There, I punched a hole in a window wide enough for the gun barrel and tall enough to give clearance for my sight. I had to be careful that no vapor from my breath escaped.

The snow was coming down hard, but I could still make out the spot where I figured Gray Wolf would stand to take his shot. Across the road and slightly to my left was a short alley that led to the back street, and next to it was the stone wall enclosing the playground for children. On the far side of the playground and across another narrow alley was The Dragon's Egg. The subject would come out of that building and come back up toward the playground area, right under a streetlight.

Gray Wolf, when he did a wet job, tried to control four shooting parameters: a clear field of fire, good cover, good target sighting, and multiple escape routes in case things went sour. The distance to the subject would be no more than five yards in a clear field of fire, the subject would be walking right toward him where he could be concealed with good cover, the light would be good, and there were four ways to get away from the firing position. Perfect.

And for me it would be perfect, too. Gray Wolf would be almost below me, perhaps three yards away. When he took aim, I'd have a perfect shot at the side of his head.

I opened the mahogany case and took out the pieces of the rifle and fitted them together. The pieces snapped in place with reassuring little clicks. I pulled a bullet out of its container and held it in my hand. The old tingling feeling swept over me. The feeling of power I always got just before a shoot. I rammed the bullet into the chamber and closed the bolt. As I looked through the nightscope, the night turned to gray, shimmering day.

I closed my eyes and thought of Gray Wolf crouched behind the stone wall and in my mind I could see his ear in the cross

271

JAMES N. FREY

hairs and I could see his head exploding. I pulled back in from the window and waited.

My feet were cold from walking in the wet snow. I checked my watch. Still forty-eight minutes to go.

I started thinking of another time I was hunting somebody who'd turned—only Gray Wolf and I were still a team then. It was in the summer of 1981. We were sent to Brussels where the Russians had gotten to one of the code clerks in the CIA's European command center that was then in a sixteenth-century house covered with ornamental iron on the Rue de la Loi, two blocks from the Belgian Ministry of Defense. We were called in because the CIA had a staff shortage at the time—at least that's what they told us. Later we heard it might have been because their personnel section had been compromised.

It was great duty: Gray Wolf and I took an apartment on the Rue de Flandre near the market square and went to work at the embassy every day as "efficiency experts." We wore white coats and carried clipboards, we measured the work space, sat around taking notes, timed phone calls, looked officious. We quickly narrowed our suspects down to three: the supervisor of the code clerks, a matron in her forties, a no-nonsense type who breathed fire whenever there was a screw-up; the security chief for that section, a little runt of a man close to retirement, and a code clerk named Terri Call.

The matronly supervisor, we found out, was supposedly a devout Jehovah's Witness. Gray Wolf joined her congregation and took up Bible study, hoping to get close to her. The runt security chief liked to drink at a café near the Church of Saint Peter. We joined him there every night after work and we all became great buddies.

I started dating Terri Call.

272

She was small boned and five feet four or five, bouncy and cute, with auburn hair tied in a ponytail. She was ten years younger than me and sweet as Grandma's molasses cookies. She was from Newton, Iowa, where they make Maytag washers, and swelled with pride every time she mentioned it. Her parents had been farmers. Her brother got blown away in a rocket attack twenty-two days before the end in Vietnam, and she was bursting with pride about his posthumously awarded Silver Star.

We kept up surveillance for six weeks and still didn't have a clue as to which one it was. We started getting bugged from upstairs. They wanted whoever it was taken care of because of some very sensitive SALT talks that were going on. We were given a deadline. If we couldn't find out which one it was in forty-eight hours, we were to eliminate all three of them.

By that time, I'd grown fond of Terri Call. A dangerous thing in our business. You aren't supposed to make friends with your targets. I certainly didn't want to do her if she hadn't crossed the street. I fumed about it, and told Gray Wolf I'd quit the Exchange before I'd pull the trigger on her.

Gray Wolf tried to cool me down. "It's just one more job, Coldiron, one more job. You fell into a fool's trap. Never get the hots for a woman you might have to put down." He scowled at me with a shaking finger, laughing.

"I never said I had the hots for her, because I don't. I'm fond of her. I'm a human being, can't I have human feelings?"

"Human feelings? No. You can't have human feelings. You're a player, a player isn't human."

"We're not killing her, that's all there is to it," I said.

"All you've got to do is prove she's clean, she's off the hook."

"What if she's our bogeyman?"

"She's not."

"How do you know she's not?"

"Because I see the proud look when she talks about her brother and how he gave his life for his country."

"So you're sure she's clean?"

"Absolutely. It's one of the others. I know it."

He shook his head. "Poor little Boy Scout." He patted my cheek. "Don't worry, Uncle Gray Wolf will take care of everything."

That night we sent messages to all three of them in a code we knew the local KGB guys were using. The message said their cover was blown. That's all. Then all we had to do was wait and see which one of the three took off.

Gray Wolf went to church with the Jehovah's Witness and I watched the runt security man. We got a man from the pool, a trainee named Daniel Yont, to watch Terri Call.

The security man caught a train to Berlin the next morning, and I went right along with him. I figured he was our man for sure. He checked into a hotel, then went to the bar, had half a dozen drinks. I figured he was going to make contact. I figured to put him down when he left. He stayed there all day. The next morning I followed him to the airport. I was certain he was going east, but he didn't. He got on another train to go back to Brussels. When I got on the train I took the seat next to him. He seemed surprised to see me. I asked him what the hell he was doing; he said he'd gotten a strange message in a code he couldn't understand, then he got a telephone call from Terri Call to meet her in Berlin, that she'd explain.

That's when I knew it had to be Terri Call and I'd been made a fool of.

Gray Wolf and I found Daniel Yont's body dumped into a trash can in front of Terri Call's place. She'd killed him with a stiletto shoved between his cervical vertebrae, a very professional method that requires a high degree of speed and skill.

"We all make mistakes," Gray Wolf said, slapping me on the back.

"I guess this isn't going to look so good in my personnel jacket." I was a good little soldier then, did everything by the book.

"I'll take care of it," he said.

He wrote up the report and never mentioned my involvement with Terri Call. He was called to London, where the Exchange had its European Base of Operations headquarters, and there the brass grilled him about how we bungled it. He put all the blame on Yont, who was dead and couldn't defend himself, but when that didn't work, he blamed himself. It lowered his rating—he was the number-one field operative at the time—and hurt his chances for promotion. He said he didn't care about a promotion, and maybe he didn't. But I remember thinking I'll never have another friend like this.

And now here I was in a church waiting to kill him. If only he had trusted me. If he had realized that I was as much his friend as he was mine.

I hadn't eaten anything since the day before and my stomach growled. You don't eat anything before a show like this. If you're belly shot, you're a lot worse off if you've got food in you. I took another look at the street, trying to figure out if I'd made some miscalculation, if there were some better place he might pick to take his shot. There wasn't any.

I started thinking of Brussels again, and that summer dating Terri Call. Until Meredith and maybe Rita O'Tool, it was the best time I'd ever had. That was before El Salvador, before he started to change. Before he was headed on the road that would take him to this little village in Ireland to be killed by the best friend he ever had.

I paced around, keeping an eye out for his arrival. I didn't really expect him so soon. He usually arrived just a few minutes before a job. He didn't like waiting. A Volkswagon bus with the name of a medical supply company on the side came by.

I pushed the button on the radio.

"Vanders?"

No answer. I tried again: "Vanders?"

"Sir?"

"See anything?"

"A VW bus. It kept on going."

"Stay alert."

"No need to say that, sir."

I clicked off.

I glanced out the window. Up the street I could see lights coming on in the house where Sean Rohan would be.

I paced back and forth, trying to keep my feet warm. Any minute now Gray Wolf would appear. He would drive around a bit to make sure everything looked clear. Vanders was two blocks away, and by now his car would be covered with snow. Everything was going exactly right.

Come on, come on.

I kept pacing. I kept thinking of Meredith, but I didn't want to think of Meredith. I had to keep my mind on something else or I'd go crazy.

I thought of the time we went after Giap, the first time I'd met Gray Wolf. If we'd gotten Giap, we'd have been heroes. We'd have been flown to the White House and had medals pinned on us by the president.

A car came by, a Japanese job, going too fast for the slippery road. It slid a bit on a curve in front of me and went on down the road, fishtailing. Late for work, maybe.

I could see a milk truck making its way up the street from south to north. It stopped in the middle of the block. I took a look through the night scope. Looked like a milkman delivering milk.

Still no Gray Wolf. Fifteen minutes to go. I was tight, like a kid waiting for a bicycle for Christmas. I was sure I was going to get my bicycle . . . I had it all figured out . . .

I was suddenly shaken by the notion that somehow I'd figured this all wrong. This had gone too easy, it was too perfect.

And then I remembered the fear in Paddy's eyes. I thought he had been afraid of Gray Wolf, but what if it wasn't Gray Wolf, what if he had been afraid I might figure out he was lying?

But why would he lie? He hated Gray Wolf . . .

That's how Gray Wolf knew I'd trust him. Not only had we worked together and fought together and gotten drunk together, he hated Gray Wolf. Paddy was one of the few men in the world who I'd believe wasn't working with Gray Wolf.

All Gray Wolf had to do was grab his mother or his wife or his daughter and Paddy would sell me out. I wouldn't suspect he'd do that, because Gray Wolf had never snatched civilians before, which would be the smart thing for him to do.

So where would he be?

The answer. Taking care of my backup. I looked back down the street and there was the milk truck about even with Vanders. Milfred Dairy was the name on the front of the truck, over the windshield.

Gray Wolf always went for the quick stuff—fast cars, motorcycles, speedboats. He never came in slow. Who'd think he'd come in a milk truck?

I grabbed the radio. "Vanders! Come in! Where the hell are you, man? Gray Wolf might be in the milk truck!"

277

No answer. I looked through the night scope for the milkman. He wasn't leaving off any milk now, he was just slowly
driving up the street.

"Vanders! Can you hear me?"

The radio crackled. "Hello? Sir? This damn radio . . ." His
voice faded.

"Hit the milkman! Now! Open fire!"

"But, sir, how do we know it's him—he looks like a milkman."

"Open fire!"

"I've got to make sure!"

The radio clicked off.

"Vanders!"

No response.

Suddenly there was the rattle of automatic weapons fire.
Heavy stuff. Vanders's Heckler and Koch, maybe. Through the
scope I could see the milk truck parked in the street. It looked
like its windshield was smashed out.

I dropped the radio and the sniper's rifle and ran down the
winding steps and out the front door of the church and sprinted
across the street. In the swirling snow, I was barely able to make
out the outline of the milk truck.

I ran up an alley to the back street and headed toward where
I'd left Vanders. When I got there, out of breath, I peered around
the corner of a building and looked down the alley. Vanders's car
was sitting where I'd left him, steam pouring out of its radiator.
A woman in the window above shouted something and slammed
the window shut. Lights were going on all over town, but no one
came out.

I pulled out my automatic. Sticking close to buildings, I
moved swiftly to the car. Beads of safety glass lay everywhere. I
looked inside. Vanders sat at the wheel with the Heckler and

Koch assault rifle in his hands, his head tilted back against the headrest. His face had been shot away.

I took the Heckler and Koch.

From the direction of fire, I took it Gray Wolf let him have it from across the street where the milk truck sat, its motor running, one headlight on. The truck was riddled with bullets, so Vanders might have hit Gray Wolf. I couldn't see any footprints in the snow; Gray Wolf hadn't checked to make sure he'd taken Vanders out. That might mean he was wounded or killed. A wave of disappointment washed over me. I wanted him. He was mine!

I moved back down the alley and around the buildings and around the block to approach the milk truck from the back. I crouched behind a car and looked up the street. The milk truck hadn't moved.

I took a deep breath and sprinted across the street, then quickly up the sidewalk on the other side. The wind howled and snow whipped my face and suddenly I was next to the car behind the truck. Raising Vanders's assault rifle, I opened fire, spraying the truck. Quickly, I moved up on it, rolling under it. I came up on the other side, firing through the door.

I rolled under the truck again and came up on the right side—the driver's side. The door was partway open. I slid it back and pushed the muzzle of the Heckler and Koch inside and sprayed it. Then I climbed in and shined my flashlight around.

A man's body lay in the back, splashed with milk and shreds of paper cartons. The milkman, no doubt. He was naked to the waist and full of bullet holes, dozens of them.

I took a quick look around and found blood on the left side of the front seat, where Gray Wolf must have been when Vanders opened up on him. There were sprinkles of blood on the dashboard. Judging by the spray of blood, I figured he must have been hit in an artery, probably in the neck above his vest.

I had a moment of panic. He might be dead before I caught up with him.

He'd be heading for his car, I thought. That Jaguar that was supposed to belong to Sean Rohan.

I ran back down the alley and made a left. The snow came so hard I couldn't see more than ten or fifteen feet in front of me.

Gray Wolf would be looking for me to follow his footprints and he'd be waiting for me. I went down an alley to the back street and made my way around the playground to the Jaguar.

I broke in and pulled the wires out from the ignition, then went into the woods next to the playground and waited, expecting him any minute. I watched the minutes tick by. Three, four, five . . . still no Gray Wolf. Sitting there in the snow I thought of the day I'd had the snowball fight with Meredith. Superior generalship, I told her.

He must have known by now that I wasn't behind him. He was either too weak to make it, or he had figured out that I had gotten ahead of him, and then what?

He'd know I was here laying for him. He'd come around me in a wide circle. The wisest thing for me to do was to cut him off. I moved deeper into the woods.

Out of the corner of my eye I caught a glimpse of a dark figure moving in the snow. I dropped to the ground as a spray of bullets raked the trees. I returned fire with a small burst and saw him disappearing into the swirling snow.

Then I was up and running, crouching low, circling to my right. I came up to a stone wall. I moved along the wall until I came to footprints. They led over the wall. And next to the footprints there was blood on the snow.

I peered over the wall and could make out the gray outline of the kid's playground. I slipped over the wall and crawled across the snow, following the tracks now. Ahead of me, I could make out a stone playhouse made to look like a castle. The wind whipped at my back. Suddenly I heard a voice coming from behind another little playhouse a few feet from me.

"Thomas, is that you?"

The voice was weak, hollow, but it was Gray Wolf's voice, no doubt about it. "Thomas?" he asked again.

I didn't answer him.

"If we don't get this over with soon, I'm going to fucking bleed to death. Come on, man. Come and get me."

I said nothing.

The wind gusted. I waited. Patience, patience. He wanted me to come at him, did he? Go in for the kill. But what if he wasn't where I thought he was? I looked to my right; there was a low sandbox, half covered with snow. If he was in there, he'd be in perfect position to drop me as soon as I moved in on the playhouse.

I circled around to my right, making a sprint for some cover behind a bench. I dropped to the ground. I was on a small rise above the box. I aimed at a hump of snow that just might have been big enough to hide a man, but before I could fire the hump moved and I saw him bring his gun up. We fired simultaneously. I ducked as the bench disintegrated above me.

I rolled and came up firing. I caught a glimpse of him moving around the castle. I fired again and saw him pitch forward.

I ran to the other side of the castle and went around the far side, ready to fire.

Gray Wolf was on his knees, his back hunched, his head in the snow. He'd dropped his assault rifle. I could see the two-way radio in one hand. He must have tossed the receiver into the other playhouse to make his voice come from where he wasn't. He tried to raise himself, but couldn't. He fell on his side, unmoving, blood pumping from a wound in his neck.

As I came closer he raised his head. "You never used a backup before," he said, coughing. His voice sounded weak, far away. He was dying quickly. He coughed some blood up into his hands. "Who was he? The guy that got me, tell me his name."

"Vanders. Bill Vanders."

"He a top shooter?"

"The very top."

"Did I get him?"

"Yes."

He coughed again and shut his eyes, then he opened them again. He was fighting death and death was winning.

"I knew they'd get you to come after me, somehow," he said. "They're good at things like that." He coughed, his face contorted in pain.

"Not before Meredith, they didn't get me to do it," I said. "Not for money, not for anything."

He got a puzzled look on his face and started to say something, then he coughed hard, and rolled to his side.

I stood over him for a moment, watching the snow collect on his forehead. The blood flow ceased from the wound in his neck. I reached down and checked his pulse at his carotid artery. There was none.

I didn't feel like I thought I would feel; there was no joy in this, only anguish that we had come, he and I, to be in this place. My gun fell from my hands, and I found myself running from that place, running through the blinding snow.

Frank Webb met my plane in New York. We went into a cocktail lounge and found a secluded booth where we could talk.

"You did a good job, Tom."

"Yeah, I'm real good at killing people."

He looked at me. He was lighting his pipe and he held the match over the bowl and just stared with a blank look on his face. Then he leaned back, looking down into his drink and sloshing it around. "It's all behind us now," he said. "It's all settled. The score's evened up."

I gulped down my drink. I'd had plenty to drink on the plane, but it didn't seem to affect me any. "What are you doing here, Frank?"

"I just wanted to congratulate you. And give you your money." He reached into his coat. I stopped him.

"No charge for this one."

"You sure?"

"I'm sure."

"Okay." He signaled the waitress to bring us a couple more drinks.

"You're not here just to congratulate me," I said. "I know you, Frank. What's on your mind?"

He leaned forward and folded his hands on the table. A soft smile came to his lips. "I've been authorized by the Director himself to make you an offer . . . the best offer you've ever had in your life."

"What kind of offer?"

"How'd you like to be head of field operations? It's not a desk job, you'd be right out there with the men in the field. You'd be in on all the big ones. Planning, logistical support, operations control. It's a big job, and it needs a big man. You, Coldiron."

"Not interested."

"You haven't heard all of it. You'd be groomed for the top spot some day. You could end up Director."

"Tell them no. Okay? Just no."

The waitress brought us our drinks. Frank Webb paid her and gave her a five-buck tip. When she'd gone, he said: "Things settle down, you'll change your mind, Coldiron. You'll get antsy, you'll want to get back in the saddle."

"No, I won't, Frank. And you'd better make it clear to them that I won't. They send anybody around, I just might put a fucking bullet in their brain. You tell them."

He nodded, then sighed, as if to say my attitude was beyond human understanding. "What you going do?" he asked finally.

"I'm going back to Amber and be a nobody."

I arrived in Amber at eleven at night driving an old pale yellow Bronco I'd bought used out of the paper in Schenectady. There was snow on the ground, but it was old, dirty snow.

I went first to my house. It was dark and the snow was deep in the driveway. I didn't go in. I just sat in the Bronco and stared at the house for a long while, aching inside.

Then I drove by Meredith's old place. There were half a dozen cars parked in the driveway and it made me feel sad as hell to have strangers living in her place. I parked in front and heard laughter and felt suddenly angry, like someone wasn't giving proper respect to a shrine. But how were they to know? I guess they couldn't. I drove into town.

Jenny's Diner was closed when I got there, so I went over to Willy and Martha's place and had a beer and Willy told me he and his wife were packing up and going back to New York. Martha's paintings had been shown at some prestigious gallery and were selling for five to ten grand each. He didn't seem too happy about it. She'd already left for New York because she was being interviewed for a spread in the *Sunday New York Times Magazine.*

He said under his breath that he'd rather stay in Amber with real people, but Martha had stars in her eyes. He asked about Meredith and the sudden disappearance and I said we went off on a sudden whim to maybe get married, but we had a fight and split, and she'd gone back to Arizona.

He shook his head. The fickleness of women.

I had a couple of shots of bourbon and a beer chaser. Didn't help much.

That night I slept in my house, sitting in a chair in the living room while a fire roared in the stove. I kept getting up and pacing. I found a quart bottle of bourbon in the kitchen cupboard and started drinking it about two in the morning, and by the time the sun came up I had just about finished the son of a bitch.

I finally flopped down on the couch. I could hear a dog barking and in my drunken stupor I thought maybe it was

Prince's ghost, but I didn't believe in ghosts. I didn't believe in anything. I woke up and finished the bottle. All I could think about was Meredith and how she smelled and how she felt when I held her and how soft and warm her lips were when I kissed her.

Later that morning I drove into town to Maxie's Convenience Store for more liquor and cigarettes. I went back home and started drinking and kept drinking, losing all track of day and night, and myself.

I opened my eyes and there was Jenny standing over me with a cup of steaming coffee in her hand.

"I'm a little disappointed you ain't come to see me since you been back."

I was stretched out on the couch feeling bone cold. I felt stiff and sore and my head throbbed. Light filtered in through the sheets I must have put on the windows. I sat up and took the cup from Jenny. It shook in my hand. I took a sip of strong, bitter coffee.

"You look like something a truck run over," Jenny said.

"How'd you get in?"

"The door was wide open. Damn, it's cold in here." She opened the stove and peered inside. Then she balled up some newspaper and tossed it in, threw on some kindling, and lit it.

I stumbled into the bathroom and ran some cold water over my face. I had a week's growth of beard. In the mirror I looked bleary eyed. I took a leak and got cleaned up and came back out into the living room.

A fire roared in the stove and I could hear something sizzling in a pan in the kitchen. Jenny was setting up some eating utensils on the coffee table.

"Sit," she said.

"I'm not really hungry," I said.

"I don't doubt it, but I'm gonna make you eat if I have to hit you with a frying pan."

She went into the kitchen. I looked around for the bottle of bourbon I'd been keeping company with the night before and it was gone. I wondered vaguely what I'd done with it. I looked behind the couch.

My feet were cold and numb. Jenny came back with a steaming plate of ham and eggs and potatoes.

"I put your hootch in the kitchen cabinet," she said. "I didn't steal it."

She put the plate in front of me. The look and smell of it nauseated me.

"Come on now," she said, "take a bite."

I tried a little potato and was surprised to find it wasn't bad. My stomach growled a little, but it accepted the food.

Jenny sipped a cup of coffee and smiled at me while I ate. "You're doing fine," she said with a grin. "You're gonna be a-okay."

When I finished breakfast I lit a cigarette and leaned back and felt warm all over. Strength returned to my limbs and my head felt semiclear.

"You've been holding something inside you, haven't you?" Jenny said. "Something vile and poisonous."

"I just been hitting the sauce a little heavy, that's all."

I could tell she didn't believe me. She brushed some hair across her forehead. She looked at me with a disapproving expression as if she were trying to figure me out. Then she said, "You aren't like the rest of us, are you?"

"You think I'm from outer space?"

"I don't want to know, really. I don't care. I like you. I don't want to see you go down the shitter, that's all."

She got up and took my dishes into the kitchen and a moment later I could hear her running water. I called out to her that I would do the dishes, but she answered that it was no trouble. When she came back she had another cup of coffee for me.

"I got to be getting on into work," she said.

"Thanks for the rescue mission," I said.

She stood in the center of the room for a long moment. She'd put on her parka and was holding a box with the stuff she'd brought to make breakfast and there was a serious look on her face.

"She's dead, isn't she?"

I felt a little stab in the heart. I nodded.

"I figured she was. I'm sorry. I didn't know her well, but what I did know of her, I liked. You were in love with her, I guess."

"I guess."

She looked at me for a long minute like she had something else to say, but she didn't. Instead she turned and said, "See you." Then she walked out the back door. A couple of minutes later I heard her car start up and drive away, the wheels crunching on the gravel. I got up and went into the kitchen and poured myself a drink of bourbon and drank it at the kitchen table watching fine, powdered snow fall in the backyard.

After a while I went into the bedroom and got on my coat and walked over the back trail through deep snow, trudging, legs aching, to the house where Meredith used to live. I had this feeling all of a sudden that if I could somehow touch things that she touched, that she would still be there. Part of her, anyway.

I went up on the porch and knocked on the door. A brawny, balding fellow wearing overalls opened the door.

"Yessir," he said, "how can I help ya?"

"I knew the woman who used to live here."

"Yeah?"

"She and I—well, we moved out in sort of a hurry, and she left a lot of things behind and I was wondering if the paintings and furniture she left behind might still be here."

He scratched his head. "We didn't touch it, but the owner, he came and packed it up and put it all out there in the garage. We didn't bother it, honest."

He gave me a key to the garage and I went out there. It was all there, the couch, the bed, her clothes, her paintings. I looked at it all, and all of it brought the memories flooding back. And then I found her albums and it struck me that her mother should have these things.

That afternoon I drove down to Albany and took a flight to Arizona, feeling like I was doing something for Meredith and maybe something for myself, too. To be where she grew up was a little like being with her.

I arrived in Phoenix late that night and caught a commuter going to Flagstaff, where I rented a car and drove out to Bakerstown and rented a room at the same Holiday Inn I'd stayed in before. It was well past midnight. I drove over to the house Meredith grew up in on Sagebrush Drive. I guess I was anxious to see it. Restless. I don't really know why I didn't wait until morning.

The place looked pretty much as it did before. Leaves and debris covered the walks. One light on inside. No cars in the driveway. The name Todd was still on the mailbox, but it didn't look like anyone was home. I guess the guy who told me Mrs. Todd was coming home didn't know what he was talking about. Then again, maybe Mrs. Todd decided to stay in Hawaii.

I parked in the street and got out of the car. Icy desert winds blew and I turned up my collar. I walked up to the door of the house. A couple of old advertising circulars, yellow with age, had been thrown on the steps. I took a peek inside. As before, the place was empty except for a few boxes and an occasional piece of furniture.

There was no reason for me to go in, except I wanted to see Meredith's kid pictures again. Stupid sentimentality, I guess. Anything to fill up the big hole that had been blown in me.

The red light for the burglar alarm was on inside. I checked behind the potted plant where I had disabled it before and found the wires had been spliced together and taped, but they hadn't bothered to fix it where I'd chipped away the stucco. It took maybe ten seconds to disable the alarm.

Then I went around the back. The old alarm was still there, but the wires were loose beneath it. It probably hadn't been functional in years and I need not have bothered with it the first time.

The hole I'd cut in the glass had been taped over. I peeled the tape off and went on in.

The place had the same closed-up, musty smell. I found the box with the picture albums and took the albums into a back room and sat down on a chair and opened the first one.

There was the house, and the same old couple and old car, only the little girl in the pictures wasn't Meredith. It was another girl, with dark hair and dark eyes and a crooked smile.

I felt like I'd taken a million-volt jolt of electricity to the brain.

I quickly went through the other pictures. The same dark-haired girl. Even the wedding pictures: the same reception, the same people at the table, the same groom—only the bride was the girl with dark hair and the big dark eyes and crooked smile.

Somehow they were able to insert anybody's picture into the

290

same background. Phony up all the backgrounds you want using one house, one ex-husband.

The albums fell from my hands. I got up and stumbled out the back door and headed for my car.

It had all been a setup. Meredith had been a player all along. There was no other explanation. She worked for the Exchange. How perfect! The Exchange knew everything there was to know about me, including the kind of woman I'd fall in love with. And they'd sent her to me. She'd tried over and over again to get me to kill Gray Wolf, and when I wouldn't they simply went to plan B.

They killed her.

No wonder Gray Wolf had such a puzzled look on his face when I said I did it for Meredith. He'd never heard of Meredith. He had no idea I was after revenge. The Exchange had a Gray Wolf look-alike teamed up with Viktor Dukas. That's why they didn't want me to kill Viktor Dukas, he was one of theirs. Gray Wolf had never been after me, and had only turned on me because I was after him at Lintz's place in Indonesia, which explained why he was there in the first place. If he'd known I was after him, he would never have gone there.

I thought of looking up the guy who played the part of Meredith's husband at Kellerman Kamera, but I realized it would be a waste of time. He was no doubt just some stooge they got to play one part. No, I needed to get to the script planners, the brain trust at the Exchange who thought this all up.

Then I remembered how it all began, with Langston. He'd know who'd engineered it. I knew fifty ways to make him tell me all about it.

At six in the morning I was at the airport in Phoenix. I called a woman I once knew in Washington, D.C., Carri Bullen, who worked for the Pentagon's retirement section but did a little recruiting work for the Exchange on the side to help keep her in Cadillacs. I told her I had to see her and was flying in. She said sure, so we made an appointment for a late lunch.

Then I called a private spook I knew in Washington, Stan Waller, and had him check up on Carri Bullen. I knew where she worked and I knew she lived in Georgetown. I remembered she had a son and a daughter. I told Waller to find out who she loved best in all the world.

I called Waller as soon as I got off the plane at Dulles. Carri Bullen was very attached to her granddaughter, Betsey, he said. She took her to the park or the movies every week, bought her a shiny new bike for Christmas last year.

Waller told me where the granddaughter lived, her school, her friends, everything. She was seven years and four months

WINTER OF THE WOLVES

old, with corn-yellow hair and big blue eyes, Waller said. A real
cute kid. Liked to chew gum.

Stan Waller was always a very thorough man.

I met Carri Bullen at a place called the Peppermint Tree on
New York Avenue off K Street. It was wet and miserable outside.
We got a booth in the back and started lunch with a couple of stiff
scotches. Carri had a fondness for scotch.

Carri was maybe fifty, but looked sixty. Tiny capillaries
showed along the sides of her nose and her face was dry and stiff
as cardboard. Her makeup caked on her chin and made her look
even older. But I told her she looked well.

She downed her scotch and lit a cigarette. "I look like a
week-old corpse and I know it, so let's stop the bullshit." She
shot a glance at the waiter. He nodded. She was a regular, so he
knew what she wanted and headed toward the bar to get it.

"I heard about Gray Wolf," she said dryly. "Who pulled his
cork?"

"I've been out of the game," I said. "Did something happen
to Gray Wolf?"

She glared at me across the table, frowned, and bit into a
breadstick. "We're going to play games are we? First you flatter
me, then you bullshit me."

I smiled. The waiter brought her two more scotches and took
out his pad. "Would you like to order now, Miss Bullen?"

"I'm not having lunch. A couple more of these ought to do
it." She waved her hand over her drinks and gestured toward me
and I ordered a steak. Rare, with french fries. The waiter glided
off toward the bar again, his round tray with our empty glasses
perched next to his shoulder.

She swished her drink around in her glass and rattled the
ice cubes, then drank down half of it without coming up for air.
Then she looked at me and said, "Gray Wolf wouldn't go down

from my pockets and handed it to her. "Ten thousand dollars," I said. "All you have to do is make one phone call."

She sloshed her drink around in her glass while she eyed the envelope, but then she pushed it back at me. "Not for a hundred thousand. I've got a strong sense of loyalty to the hand that feeds me. That's how I've lived long enough to become an old lovable drunk."

I pushed the envelope back at her. "I know where your granddaughter, Betsey, goes to school, Carri. Marshall Elementary in Georgetown. She lives part-time with her mother, part-time with her father. You want me to give you their addresses?"

"No," she murmured. Her eyes registered terror.

"I'll phone you tonight at nine o'clock. If everything isn't arranged, you better call an undertaker. Tell him you're going to need a box about three feet long."

She closed her eyes. Then she nodded. I left her the ten thousand.

I called Carri Bullen at exactly nine o'clock that night from a bar on New York Avenue.

She said: "It's all set. Langston thinks he's meeting a new recruit. The meeting is set for eleven tonight at a warehouse, 5509 Tennyson in Marsden, Maryland. Marsden is fifteen miles north of Baltimore on I-95."

"Okay," I said.

She hung up.

I had a rented Honda. I headed for Marsden immediately.

Entering Marsden from the south, you come over a little rise and down a long grade. There's one exit for Marsden off the Interstate that leads to the center of town. All that was open was a Shell station, a 7-11, and a bar that had a couple dozen cars parked around it. Tennyson Street was three blocks up, and it went off at an oblique angle. As soon as I made the turn I passed a couple of warehouses and a brake shop. Number 5509 had a large sign out in front: Sampson Structural Steel, Ltd. The building was dark and looked deserted.

I drove around the corner and parked. No traffic on the street. It dead-ended in the next block in an industrial park. A light rain sprinkled on the windshield.

I could feel Langston's neck in my hands. I wanted it there more than I'd ever wanted anything in my life.

But I was still clearheaded enough to know that even an idiot like Langston might smell something and be ready for me. I got out of the car and went around the back of the building. The place didn't seem to have an alarm system. I found a back window and pried it open and climbed in.

Inside was a large empty warehouse with offices in the front, cool as a glacier. I stayed close to the walls as I moved around, checking through an infrared lens to make sure there were no infrared lights on me. I came around to the offices in front. They were on two levels, connected by a steel stairway. I went up to the second level.

The offices had furniture in them, old wooden stuff, but there was nothing on the desks. The place looked like it hadn't been used in a while. I went to the window, wiped away the dust, and looked out on the street. The rain was coming down harder, swirling in the light of the yellow street lamps.

I wanted a cigarette badly, but of course I couldn't have one. I just stood there, listening to my own heartbeat in my ears.

After ten minutes or so, a car came slowly down the road and turned into the driveway. A Japanese sedan. It stopped close to the building and two men got out. One was Langston and the other was a younger man: thin, lanky, well barbered, and neat.

His tie was tight at the collar. Another new man. Maybe one to take Vanders's place.

Ah, the fish have arrived at the fish fry.

I heard the front door open below me. "Chilly in here," Langston said. "Find the thermostat, Henry. Then you better get set up—the usual place."

I heard another door open, then close. I took off my shoes and put them in my overcoat pocket. Then I tiptoed across the room and gently pushed the door open. Light from the office below where Langston was filtered through some windows into the warehouse. I pulled my gun out and looked over the edge of the stairs.

I could see Henry's legs and part of his torso. More light flooded in. I heard Langston's voice: "You all set?"

"All set."

The voices echoed in the huge room.

The light dimmed somewhat, but I didn't hear the door click. I figured Langston or his flunky must have left the door partway open. Then I heard a chair squeak in the office. Langston was making himself comfortable. I started down the stairs. When I got about halfway down, I could see Henry standing by the door in the gray light, his hand on an Uzi. He was concentrating intently. A good man, Henry.

I continued around down the stairs and came out on the cold concrete floor. I moved swiftly and silently toward him and hit him hard on the back of the neck. He slumped to the floor. I took his gun and tied him to a rail with his belt.

I took a look through the small crack in the door and could see Langston in a chair behind a desk, facing the front door, his hat tipped back on his head. He had a cigarette in his hand and he was going through some papers.

I went back across the warehouse and slipped out the

297

window, put on my shoes, and crept around to the front of the building and burst in, pointing my gun at Langston.

Langston sat bolt upright. His hands went straight up into the air.

"Croft—what are you doing here?"

"Whose plan was it?" I said.

"Whose plan was what?"

"Don't be cute."

"Oh, you mean motivating you to do Gray Wolf? We had to do it somehow, you didn't seem to be going along with the program."

"Who's 'we'?"

He shook his head. "Classified." He didn't seem too scared, but then he was operating under the wrong set of assumptions. He thought Henry had his Uzi trained on me.

"You ever gut a catfish, Langston? You know how long a catfish can live with its guts hanging out? Two days. Wonder if you could beat that."

"You can't intimidate me, Croft. I won't let you." He smiled. He sure was sure of himself.

"I asked you a question, Langston." I stepped a little closer; he stiffened. He kept his eyes on me.

"I suggest you put the gun down," he said.

I fired the gun into the wall behind him. He jumped with a start. He wasn't smiling any more.

"Start talking, Langston."

He clenched his teeth like he'd just come to some decision that filled him with resolve. He touched the brim of his hat. I guess that was the signal for Henry to hose me with his Uzi.

Nothing happened.

He glanced again toward the door, then touched his hat again. Then he grabbed his hat and shook it and his eyes went big as golf balls. I stepped up to the desk, close enough to shove my gun up his nose.

"Your man is asleep on the job," I said. He shook his head a little like he couldn't quite believe it.

"You ready to start telling me the whole story?" I said.

"I—I can't, Croft, you know what they'd do . . ."

I fired at his ear, splitting it down the middle. He grabbed his ear without taking his eyes off me.

"Swear to God I had nothing to do with it, Tom. On my oath!"

I fired again, cutting his other ear in half. He held both ears now. Blood ran down his face and neck and arms. I came around the side of the desk and grabbed him by the throat with my left hand and shoved the gun into his mouth, pushing the chair over backward and onto the floor.

"Who?"

He didn't answer. I pulled the gun out of his mouth and hit him with it square in the face. Blood gushed from his nose. "Who, damn it!"

"Please, Tom," he whined. "Please, I didn't do it—they don't tell me anything."

Then from behind me: "That's enough, Coldiron."

It was Frank Webb.

Frank Webb had two guys with him, both with Uzis, and both had them pointed at me.

"Put the gun down," Frank Webb said.

I let it drop to the floor.

"I didn't tell him anything," Langston said.

"I know you didn't. I can see you were jus' a cool one, you were."

Frank Webb had his hands jammed in his overcoat pockets. A trickle of water ran off the brim of his hat. He turned to his men and said, "Why don't you fellas excuse us for a minute or two. Just wait right out there. Run along with them, Larry."

Langston scrambled out from behind the desk and beat the other two to the door. Frank Webb reached down and picked up my automatic and put it in his pocket. Then he leaned against the desk.

"You and me, we go back a long way, Tom. We were in it from the start. We were going to pull the goddamn Communist empire down around the fucking Commies' ears—and I guess we did it. Helped anyway. Now here you are, pointing guns at your own people."

"Maybe I had good reason."

He scuffed his foot on the floor. "Okay, you're royally pissed because you think we did you wrong. Was it our fault you got all mushy over a woman? You know a player can't afford to lose his head over a woman."

"I wasn't a player anymore."

"You'll always be a player, Tom. That's just the way it is. Once you sell your soul to Mephistopheles, it's sold, there ain't no redeeming it thereafter." He took my gun out of his pocket and looked at it, then laid it on the desk. He looked at me. "We're the same, you and me," he said. "We're in this thing, there's no getting out of it. It's like you're part of something that moves by its own laws of motion. Those things you wanted—a happy home, love, all that—it isn't for us."

"For me, it was."

"You poor, misguided son of a bitch," he said, shaking his head. "They were thinking of making you head of the whole shebang. Unlike most of the pencil-necks in this outfit, you had something upstairs in that melon of yours. And natural-born instincts. For ten, fifteen years there, boy, you were something magnificent. You had real commitment. Then, because of some fat, fucking worthless turd named Benevides, you throw it all away." He shook his head sadly.

"Who's scam was it, Frank? Who figured to have her killed? I've got to know, Frank."

"What difference does it make?"

"Give me his name, Frank."

He turned around and kicked a piece of litter on the floor with his foot. "You still don't get it, do you?" he said.

301

"What do you mean?"

"She ain't dead."

I stared at him.

"We didn't kill her, Tom."

"I saw her die!"

"No, you didn't. We had some technical people switch somebody else. Some corpse, I don't know where they got it."

My heart beat fast. I couldn't believe it. I wanted to believe it, but I couldn't. "This isn't possible," I said.

"Not only is it possible, it happened. Those guys can make you see anything they want you to see. You've worked with them before, you know what they can do."

I backed away from him. The room seemed to be rocking. My mind seemed out of whack. My heart was going berserk in my chest. My palms were sweaty as grease.

I got the words up: "Where is she?"

"You sure you want to see her?"

"More than anything."

He motioned for me to follow him outside. Rain was beating down. We went around to the side of the building, where there was a small annex and an office with a sign that said Receiving. There was a light on inside.

"She's in there," Frank Webb said. "She wants to see you, too. Ever since you dumped Gray Wolf she's wanted to see you, but didn't think it was wise. Go on in, talk to her."

Shivers ran up and down my back. I opened the door slowly. A woman, her back to me, sat on a desk, long flaming red hair flowing over her shoulders. "Meredith?"

She stood up and turned slowly and I could see the slope of her cheek, the softness in her eyes, the freckles.

My legs were weak under me.

"It's true," I said, tears flooding up into my eyes. "Oh God, it's true."

She nodded. Her mouth was tight and there was fear in her eyes. I didn't move toward her. I didn't know what to do, what to say. I just stood there like an idiot, trembling.

"I have much to say," she said.

"I do, too," I said.

"You see," she said, her voice breaking, "you were my assignment and I . . . I tried, didn't I try to convince you to do it? Didn't I? In New York, on the road when we were running from New York, and then again in Mexico, I practically begged you."

I could smell the sweetness of her.

"It was terrible," I said. "When I saw you die, it was terrible. It was like when my mother died, it was like my mind snapped. All I could think of was killing Gray Wolf."

"It's over now," she said. Tears streamed down her face, but she was smiling. "Everything's over," she said. "You're alive and I'm alive. And we can get free of all this. We can go back to Mexico, maybe, and just be ourselves, clean and new."

"Your name," I said, "I want to know your real name."

"Meredith is my real name. Meredith Thayer. We have so much to talk about—I have so many things to tell you."

She put her arms around me and held me tight. I put my arms around her and felt her warmth flowing into me.

"I wanted to tell you a million times," she said. "That day in Mexico, when they told me what they were going to do, I begged you and begged you . . . I didn't want them to do it. But I had to go along with it, they'd put so much into it, so much planning, so many resources."

I eased her away from me. I wanted to see her face. "Why

did they do it?" I said. "All this, just to get me to kill one man? They could have hired a small army."

"It wasn't just to kill one man. They wanted you back. You'd turned on them. You'd taken your humanity back and so you were no good to them anymore. They had to turn you back, just like they had you try to turn Benevides back. Don't you see? They need you to do their dirty work. They lost you and, damn it, they were going to turn you back. They figured once they got you to do Gray Wolf, you would be theirs again."

"I loved you so much," I said. I looked at her and I wanted her like nothing I'd ever wanted—but then all of a sudden all I could see was Gray Wolf lying in the blood-covered snow. I stepped back from her.

"What's the matter?" she said.

"I've got to think, sort this out."

"What's there to think about? It's over now. We can both walk away from this like it never happened. We can tell the Exchange to go screw itself."

"But don't you see, Meredith? It did happen."

"The only thing that happened was that two people in a dirty business who had their emotions frozen got them unfrozen. We found ourselves when we found each other, don't you see that? We can have all the things we dreamed, we can be the kind of people we wanted to be. Just a regular couple doing regular things."

"You do love me, then?" I asked. My voice sounded far-away. Strangely hollow. I couldn't get the image of Gray Wolf lying in the snow out of my mind.

"I do love you," she said. "Crazy, isn't it? I really fell for you. Right from the very first."

I could feel a terrible anger rising in me. "I killed Gray

Wolf," I said. "He was my friend, and I killed him because of you."

"I know," she said softly, her voice choking. "I'm sorry. Believe me, I've never been so sorry about anything in my life. I anguished over it for all those weeks we were together."

"Yet you went ahead with it," I whispered. I was feeling cold all over, like the thing, whatever it is—the spirit, the soul—was dying within me.

"It was your duty to kill Gray Wolf," she said. "We are people of duty, are we not? I had orders. I had to do something terrible, something I didn't want to do, something that I had to do because I was a soldier and I did it. I'm not proud of it. It was painful, but now it's over."

I reached out and touched her arm and drew her to me, like I was going to kiss her. My hand trembled like a drunk's.

"Did you love me?" I asked.

"Yes."

"And yet you could do this thing? Gray Wolf was my friend."

"Damn it, Tom, he went over, he had to be put down."

I made a fist and struck her on the face. Her head snapped back. She stiffened and stared at me, but she didn't raise her arms to defend herself.

"Forgive me," she said. "I beg you."

"He was my friend and I killed him because of you."

"What choice did I have?"

"In bed, you could have whispered the truth."

"Did he really mean that much to you?"

I twisted her arm and bent her over, then I brought my fist down on the back of her head, simultaneously bringing my knee up. Her neck snapped.

A single gasp escaped her lips and she tumbled forward

onto the floor, her head at an angle to her body; she quivered once, then the light went out of her eyes.

I turned and walked outside.

I took a deep breath and looked upward, letting the cold rain hit my face. I felt an inner rage, something deep, something terrible. The way I felt for all those years fighting the enemy.

Frank Webb was waiting for me, the collar of his overcoat pulled up around his ears. We walked down the driveway, pebbles crunching under our feet. At the end of the driveway his car and chauffeur were waiting.

"I ought to kill you, Frank," I said.

"Maybe you ought to, but you won't."

"Why won't I?"

"Because of who you are. We did no worse to you than you've done to a dozen others. We're men with a mission, and we do what we have to do to fulfill that mission."

"You know, as fucked up as that is, it makes a crazy sense."

"You forget about bothering Langston, we'll forget about the girl. It makes no difference who in the organization came up with the script anyway. We're a force of nature, nothing more. What say you?"

"All right, Frank."

I was feeling cold inside, clear through. And full of hate. As full of hate as I could ever remember feeling.

"I should have made her, Frank. There were a thousand clues. The funny way she acted in New York, her trying to talk me into killing Gray Wolf. I should have smelled her. She had me blinded."

"It happens to the best of us at least once."

"It's never going to happen to me again."

"No, I don't reckon it will."

We were at the end of the driveway. Frank Webb's driver was standing with the door to the Lincoln Town Car open.

"Are you coming back to reality," he said, "or you gonna try to keep living a dream?"

"Can you keep me real busy?"

"Guarantee it."

We got into his car, the chauffeur started up, and we drove away into the night.